Dear Reader,

Parades have always been one of my favorite things. To me, parades seem to show any community, and the people in it, at their very best. People put an extra shine on their classic cars, kids tie bandanas on their reluctant dogs, town leaders dress up in ridiculous costumes to celebrate their community spirit—and float-makers create all kinds of magic out of nothing more than some colored tissue paper and chicken wire.

But even more special than all the pageantry of a parade is the way a parade brings a family together. I remember shivering on the makeshift perch my grandfather always built us kids out of a board and some ladders every year at the Thanksgiving parade, but my fondest memory is of him. And I remember catching candy thrown from the floats that celebrated the fair in my town every summer, but my fondest memory is of pocketing some of my mom's favorite candy to take back to her at home.

Missing Pages is about both of these themes. It's chock-full of all the fun, excitement, and community pride of an Ivy Bay parade and holiday weekend. But at heart, it's about the fact that no matter what spectacle is going on around us, or how mundane our lives might feel, nothing matters more than family. Even long after the band plays its last note, and the final float disappears down the street, if we've still got family, we've got everything.

Vera Dodge

SECRETS *of* MARY'S
BOOKSHOP

Missing Pages
Vera Dodge

Guideposts
New York

Acknowledgments

Every attempt has been made to credit the sources of copyrighted material used in this book. If any such acknowledgment has been inadvertently omitted or miscredited, receipt of such information would be appreciated.

"From the Guideposts Archives" originally appeared in *Daily Guideposts 2003*. Copyright © 2002 by Guideposts. All rights reserved.

Cover and interior design by Müllerhaus
Typeset by Aptara, Inc.

Printed and bound in the United States of America
10 9 8 7 6 5 4 3 2 1

Missing Pages

ONE

◆◆◆

"Mommy, look!" A little girl with wide dark eyes and a mop of dark curls stood in the gutter on the side of Main Street, pointing up at a giant paste and paper elephant. As she did, a clean-cut member of the Ivy Bay swim team tossed a handful of Tootsie Rolls from the back of the float the elephant was perched on. They rained down on the little girl's head. She squealed with glee.

As the little girl scrambled in the street to collect all her candy, the float, built on a partly disguised boat trailer, drifted on down the street, pulled by a fisherman's powerful pickup truck. When the little girl looked up, her fists full of chewy chocolate candy, the elephant had been replaced by a new float. This one was based on the story of *Goldilocks and the Three Bears*. It featured several members of Ivy Bay's high school theater group dancing clumsily but exuberantly in rented bear suits. The girl's eyes grew even wider at this new apparition. She raised one hand to wave, remembered that it was still full of candy, and compromised on pointing instead.

"Mommy, *look!*" she cried again.

As Mary moved past them, picking her way through the friends and neighbors gathered in lawn chairs and on plaid blankets along the parade route, she smiled. Her excitement almost matched the little girl's. It was wonderful to see Ivy Bay all decked out for the Fourth of July, with bunting hung over the door of the Tea Shoppe, dozens of American flags on short dowels crowding the windows at the Black & White Diner, and patriotic historical items on full display at Gems and Antiques.

She'd always loved the Ivy Bay Fourth of July parade, and every time she went, she was reminded of when she and John were much younger and had come down from Boston to spend the Fourth of July weekend with Betty and her family. Yet in a way, this year's parade felt even more special.

Part of that was because her son Jack, his wife Christa, and their daughter Daisy were in town from Chicago for the weekend. She'd watched part of the parade with them, and everything seemed sweeter when she got to share it with her family. Jack and his family made occasional trips out to Ivy Bay to see Mary, and Mary did her best to get to the Windy City as often as she could, but when there was a grandchild in the picture, there was no such thing as often enough. Especially now that Daisy was sixteen and growing so fast, Mary treasured each moment with her. She'd been delighted when they arrived to visit for the Fourth of July weekend.

This weekend also felt more special than usual because Betty had a hand in just about every float in the parade this year. Her interior decorating skills translated directly to float building, and over the past decades, just about every high school club, retirement home, and ladies' auxiliary group in Ivy Bay had figured that out. Ever since May, when the float planning began, Betty had been in high demand, consulting on everything: new float concepts, the safest way to fasten a tree made out of chicken wire to the cab of a truck without damaging the truck's paint job, the delicate process involved to create a flower from a fistful of crepe paper. Everywhere Mary looked, she could see her sister's eye for beauty and painstaking handiwork. It was almost like Betty had gotten to use the entire Main Street of Ivy Bay as her studio for the afternoon.

But Jack and Betty weren't the only ones on Mary's mind that afternoon. When her old friend Henry had dropped by her bookshop earlier that week, Mary had bubbled on for a few minutes about Betty's plans for the parade, and how she couldn't wait to see those plans come to life. But she'd quickly realized that he seemed more subdued than his usual cheerful self. She wasn't sure exactly what to ask, but she'd switched the conversation to him and asked if he was looking forward to the parade that year.

He'd tried to muster some enthusiasm for it, because he could see how excited Mary was to see all of Betty's creations, but after a few more gentle questions, he'd admitted that the Fourth of July had always been a special time for him and his wife, Misty. In fact, one of their first dates had been to the Fourth of July fireworks, when they were both in high school, decades ago. He knew Misty would want him to enjoy everything there was to enjoy about life—especially this holiday that had meant so much to both of them. He just still wasn't sure how to do that.

Mary knew from her loss of her husband, John, that there wasn't anything she could say to make any of this better, so she'd just listened. But from the moment she woke up on the Fourth, she'd been thinking of Henry.

So after spending some time with Jack and his family, who'd taken up a spot on the curb to watch the floats pass by, she started to drift through the crowd just a bit ahead of the pace of the parade, keeping an eye out for Henry.

She hadn't glimpsed him yet, but as she wound her way between blankets and families, she caught sight of someone else she recognized: Amanda Branson—not in the crowd, but on a float.

It actually took Mary a moment to recognize her. She'd gotten to know Amanda, a rising senior at Ivy Bay High, when Amanda took an independent study in writing and publishing. As part of learning the ins and outs of the publishing world, from putting the pen to paper to seeing a book in an actual store, Amanda had spent a week of afternoons in Mary's shop, learning about the kinds of people who eventually bought the published titles and took them home to read. Mary had enjoyed getting to know her during that week. And she'd gotten a kick out of the way Amanda's boyfriend, Jared Wilson, had showed up daily at the store, a few minutes before Amanda was supposed to leave, to walk her home.

During her visits to the store, Amanda had always looked pretty and presentable, but dressed down in casual wear, khakis and simple tops. Today, however, she looked like the July Queen she was. Her glossy brunette hair was piled high on her head, and she wore a modest but striking red gown, covered with sequins, with a high neck and three-quarter-length sleeves that glittered as she lifted her hand to wave to the crowd.

As soon as Mary saw the float Amanda rode on, she remembered Betty talking about it. It was one of Betty's favorites: a fairy forest theme, with Amanda and her court of girls styled as the fairy queen and her attendants. The whole bed of the trailer was covered with real tree branches that had been fastened to a makeshift wooden floor so they stood up like the trunks of trees. Betty hadn't been able to secure them to the float herself because of her rheumatoid arthritis, but she'd supervised closely while Jimmy Shepard, owner of Jimmy's Hardware, fastened them for her, one by one. Then she'd wrapped the branches in diaphanous swaths of glittered tulle, creating a glimmering fairyland feel. Betty had given Mary the complete play-by-play of the construction of the forest when she returned home. But as beautiful as the fairy forest was, the crowning achievement of the float was actually a special addition by Jimmy, who had sponsored the float and was now slowly driving it down Main Street.

He'd been enthusiastic about all of Betty's plans for decoration, but he'd kept insisting that kids today had a lot more fun when things involved some motion, like a video game. Betty hadn't warmed to this suggestion all that quickly. "I'm trying to make a thing of beauty!" she'd complained to Mary after her first meeting with Jimmy. "Not a video game!" But eventually, Betty and Jimmy had come to a meeting of the minds and imagined the most spectacular feature of any float in the Ivy Bay parade that year.

This was a giant tree trunk, big enough to contain the armchair that Amanda sat in as she waved to the crowd and decorated with silk flowers and vines that clearly marked it as the most "enchanted" tree in the forest. Jimmy had rigged it up to an ingenious lazy–Susan platform, which turned as the truck moved down the street, so that from time to time, Amanda's chair would disappear into the tree trunk, and then emerge again, each time with a convincing puff of dry-ice smoke. These kinds of effects in the Ivy Bay parade were unprecedented, and Betty and Jimmy were understandably proud. As Mary slipped through the crowd, keeping pace with the float, she could hear the gasps and comments. She listened, noting a few of them to tell Betty later. Then she glanced over at the faces of the two girls who were riding with Amanda in her "court," and recognized one as Paige Bailey, Tess's daughter. She watched Paige toss candy and glimpsed Amanda's wide smile before the lazy Susan turned again and Amanda disappeared into the tree.

By that time, the parade route had approached Shore Drive, just off Little Neck Beach, where fireworks were being readied for the big display over the water that always marked the end of the Fourth of July celebration.

Still, Mary had seen no sign of Henry. So she headed toward the docks, turning left on Shore Drive, enjoying the way the sound of the crowd began to fade. As she walked, she used the bottom of her blouse to wipe a smudge off her glasses, then eventually caught sight of a narrow alley that led away from Main Street and snaked through the backs of the commercial district, out toward the docks. Maybe, she thought, Henry had decided the parade was just too much this year. Maybe he was down near the *Misty Horizon*. Maybe he had wanted to find an isolated spot to watch the fireworks he and Misty had always loved so much. She ducked down the alley, heading for the docks.

There was often a hubbub of activity around the docks, but in the gathering twilight tonight, they were eerily deserted, probably because almost the entire population of Ivy Bay was watching the parade go by, or gathering by the water for the fireworks display.

She walked through the dusk that had begun to shroud the hulls and masts of the ships, the fishing shanties, and the proud docks that had welcomed so many boats back to Ivy Bay and held them fast through all kinds of weather. But she kept a sharp eye out all the way, and she didn't find Henry—or anybody.

Lord, she prayed as she turned back toward the beach, *I've done my best to find Henry, but You already know where he is. Please take care of him, whatever he might be going through tonight.*

As she prayed, something whirred and hissed overhead. Then a beautiful burst of white sparks erupted in the sky: the first firework of the night. Mary smiled as another joined it, this time red and blue. The parade must be over. And Betty would be excited to share all the disasters she'd had to avert and battles she'd had to fight to make sure all of the floats she'd been involved with came out perfectly. Mary decided to go to the old warehouse in town where the high school band and all the floats wound up, and where the volunteers who had built them dismantled each year's creations.

As she started to walked back along the narrow road that led to and from the docks, she caught sight of a familiar figure: a girl in a tank top with a gait that Mary had learned to recognize from the week Amanda had spent working among the shelves at her bookshop.

"Amanda!" Mary called as the girl walked toward her. "Wonderful job!"

To her surprise, the girl averted her face. Then she turned, ducked into an alley that ran between two shanties, and hurried off.

Mary was so startled by this that she stopped in her tracks, then turned to watch the girl go. When she did, she realized her mistake: the girl had the same build as Amanda, but this girl's hair was long and blonde. Nothing, Mary realized, like the fancy updo she'd just seen Amanda sporting on the float. In the dim light, she'd mistaken a girl she didn't know for Amanda. And with a stranger shouting greetings at her, there wasn't much of a mystery about why the girl would hurry off.

As Mary approached Main Street, figures headed past her in the opposite direction, heading to the beach or docks, which would soon be almost completely swarmed with spectators for the fireworks. As she passed through the crowd, Mary scanned their faces, still keeping an eye out for Henry. She nodded at a few strangers and smiled at customers or friends she recognized as they straggled past.

Still slightly embarrassed about her encounter with the young woman, Mary upbraided herself ruefully over her lack of sleuthing skills. Not only did the girl have different hair than Amanda, and in a completely different style, but she also wasn't wearing the beautiful dress Amanda had been wearing on the float. And the queen and her court traditionally wore their dresses all night after the parade, providing a little dash of glamour to the dressed-down vacation garb of the rest of the revelers. She hadn't just made a bad guess when she'd called out to the girl, she told herself. She'd been off by a mile.

Mary knew she was getting a reputation around town as a solver of mysteries. *I guess this a little lesson in humility, huh, Lord?* Mary prayed. But incidents like this should keep her humble, if she was getting any unwarranted ideas that she was some kind of expert. Still, she was glad it had been a private lesson. It would have been even more embarrassing if anyone but the girl had been around to see it.

These thoughts carried her along Main Street, which was practically deserted now, but still not opened yet to traffic, and then on to Route 6A, to the old warehouse. Its big doors were thrown open, and light spilled out into the twilight. She slipped in, looking for Betty.

Mary had expected the scene to be a happy brawl of half-dismantled floats and full of the kind of joking and laughter and occasional barbs that people traded when they had the chance to work on something for fun. And the warehouse was a buzz of activity. Crepe paper streamers drifted through the air, teenagers carried around giant cardboard lollipops, and one young man still walked around wearing the head of one of Goldilocks's three bears. But the mood was all wrong.

Instead of the usual teasing and jokes, voices were hushed and worried. People glanced at each other, and at Mary, watchfully, as if they were waiting for something or looking for someone.

Quickly, Mary surveyed the big room. In the far corner, she caught the familiar sight of Betty's unmistakable fairy trees and what she thought was a glimpse of her sister, moving through the raised forest of branches and tulle.

This time, she was right about who the figure was, even though she'd only briefly spotted her across a crowded room. But when she reached Betty, she saw the same worried look on her own sister's face.

"Mary," Betty said, "there you are. Have you heard anything? If anyone would have a lead by now, it'd be you."

Mary came to a stop at the foot of the trailer and looked up at Betty. Betty's fingers were covered with glitter, but her face was dead serious.

"What are you talking about?" Mary asked. "A lead on what?"

Betty looked down at her, incredulous. Then she held out her hand, asking Mary to help her down from the trailer. Mary held her hand up and braced while Betty leaned on her for balance as she eased herself off of the trailer bed.

"Betty," Mary insisted when they stood side by side near the cab of Jimmy's truck, "did something happen?"

Betty studied Mary's face as if she wasn't sure how to break the news to her. Instead of answering, she asked her own question. "Did you just now get here?"

Mary nodded. She wasn't just impatient now; she was worried herself.

"Where have you been?" Betty asked, as if she was still trying to understand how Mary had missed whatever had happened.

"Down by the docks," Mary said. "I took a walk to look for Henry."

"So you...haven't heard," Betty said.

"Heard what?" Mary asked. "Betty. Tell me what's going on."

Betty shook her head. All the satisfaction Mary had hoped to see in Betty's expression after the parade was gone, replaced by worry—and maybe even fear.

"It's Amanda," Betty said. "She's missing."

TWO

M issing?" Mary repeated.
Betty nodded.

Mary looked around the warehouse, in shock. The spot on the parade route where Amanda had been when Mary had last seen her was only a few hundred yards from here. And almost everybody knew Amanda, a popular, outgoing high school student. How could Amanda have gotten lost between here and there, especially if people were looking for her? It didn't make sense.

"What do you mean, missing?" Mary asked.

Betty shrugged. "She's just—" she began, and then spread her hands. "Gone," she finished. "We can't find her anywhere."

Immediately, Mary thought back to the girl she'd seen by the docks. She'd convinced herself that couldn't have been Amanda. Now she wasn't so sure. But she wasn't ready yet to mention it to Betty until she had more information.

"Start at the beginning," Mary said, leaning against the trailer.

"It's not much of a story," Betty told her. She looked back up at the giant enchanted tree. Some of its branches still stretched over them, but a hidden door had been opened in it, showing the makeshift chamber within. The chair Amanda had been seated on was clearly visible inside, but there was no sign of Amanda.

"As Jimmy reached the end of the parade route, the mechanism pulled Amanda into the tree again," Betty said.

"I saw how that worked," Mary said.

"Everyone there on the street saw her go in," Betty said. "And about a minute later, she should have come out. But the tree didn't open again the way it should have. Jimmy caught that in his rearview mirror. One of the girls went to the back of the float and tried to make sure nothing had gotten stuck, but it's actually a pretty sophisticated machine." Even in the midst of the story, a hint of pride crept into her voice at this. "She wasn't able to get it working. But they were so close to the end of the parade that nobody thought it would be much of a big deal. One of the girls said she could hear Amanda inside, and she said she was fine. They just thought it'd be a funny story, at the most. You know, how the July Queen got stuck in the float for a few minutes at the end of the parade. And that tree isn't exactly made from Kevlar. Worst-case scenario, we'd just have to cut through some chicken wire to get her out and rebuild something better on the lazy Susan for next year."

"You and Jimmy are already planning the float for next year?" Mary asked.

Betty gave her a look as if to say that question didn't even bear answering. Then she went on. "But when Jimmy pulled in here," she said, "Amanda wasn't answering anymore. The girls were afraid she'd fainted, maybe from being overheated or dehydrated. Jimmy had the lazy Susan working in no time. Turns out it was just a minor jam in the system—a piece of paper from the street that flew up in the works. But when he and the girls finally broke the tree open, she wasn't there."

"Wasn't there?" Mary repeated, trying to understand how a thing like that could happen.

"That's what I said," Betty said, sounding both worried and exasperated with her sister's obtuseness.

"But how—?" Mary began.

"That's what nobody knows," Betty said. "All we know is, she wasn't there. No Amanda, and no sign of her. And now the real question is, where is she? Why would she leave town, in the middle of the July Queen competition? She's always been a great girl—never been in any trouble. So I'm afraid Chief McArthur is wondering if there might be some foul play involved."

"Chief McArthur?" Mary said. "He's involved already?"

"He was running traffic for the parade, directing the last floats into the warehouse," Betty said. "So he was close by when we broke into the enchanted tree. He was just as surprised as Jimmy and me. So the chief led the search through the warehouse. And when we didn't find her here, he sent the traffic detail back out to look for her in the crowd by the water."

At the mention of the shore, the girl Mary had seen as she came back from the docks sprang to mind again. "Bets," she said, "I think...I may have seen her."

"You *saw* her?" Betty asked. "Are you sure?"

Mary shook her head. "I was at first," she said. "But then I thought I must have made a mistake, because I'd just seen

Amanda at the parade. But if she'd already disappeared from the parade, then maybe—"

"Wait," Betty said. "You thought you'd made a mistake. Why?"

"Well, the girl didn't answer me when I called out to her," Mary said. "And then when I looked back to see why, I realized she had blonde hair."

"Amanda's a brunette," Betty said.

"I know that," Mary said, now with some of her own sisterly exasperation. As she tried to tell the story, she could hear how unconvincing it sounded. But now that she'd heard about Amanda's disappearance, her initial feeling that the girl she'd seen had been Amanda got even stronger. And Betty wasn't the one to convince. Chief McArthur was the one in a position to do something with the information.

"Where's Chief McArthur?" she asked.

"Just outside the doors," Betty said, pointing. "He's got some kind of station set up, over by his car."

"Thanks," Mary said. "I'll be back."

She found Chief McArthur just where Betty had said. The station Betty had described seemed to consist of a pair of lawn chairs, possibly commandeered from a parade goer. But despite the makeshift setup, the chief was pacing by the chairs, and his expression was deadly serious when Mary approached.

"Chief, hi," she said. "I heard about Amanda's disappearance."

Chief McArthur nodded as he stopped moving. "Thanks for coming over, Mary," he said. "I'm afraid we're in the midst of a full-scale investigation. Can we talk later?"

"Well, I think I may be of help," Mary said.

The chief sighed. "You've been a lot of help in the past, Mary. But the disappearance of a child is serious business, and we've got to find—"

Mary interrupted him before he dismissed her altogether. "That's the thing," Mary said. "I think I saw Amanda."

"Saw her?" Chief McArthur said, obviously startled. "Where?"

"Near the docks," Mary said.

"When?" Chief McArthur asked.

"A few minutes after the parade ended," Mary said.

Chief McArthur shook his head, slowly. "That doesn't line up with the timeline we've established," he said. "She was still in the tree at that time."

"But the tree had broken by then, hadn't it?" Mary asked. She'd done the math as Betty was telling the story. If the mechanism had broken when Betty said it had, then Mary had watched Amanda disappear into the tree for the final time just before Mary headed toward the docks. "She could have disappeared sooner than anyone knew."

"*Hmm.*" Chief McArthur tilted his head to indicate he was willing to listen. "Well, where was she when you saw her?" he asked.

"On the back path down to the docks," Mary told him. "She was maybe forty feet away from me. I called her name, but she took off without answering, into an alley between two shanties."

As they were speaking, one of the chief's deputies came up. He nodded at Mary, then the chief. "Sir," he said.

"What have you got for me?" Chief McArthur asked.

"Tracking the cell phone won't work," the deputy said.

Chief McArthur frowned. "Nonsense," he said. "Have you still got the number? Get them back on the line for me. I know they don't like to pursue missing person cases this early, but Joan owes me. She can at least track a cell phone for—"

The deputy shook his head and pulled a clear plastic evidence bag from his pocket. When he held it up by the corner, the contents were visible: a slim cell phone in a purple case studded with pink crystals. "Joan was glad to do it for us," he said. "But before she could get back to me, I talked with the boyfriend. She left this with him. Along with everything else in her purse. Credit card, money, keys. Apparently, there was no place for them on the float."

"This is looking less and less like a voluntary disappearance," Chief McArthur said darkly. "The boyfriend see anything?"

The deputy shook his head. "Says he didn't," he said. "He came down to the warehouse to help tear down the float. That was the first he heard of anything. He's pretty shook up."

"Did you take a statement from Jimmy?" Chief McArthur said. He had clearly all but forgotten that Mary was still there.

The deputy nodded. "Yep," he said. "Nothing new. Same story he told you and me earlier. He was driving the float the whole time. No idea what happened."

The deputy shifted restlessly. "You need anything else from me?" he said, looking into the crowd. "I'd kind of like to get back out looking...."

"That's where you belong," Chief McArthur said. "Get out there."

Gratefully, the deputy took off.

Chief McArthur looked down and rubbed his temples, then turned back to Mary. "So you may have seen Amanda. You recognized her by the dress?" he said.

Mary hesitated. "No," she said. "Not exactly."

"Not exactly?" Chief McArthur repeated. "What do you mean?"

"She wasn't wearing the dress," Mary explained. "She was wearing a tank top and shorts."

"So you recognized her by her hair, then?" Chief McArthur said. "It's pretty unmistakable."

"No," Mary said. "Actually, this girl had"—she looked down—"blonde hair."

"You got a good look at her face, then?" Chief McArthur said, growing more dubious.

Mary had to shake her head again. "No. The fireworks had just started, and she wasn't really looking my way. It was more…" She hesitated, searching for the words. "It was more the way she walked," she finally said, somewhat lamely. "I was sure it was her."

Chief McArthur was obviously trying to be patient, but his patience was stretched a little thin by now.

"But this girl wasn't wearing the dress Amanda was wearing. And she didn't have the same hair color. You're basing this on a walk?"

"Amanda worked in my shop for a week," Mary told him. "This girl I saw, she just…moved like her."

Chief McArthur shook his head. "I'm sorry, Mary," he said. "We'd all love to have a lead in finding Amanda, but this sounds like a case of mistaken identity to me.

It was getting dark. This girl doesn't match Amanda's description—"

"Well, yes," Mary began, "but—"

Before she could collect her thoughts, another deputy came up.

"Just talked to the girls," he said to the chief. The deputy looked at Mary as if wondering if he should continue in front of her. The chief hesitated, then nodded for the deputy to continue. Mary's ears pricked up to listen in.

"The girls are pretty upset," the deputy went on, "but they didn't see anything. They both said they didn't know why she'd want to run off. Didn't think she would. She's been talking about the July Queen thing for weeks. One of them did say something that was kind of strange—she saw a man carrying a big package by the bank. She'd never seen him in Ivy Bay before, and he seemed like he was watching Amanda pretty close. I guess he even seemed to be following the float along the route for a little while, instead of just standing in the crowd."

"You get a description on him?" Chief McArthur said, his eyes lighting up.

"Yep," the deputy said. "Middle-aged. Forty, forty-five. Curly hair, cut short, going gray. Average height. Blue T-shirt. Jeans. She said she noticed him because he looked nervous."

"Interesting," Chief McArthur said.

"The girls weren't the only ones who saw him," the policeman went on. "I also canvassed the crowd. People weren't paying too much attention to each other. The floats were just so great this year. Did you see the one with the paper elephant? I never saw anything like that in parades up in Boston."

Betty would be gratified to hear her work compared so well with the big city, Mary noted as the policeman went on.

"But I asked around, anyway. You seen anything strange? Anything out of place? And two people mentioned this guy, curly hair—"

"Over by the bank?" Chief McArthur broke in.

The policeman nodded.

"What did they see him doing?" Chief McArthur asked.

"Not much," the policeman said. "But he didn't seem to be paying much attention to the parade. Just kind of following it along. Seemed real nervous."

"Yep, yep," Chief McArthur said. He was showing much more enthusiasm for this lead, Mary noticed, than for her own.

"I talked to two or three more people down the block," the policeman said. "They all said pretty much the same thing. And then, it's like he disappears. At one point in the parade, several people remember seeing him. Then all of a sudden, nobody does."

"What about this package?" Chief McArthur said. "What do they say about that?"

"I guess"—the policeman rifled back through his notes—"it was pretty big. Like the size of a grocery bag. Maybe a little bigger. Brown paper. Taped up, or tied up. They don't all agree. Didn't seem like it was real easy for him to walk around with it. Seemed like it might be kind of slowing him down."

Chief McArthur frowned. "What do you think was in it?"

The policeman shrugged. Then he looked at Mary. "You seen anything like that?"

"No," she said. "I was down by the docks."

"She thought she might have seen Amanda," Chief McArthur said quickly. "But the girl she saw doesn't match the description."

"Well, yes," Mary said. "But she was the right height. And the right age."

"I figure she ought to be pretty easy to recognize," the policeman said, as if preparing to side with Mary. "In that dress."

"Well," Mary was forced to say, "she wasn't wearing the dress."

"And she was a blonde," Chief McArthur said, with a meaningful look at the policeman. The interest that had lit in the policeman's eyes when he first heard Mary's story flickered out. And to be honest, she couldn't blame him. After Betty's and the chief's reactions, the story didn't sound plausible even to her anymore. Still, she couldn't shake the feeling the memory gave her even when she thought about it again now. Something in her *had* recognized the girl as Amanda, even if nothing in the description she could give lined up.

"Well," Chief McArthur said, "one thing that's nice about this town: Everybody's always willing to help. And it's our job to sort through all these leads people bring us and figure out which ones pan out. So thanks for bringing your story to us, Mary. We'll make sure to check it out."

"I understand how it sounds," Mary said. "I just can't shake the feeling. I wish you'd at least send someone down to the docks to look around."

"That's where some of my men are right now," the chief said. "Looking for Amanda."

"Get on the radio," Chief McArthur said to the policeman, nodding at the car. "Get that description out. Let's see if we can't track him down."

Mary glanced at the deputy as he got on the radio in the car. "Maybe it would help for them to have the other description?" she suggested.

Chief McArthur barely seemed to have heard her. "We'll pass it along," he said.

Mary sighed and turned away, still uneasy. She couldn't promise Chief McArthur that the girl she'd seen was Amanda. And she had to agree with him that the girl she'd seen didn't fit Amanda's description. The problem was, none of those facts shook the weird certainty she'd had the first time she saw the girl, when she'd recognized her instantly as Amanda. And now that Amanda was gone, that feeling was even stronger.

THREE

Mary headed back into the warehouse, winding her way through the eerily subdued volunteers and parade participants, until she reached Amanda's float. To her surprise, it was still largely intact.

To her further surprise, her granddaughter Daisy stood near the door of Jimmy's cab, carefully pulling off the wads of masking tape that had fastened the vines and flowers to the bed of his truck.

No matter what the situation, the sight of Daisy always raised Mary's spirits. "Hey, honey," Mary said, going over to tousle Daisy's hair.

"Hi, Grandma," Daisy said. She didn't object to Mary's touch, but her hand came up to smooth her hairdo back into place where Mary had disturbed it. Mary suppressed a smile, but she also felt a pang. Daisy wasn't a little girl anymore. She smoothed Daisy's hair down again herself.

"This is a nice surprise," she said.

Daisy didn't really meet her eyes. "Yeah," she said.

Betty came around the front of the cab. Mary gestured up at the float. "I thought you'd have this all taken down by now," she said.

Betty shook her head. "Nope," she said. "Just after you left, we got a visit from one of Chief McArthur's deputies. Turns out, this float is evidence. We're allowed to pull the tape off so it doesn't ruin the paint job. Other than that, it stays as it is."

Jimmy followed Betty around the wide grill of his big truck. "They tried to tell me the truck was evidence too, but we talked them out of that. I can't do my deliveries for the store if I don't have this truck."

"So we're cleaning up the truck," Betty said.

"I just don't know how my hardware-store customers would take deliveries from a truck covered with silk flowers," Jimmy joked.

"Some of them might like it," Betty said. "There are a lot of handy ladies in this town. And a lot of good men like to see a flower or two here and there. You never know."

"I guess not," Jimmy said. He smiled at Mary. "I'm just glad we kept the truck out of the impound lot, silk flowers or not."

"And Daisy's doing a great job of removing them the way I showed her," Betty said.

"Without ruining my paint job," Jimmy added.

Mary took up a spot beside Daisy. "I'm not sure the best way to do this," she said, looking at the wads of tape, some still sporting little flags of crepe paper. "Would you like to show me?"

Usually, Daisy was enthusiastic and quick with a smile, but tonight when she answered, her voice was subdued. "It's no big deal," she said, reaching for a clump of tape to demonstrate. "You just peel it off slowly, like this." The tape came free in her hand.

"I think I've got it," Mary said, gently dislodging a sticky clump from beside the one Daisy had shown her.

"That's right," Daisy said.

Side by side, Mary and Daisy removed the wads of tape, one by one.

"So did you enjoy the rest of the parade?" Mary asked. "Weren't Aunt Betty's floats great? Did you know she had all that in her?"

Daisy shrugged.

"Did you see any favorites?" Mary pressed.

Daisy shook her head. "We didn't really see much of the parade after you left," she said.

"Oh?" Mary said. "Why not?"

Mary glanced at her granddaughter. She looked upset, but stubborn. Mary held her tongue, giving Daisy the chance to go on.

"We had a big argument after you left," Daisy said, after a minute.

"*Hmm*," Mary said, to show she was listening, but without coming down on anyone's side.

"I wanted to go hang out with my friends. But Dad wanted it to be some big family thing," Daisy said. "I'm sixteen years old now. When do I get to do some things on my own?"

"That's too bad," Mary asked. "I would have thought watching the parade with your dad might seem like fun."

Daisy looked a little abashed at the prospect of having to answer to her grandmother. "It wasn't the parade, really," she said. "I just didn't feel like doing much of anything. Not with them, anyway."

Mary thought back over the day since Jack and Christa had arrived, with Daisy in tow. Everyone had been polite to each other, and they'd all seemed happy to see Mary. But she had noticed a bit of a frosty feeling between Daisy and her parents. She saw them only occasionally, though, so it could be hard to tell. Especially since Daisy was growing up now, and kids and their moods changed so fast at her age. But did all of this go deeper than a passing mood for Daisy?

"Is everything all right, honey?" Mary asked.

Daisy didn't answer. When Mary glanced at her again, she saw that Daisy's lip was trembling. Mary put her hand on Daisy's shoulder.

"It's just not fair!" Daisy burst out.

"What's not fair?" Mary asked gently.

Daisy shook her head and swiped at a tear that had escaped from her eye. "You'll think it's stupid," she said. "Just like they do."

"Maybe," Mary said. "But maybe not. You can't know that until you try me."

Daisy looked at her grandmother. "There's a big party this weekend," she said.

"A party?" Mary repeated, wondering how Daisy had possibly connected so quickly with the other teens in town. She had some local acquaintances from other visits to Ivy Bay but she'd only been there for less than a day. "In Ivy Bay?"

Daisy shook her head, and her voice rose to a wail. "No!" she said. "That's the problem. It's back in Chicago. It's Angela Krepke's big Fourth of July party. They live in a big apartment building on Lake Shore Drive, and her father rents the roof for a party every year. The fireworks are so close that sometimes ash lands on everybody. And you can see the whole lake, and the fireworks on the water, and the Ferris wheel down at Navy Pier."

"Have you been to it before, then?" Mary asked.

Daisy shook her head. "No!" she said again. "But everyone who does talks about it all year. And this year, she finally invited me. Her father only lets her invite fifty kids, and I was one of them. Until Dad planned this stupid trip. I told him it wasn't fair. Angela asked me all the way back in May, and I had permission and everything. But then Dad decided we had to come out here to Ivy Bay instead. I even tried to get them to let me just stay home in Chicago. I have some money saved up. I was even going to pay for my own cab. But they said no. It's just not fair," she repeated. "I'm not a kid anymore. But I never get to decide anything for myself. Not anything important, anyway."

Mary gave Daisy's arm a squeeze. Mary still remembered what it had been like for her, and then for her own kids to live through this in-between age. It was hard to want to strike out on your own, but not have the power or the freedom. And Mary knew better than to point out all the ways Daisy was still a kid and all the things her parents still did to take care of her every day. One day, Daisy would realize all that, she knew. But that day was still a while off.

"Well," Mary said, "I'm so sorry to hear that you're missing your party. It sounds like it would be a lot of fun. But I have to tell you I'm so glad to have you here in Ivy Bay. You haven't even been here a day, and it's already one of the best parts of my summer."

Daisy looked a little abashed at the idea that she might have hurt her grandmother's feelings. "Oh, Grandma," she said, "I didn't mean I didn't want to come see you. It's just—"

Mary drew her into a hug. "You wish you could come to Ivy Bay, and go to the party too," she said.

Daisy nodded against her shoulder. "It's not even just the party," she said quietly.

"No?" Mary said.

Daisy shook her head. "Jordan Brewster is going to be there," she said.

Mary released Daisy and looked at her face, smiling. "And I take it Jordan Brewster is someone special?"

"He's so funny, Grandma!" Daisy said, her face lighting up. "And he likes to read, the same as me."

"Well, that sounds good," Mary admitted.

"I talk to him every day after school," Daisy said. "We wait on the same corner for our parents to come. And the last time I saw him, he asked me if I was going to Angela's party. And he said he'd see me there. And I haven't seen him since June!"

"Oh, honey," Mary said. "That's too bad."

"That's why I didn't want to come to the parade," Daisy said. "I just didn't really feel like doing anything. And Mom said to just leave me alone if I didn't want to go, but that wasn't good enough for Dad. He wanted everyone to come along and be one big happy family. That's how we wound up in a fight."

Mary could imagine that. Daisy came by her stubbornness honestly—Jack had been just as stubborn as Daisy is now when he was a kid, and although he'd grown into a man

Mary was proud of, he hadn't really lost his stubbornness along the way.

"Then I went off with some kids from Ivy Bay," Daisy said. "But then he called me and told me I had to come help Aunt Betty take care of the floats while I thought my attitude over."

"So what have you been thinking?" Mary asked.

Daisy shrugged. "I'm sorry I got in a fight with Dad," she said. "I don't really like to fight with him."

Mary nodded.

"But I still don't think it's fair," Daisy said. "They act like I'm still a kid, when I'm not anymore. I'm practically a grown-up. And I can do a lot of things that they can't even do themselves. My mom can't even open her e-mail account half the time if I don't fix it for her. But then when I want to do something myself, suddenly they're the parents, and I'm not allowed to make any decisions for myself."

"Well," Mary told her, "I can understand how that feels. But your parents love you a lot. They've known you since you were so little you couldn't do anything for yourself. And they've been around longer than you. It's hard to blame them for wanting to watch out for you. It can be scary to be a parent. You just love your kids so much. And you hear about all kinds of things happening, so it's hard not to worry about them."

"Like Amanda?" Daisy asked quietly.

Mary looked into her granddaughter's eyes. She wished that they lived in a world where she could just deny that anything bad ever happened, but she couldn't. And Daisy was right. She was growing up, and it was time for Mary to stop treating her like a kid. "I hope we'll find Amanda safe and sound," Mary said. "But yes. This is the kind of thing a parent worries about." She felt a sharp pang of sympathy, thinking about Amanda's mother, Heather. She'd only met her a few times in the course of Amanda's work at the shop. But she didn't need to know her well to know how a mother must feel if her daughter disappeared. What must she be going through right now?

As they were talking, Jimmy, trailed by Betty, came back around from the tail of the truck, where they'd just been clanking chains and fasteners, releasing the trailer from the back of the truck so Jimmy would be free to go home.

"You talking about Amanda?" Jimmy said, pushing his cap back on his head with a slightly worried look.

Mary's heart went out to him. He was hiding it well, but he was clearly rattled by Amanda's disappearance. "Not really," she said.

"You talked with the police for a while, though," he said. "They say anything?"

Mary shook her head. "They don't know much," she said. "I guess there was a stranger a couple of people saw over by the bank, carrying a big package. They seem to be looking for him."

Jimmy nodded.

"They said they talked to you too," Mary said.

Jimmy nodded. "I just wish I'd had more to tell them," he said, his face full of regret. "Honestly, I was just trying to keep my eyes on the road. With all these clowns and kids and pets and politicians running all over the parade route, it's harder than it looks just to point your truck down the street."

Mary smiled. "Well," she said, "I wouldn't feel too bad. It doesn't sound like anybody else saw anything more than you did. I guess they talked to Amanda's friends on her court, and her boyfriend too, and they didn't have much to add either."

"Really?" Betty said.

Mary, Daisy, and Jimmy turned back to her.

Betty folded her arms. "I'm just a little surprised to hear that."

"Why is that?" Mary asked.

"Well," Betty said, "I was working on this float right up till the last minute, when the girls were doing each other's makeup and taking their places on the float. Jared was here too. He was carrying around a bag with all her things in it, because there was no place for any of it on the float. And let me tell you, something was up. With all of them."

"What do you mean?" Mary said.

"Well," Betty said, "Amanda was not happy with Jared; I can tell you that much. He had her stuff with him, but she was not happy with him at all."

"Did you hear anything they said?" Mary asked.

Betty shook her head. "Whenever I got close enough, they clammed up. But the other girls were whispering up a storm too. They kept looking over at Amanda and Jared and then whispering again."

Mary frowned. "I don't think anyone told the police any of this."

Betty shrugged. "Well, you know kids," she said. "They think something's the end of the world one minute, and the next minute, they've forgotten it. Maybe once Amanda disappeared, none of it seemed important enough to mention."

"Her friends told the police they couldn't think of any reason Amanda would want to leave the parade," Mary said. "So they're thinking she must have been taken against her will. But if she was fighting with Jared..."

"Teenage girls in fights with their boyfriends," Betty said. "Watch out."

Mary nodded. Chief McArthur had almost had her convinced by his logic. After all, everything that she had to offer about the young woman she'd seen by the docks was a familiar feeling and a hunch. Nothing, as Chief McArthur had so amply pointed out, that really amounted to proof. But with this new tidbit of information, her mind began to work again. Chief McArthur was working the case as if it might turn into some kind of kidnapping. But what if it wasn't? What if Amanda had walked away from the parade under her own power? And if she had, what could possibly have frightened or driven her to such lengths?

Mary wasn't sure of much, but with this new bit of information, she did know one thing: She wanted to go back down to the docks and get another look.

"I think I might go down and see the fireworks," she said.

"The fireworks?" Betty said, raising an eyebrow.

Mary smiled. Her sister knew her too well.

"Yes," Mary said. "I might take a little look around."

FOUR

The sky was full of sparks of color when Mary walked out of the warehouse. It was the grand finale that marked the end of the night, and the Ivy Bay fireworks organizers had spared no effect. Giant strands of red dripped down the sky, dotted by white stars, with smaller flares of blue and green sizzling here and there. Behind it all was a towering cloud of the smoke that had been released with each successive explosion. The real stars, high overhead, seemed dim by comparison.

For several minutes, the blur in the sky was almost blindingly bright. But then, in a final burst of pops and flashes, the display winked out. As Mary turned left onto Shore Drive, just before the beach, she saw the crowd begin to head for home. A steady trickle of foot traffic began to pour from the beach and the docks.

But when Mary began to trail along Shore Drive, she felt a wave of hopelessness. *I don't know what I thought I was going to find, Lord,* she prayed. Since she'd seen the mysterious girl disappear into the maze of the docks, hundreds, if not thousands of people had passed. By now, they must have obliterated any footprints that could have given her a clue as to where the girl went after she vanished around the corner where Mary saw her last. If the girl had left any other signs, those were probably trampled or handled beyond recognition now, as well. Not to mention the fact that, with all these people in the area, there was no way to tell what clues the girl had left, and what clues had been left by everyone else who had now passed that way tonight.

Still, Mary made her way doggedly down to the docks, against the flow of traffic. When she finally reached the place where she'd seen the girl, the crowd was starting to thin out. The sun had totally vanished from the sky while the fireworks were going off in the twilight, and now true night had set in.

Mary switched on the "light" function on her cell phone, and used it to scan the ground as the last few revelers went by, eyeing her curiously.

"Lose something?" one man asked as he went by. "You need some help?"

"Oh," Mary said, laughing, "I'm just—" She didn't know exactly how to finish her sentence, but the man got her hint, smiled, and moved on.

If anything, the disruption of the crowd had been even worse than she thought. The whole road was a mess of footprints, some sandy, some damp, all impossibly mixed up together. If the girl had left any trace on the road itself, it had long since vanished.

As Mary approached the place where she had called out to the girl, though, she felt slightly more hopeful. The girl had disappeared down a narrow alley that ran between two fishing shanties, and although a huge amount of foot traffic had passed by it, there hadn't been much reason for anyone to drift off the beaten path—not with the impressive fireworks display going off overhead.

In fact, when Mary took a few steps down the narrow alley herself, holding her phone out to light her way, she realized by the weak beam of her phone that there didn't seem to be much reason for the girl to have ducked down the alley either. Mary hadn't been able to see it from the road at the time, but unlike many of the other back ways and footpaths that laced through the docks, this particular alley didn't lead anywhere. She'd thought the girl had just been going on her way. But standing in the short, blind alley between the two shanties, she suddenly realized she'd been wrong. The girl had either come down here for a very specific reason, or she'd been hiding from Mary.

Carefully, Mary shone her cell phone around the area, illuminating everything she could, looking for anything that might have drawn the girl, or any sign that anything had been hidden in the area—or removed from it. As far as she could see, the area didn't present many opportunities for stashing anything. It was just a narrow space between two unremarkable fishermen's shanties. No intriguing boxes, piles of nets, or even trash cans—just the ramshackle, weathered sides of the shanties and a small drift of sand on the asphalt between them, made eerie by the cell phone light.

Mary's heart began to beat a little faster. If the alley didn't lead anywhere, and if there was nothing here to draw the girl in, that strengthened her suspicion that the girl had been hiding from her. And why would any young girl hide from a friendly greeting, unless she hadn't wanted to be recognized? Her certainty that the girl she'd seen might have been Amanda after all increased, but at the same time, she could imagine trying to have another conversation to convince Chief McArthur, and she could already hear the skepticism in his voice. So her mysterious stranger had turned down a blind alley. What exactly did that prove? She could hear him ask it in her head, and she turned the cell phone around, scanning even the shingled walls of each shanty.

Wasn't there *any* scrap of proof here she could take to Chief McArthur? Then, in the blue light of the phone, she caught a flash of gold.

It disappeared back into the darkness so quickly that at first she thought she must have imagined it. But then she swept her cell phone light back over the shingled wall and caught the glimmer of gold again. This time, her hand froze, capturing the flash in the weak beam of her phone.

It took her another minute to recognize it: a strand of blonde hair, caught in the crack of one of the shanty's shingles.

A minute later, she was fumbling through her handbag, searching for something to collect the clue into. She briefly considered trying to retrieve it using a piece of paper torn from her weekly calendar, or a tissue, but then her hand closed on the first-aid kit she kept in her purse for emergencies. She hadn't been planning on an emergency exactly like this, but now that she had it in her hand, she realized it was perfect.

Still balancing her makeshift cell phone flashlight in one hand, she flipped the first-aid kit open to reveal a jumble of ointment, cotton swabs, sanitizer, tweezers, and a small ziplock bag of Band-Aids. Quickly, she dumped the Band-Aids in among the rest of the items, keeping hold of the ziplock bag, then pulled the tweezers free from their carrying case. She shut the lid of the case and replaced it in her purse. Then she shone the light back on the wall of the shanty again.

The delicate strand of gold hair flared up again in the bluish light. Very gently, so as not to break it, Mary used the pair of tweezers to work the single strand of hair free from the split in the wood that had caught and held it. When she'd pulled it free, she clamped it firmly between the tweezers, opened the bag, and dropped the hair in. Then, before it could fall out or blow free, she sealed the bag.

The hair was so light that it didn't add any discernible weight at all. She flashed her light through the plastic to make sure she'd captured the hair after all. When she was certain she had, she dropped it all in her bag: phone, hair, and all. Then she started back to town, in search of Chief McArthur.

After a brisk walk through town, she found him just where she'd seen him last: still at his post beside his car, outside the warehouse, which was now largely deserted, except for a few slow-moving float volunteers who were in the final throes of dismantling the last handful of floats.

This time, though, he was surrounded by a handful of the Ivy Bay police. There weren't many of them, but Mary recognized them as the bulk of the small local force, a couple of whom had been there earlier when Mary first approached the chief. Hope rose in Mary's heart as she walked up. If Chief McArthur had recalled so many of his men, maybe Amanda had already been found. That was the simplest explanation for all of this, after all—that there'd just been some mix-up: a case of nerves, a fight with her boyfriend, and that Amanda would just turn up on her own again. Especially if Mary was right that she'd seen Amanda down by the docks, there was no reason to believe that she wouldn't just eventually wander home, even if something had happened to make her feel she needed to get away from it all for a while.

But when Mary reached Ben, he didn't have the expression of a man wrapping up a case after a job well done. If anything, he looked even more worried than he had the last time she'd seen him. He was listening intently to someone who was speaking to him over a cell phone, nodding from time to time, and making notes.

"Yep," he said. "Yep, sure. And tomorrow's the earliest...? Okay, fine. Thanks."

After saying a few good-byes, he ended the connection and shook his head.

"Can't we keep looking for her tonight?" one of the deputies asked.

Chief McArthur shook his head. "You boys have been all over the town, and up and down the docks. If there was some accident or mistake, we'd have found her by now. No. Either she doesn't want us to find her, or someone else doesn't want her to be found. You all go on home. But I want you back fresh and ready first thing tomorrow morning."

Reluctantly, the other members of the police force began to drift off into the darkness. As they did, Chief McArthur looked up and saw Mary.

"Mary," he said. "How are you doing? On your way home?"

"Actually," Mary said, "I think I found something."

Suddenly, hope flared in the police chief's weary eyes. He stepped forward. "What?" he asked.

"I went back to the place where I saw that girl," Mary said, rummaging through her bag. "And I went around the corner where I saw her go. But it doesn't lead anywhere. She must have been looking for something there. Or hiding, from me."

When Mary had been lurking in the tiny alley, it had seemed obvious to her that this helped prove the mysterious girl was Amanda after all, but now that she told Chief McArthur, it didn't seem quite so convincing.

Chief McArthur was still watching her closely, though, waiting for her next words.

Her hands closed on the plastic bag in her purse. "And then I found this," she said, and pulled it out.

Chief McArthur took the plastic bag from her hands. He peered at it for a long moment. Then he looked up at Mary.

"What is this?" he asked.

"It's a hair," Mary said. "A blonde hair, just like the girl I saw."

Chief McArthur could barely hide his reluctance. "But Amanda isn't blonde," he repeated.

"I know that," Mary said. "But maybe this will tell us something. Even if the girl wasn't Amanda, she was acting suspicious, right around the time Amanda disappeared. You could test it, see what we can learn."

"I know you've been trying to help," he said kindly. "But chances are this is just a stray hair from someone who passed by months ago. Or one that got blown into the alley by somebody who was never there at all. But to be fair," he said, patting the pocket where he'd just put the hair, "this little strand of yours is just about as much as my guys and I have found to go on tonight."

"So you'll test it?" Mary asked.

Chief McArthur gave her a brief smile. "I'll have it tested," he promised. Then he stared out past the lights of town in the direction of the docks, and the dark water beyond. "At this point, I'm willing to do anything," he added. He shook his head. "Everything I do as a policeman, I think of it as trying to protect our kids. I don't like this a bit. Going home tonight, knowing one of our Ivy Bay children is missing..."

"She's a smart girl," Mary said, partly to comfort him, and partly to comfort herself. "Maybe there's just been some kind of mix-up. Maybe she's even on her way home right now."

Chief McArthur looked unconvinced, but he did manage to nod. "Well, let's hope so," he said.

"We can hope," Mary said. "And we can pray too."

"Now that kind of help I'll never object to," he said with a playful smile. Then he tipped his hat and got into the patrol car that had served as his makeshift office that night. "Good night," he said, and pulled out onto the street.

Mary stood alone for a minute, looking out toward the water as his lights faded around the corner. It was hard to believe that Amanda was really somewhere out there in that dark night, perhaps all on her own. God only knew where.

Only God knows, Mary thought. This was one of the many times when that really was true.

Lord, she prayed, *You know where Amanda is. Please be close to her, wherever she is. Protect her. Lead us to her. And bring her home safe.*

When she was finished, she felt a little more peaceful. But the uneasy feeling that she'd had since Betty told her about Amanda's disappearance didn't really go away. She looked around the empty warehouse and the empty street that had been bright with the sights and sounds of the parade and all the Fourth of July celebrants just a few hours ago. Part of her kept thinking that if she just turned in the right direction, she'd catch sight of Amanda, running up with her familiar smile and wave to explain everything. But the area remained quiet and dim.

FIVE

Mary came out of the back room of her store that night and glanced around the shadowy bookshop. Emergency or not, she'd had a new shipment come in that day. It would have been hard for her to unpack the new stock, check it against the orders, and put it out on the shelves for the holiday weekend rush, while still giving customers the personal attention Mary knew they loved. Mary may have felt exhausted after the long day, but the extra work she'd put in tonight would be well worth it.

And the truth was, she was restless, and she knew it would have been tough for her to fall right asleep. If there'd been anything more she could think of to do for Amanda, she'd have been out doing it. But she hadn't been able to think of a single thing. So she'd come here, to spend a little time putting things in order before the shop opened tomorrow. It felt good to be able to put at least some things in order: pull the books from their boxes, smell their new-book smell, and then carry them out to the shelves where they'd be displayed for tomorrow's crowds.

She'd left the light off in the front of the shop so that she wouldn't confuse customers into thinking the place was open at this late hour. That meant she'd had to pad from shelf to shelf in the moonlight to place the books where they belonged. But the moonlight was bright, and Mary actually got a kick out of padding around her store in the dark. It felt like being a kind of reverse cat burglar. Instead of sneaking into her shop to steal something, she had snuck into her shop to fill the shelves.

As she went by the register, she stopped and looked again at a small folder she'd pulled out when she first came in. She'd created it the week Amanda worked at the shop, for Amanda to hold any papers she needed in the course of her tasks there. The fact of the matter was, there wasn't a whole lot of paperwork left in the book business, except the books themselves. Most of Amanda's work had been done digitally. So Mary had only found one piece of paper in it: the receipt for a keepsake album Amanda had ordered with her employee discount. It hadn't seemed like much of a clue to Mary when she first dug it out earlier that day, and it still didn't.

She let the folder drop closed and glanced out the window.

Outside, a dark shadow filled the door.

It must be a customer, Mary thought, hoping maybe the shop was open because they'd caught sight of her inside.

She shook her head and called, "We're closed! Sorry!" through the glass.

The shadow didn't leave. Instead, it took a step closer.

Mary felt a quick thrill of fear, but she steadied herself and stepped briskly forward to shoo away the unwanted visitor.

But as she reached the door, the shadow finally stepped back, into the streetlight, and she recognized Henry's face. She felt a rush of relief, followed by a little pang of happiness.

"Henry!" she said, stepping through the door and then turning back to lock it up securely. "You almost scared me to death!"

"I'm sorry," Henry said. "I didn't realize you couldn't tell it was me until you tried to chase me away like any old customer."

"Well, you're hardly any old customer," Mary said. "And I have to say, I'm glad it was you and not someone else."

"I have to hand it to you," Henry said, "I couldn't tell you were scared. From the way you walked to the door, I was a little scared myself. What were you planning to do to your mystery visitor, exactly? Smack him with a hardcover?"

"I was going to figure that out when I got there," Mary said, and laughed. "What are you doing here at this hour?"

"I could ask you the same thing," Henry said with a smile. "I just watched the fireworks, and then I didn't quite feel like going home yet. I took a walk down Main Street and certainly didn't expect to see you in here, all lit up by the moon."

"Touché," Mary said with a chuckle. Then they stood on the warm sidewalk for a moment in companionable silence. She knew he was thinking about Misty, but she also knew how she had felt after John passed away. She didn't always want to try to put her feelings about him into words. Sometimes it was enough just to have some company. She was glad to provide that to Henry. And if he wanted to talk more about Misty, that was up to him.

"So what *are* you up to?" Henry finally asked.

"Well, actually, I was in the same boat as you. Just not quite ready to go home yet."

"Oh?" Henry asked. "Why not?"

"Well," Mary said, "have you heard about Amanda Branson?"

Henry shook his head. Quickly, Mary began to bring him up to speed on everything: Amanda's disappearance from the float, the girl she'd seen by the docks, and Chief McArthur's skepticism. As they talked, the two of them began to drift along Main Street, and before Mary knew it, Henry had delivered her to the sidewalk outside the house she shared with Betty.

"This is better than taxi service," she said, smiling.

"Door-to-door delivery," Henry said. "Unless you still don't feel like going home. We can take another spin around the block."

Mary shook her head. "Thanks," she said. "But it'll be good to be home. I just needed some time to clear my head."

"Well," Henry said, "I'm glad I ran into you tonight. It was good to see you."

"And I'm glad you were there to protect me from that person who was prowling around my bookshop," Mary said.

"Well, your prowler and I were one and the same person," Henry said. "So I'm not sure if I come out ahead in that math or not."

"It was good to see you," Mary assured him. "And my imaginary prowler just added a little excitement to the night, that's all."

"I'm afraid this night has already had more excitement than any of us might have liked," Henry said, his face turning serious.

"Well," Mary said, "there's nothing more we can do about it tonight. We'll just have to pray for her until the morning."

"You bet I will," Henry said. He watched until Mary reached the door of Betty's house. When she turned around to give him one last glance, he lifted his hand in a slight wave.

Mary found Betty nursing a cup of tea in the kitchen. When she walked in and saw her sister's tired expression, she felt a little tinge of guilt. Maybe, instead of taking care of things at the store, she should have been home, taking care of her sister. After all, even on good days, Betty's rheumatoid arthritis meant that she was pretty worn out by the end of the day. And this hadn't been any old day. Even before Amanda's disappearance, Betty had worked much harder than she normally would. And then her beloved float had turned into the central piece of a teenager's disappearance.

"Jack and company sleeping?" Mary asked Betty.

Her sister nodded, not yet looking up at Mary.

"How are you?" Mary asked gently, settling into the seat across from her sister.

Betty looked up then and gave her a rueful smile. "Well, I never thought I'd win best float in the Ivy Bay parade and still feel so deflated at the end of the day."

"Did you win?" Mary said, her voice rising in excitement. Despite everything that had happened that day, she knew that Betty had wanted to win top honors at the Fourth of July celebrations for years.

Betty nodded. "Bea Winslow came by after the parade to let me know we'd been chosen unanimously. She had no idea anything had happened with Amanda."

"Did you tell her?"

Betty shook her head. "I figured that wasn't my news to share. At least not yet, anyway. People will find out soon enough."

"Maybe," Mary said, "we'll have found her before too many other people even know she was ever gone."

"I'd like that ending to the story," Betty said. She took a sip of the tea and winced a little as she set it down.

"How do you feel?" Mary asked.

"Oh," Betty said, "you don't need to worry about me."

"I'm not worried," Mary said. "I'm curious. I just want to hear how my sister is doing."

"Well, if nothing had happened to Amanda on the float," Betty said, "I would have said it was a good day."

"I'm glad," Mary said.

"That's not to say I'm not sore," Betty said. "But sometimes that's just the cost of doing business. You can't spend all your time hiding out, worried about how your body is going to respond. It's not just about hopping out of bed like a spring chicken every morning. Sometimes it's about doing the things that make you want to get out of bed in the first place. Even if you feel it at the end of the day."

"It sounds like you've got some good memories from today," Mary said.

Betty nodded. "I do," she said. "And it's funny. When I was a young girl, maybe Amanda's disappearance would have spoiled everything. But the older I get in life, the more I realize you can't let the bad stuff spoil the good stuff for you. You've got to just take it all, good and bad, whenever it comes. And maybe sometimes even let the good stuff spoil the bad stuff."

Mary smiled.

Betty drained the last sip in her cup and stood. "I'd better be getting to bed," she said. But when she reached the doorway to the kitchen, she turned back. "You know what?" she said. "I'd like to pray for that girl before I turn in."

"That sounds good," Mary said gratefully. She'd been struggling all night with the sense that she wished she could do more. And praying for Amanda wasn't just a way to push away her anxiety. It might actually be the most important thing they could do.

Right there in the doorway, Betty bowed her head. Mary, at the table, bowed hers as well.

"Lord," Betty said, "we don't always understand everything that You do. And we don't know where Amanda is, or what she's doing right now. But You do. And we know that, no matter what's happening, all of us need You. So we just ask that You would be with Amanda right now. Protect her and comfort her. Be with her family, and be with the people who are trying to find her."

Betty paused for a moment. Mary actually glanced up, thinking that perhaps her sister had finished praying. But Betty's head was still bowed, and after a moment, she went on.

"And, Lord, this might be impossible to ask from anyone but You. It certainly looks like it might be impossible, just from what we can see now of the situation. But I want to ask that You wouldn't just take care of Amanda wherever she is. I want to ask that You'd bring something good out of this, for Amanda, and her family."

This time, when Mary looked up, she caught Betty peering at her from the other side of the kitchen. Both of their faces broke into wide grins.

"Amen," the sisters said in unison.

SIX

————◆◆◆————

Mary stepped into the kitchen and smiled at the sight of her son Jack standing by the sink, sipping from an early morning cup of coffee. She padded over to him and gave him a hug. Years ago, he'd been tiny enough to hold in one arm. Now the top of her head barely reached his shoulder.

Jack chuckled as he set his coffee cup on the counter. "I still feel like a kid sneaking sips of Dad's coffee when I drink this stuff in Ivy Bay," he said.

"Well," Mary said, stepping back to look up at him, "it didn't seem to stunt your growth."

"Who knows?" Jack said. "Maybe I could have been in the NBA. Can I get you a cup?"

Mary shook her head. "No, thanks," she said, and looked down at the day's issue of the *Ivy Bay Bugle*, which he'd already collected and laid out on the kitchen table. She sank down into a seat and scanned the front page article under Johanna Montgomery's familiar byline about Amanda's disappearance. They must have gone to press with it early the night before. It didn't contain any of the details that Mary had gathered from Chief McArthur or shared with him herself. Mostly it was just column after column of information everyone in town already knew: that Amanda was a well-liked, popular girl with a strong academic record, and that nobody who had been near the event seemed to have any idea of what could have happened or where she was now.

"Anything new?" Jack asked.

Mary shook her head. "It's old news already," she said. "It's just so hard to understand why she'd run away, or why anyone would want to take her."

"Well, teenage girls…," Jack said. "I thought they were complicated when I was a teenager. Now that I'm a dad, I realize they're even more complicated than I dreamed back then."

Mary smiled. "Hang in there," she said. "Daisy might not show it now, but one day, she'll be grateful she has a dad who wants to spend time with her."

Jack shook his head. "Some days I wonder," he said. He glanced down at the paper, with Amanda's smiling face in a recent school photo. "But then you see something like this. I can't imagine what her parents must feel like."

"Her mother must be frantic," Mary agreed.

"And her father too," Jack said, sounding a little put out.

Mary patted his hand. "I'm sure, honey," she said. "It's just that I don't know him. He doesn't live in town."

She stood as she spoke. Talking about Amanda's mother Heather had given Mary an idea. She'd gotten friendly with Heather when she'd pop into the shop to visit Amanda. Chief McArthur obviously had the criminal investigation under control. But what if there was some other explanation? Heather might be in need of some company right now. But she might also know something that would help Mary put two and two together and lead them all to Amanda.

"You know," Mary said, "I wonder if it might be good for me to go over and check on Heather. Just see how she's doing. If there's anything I can do."

Jack smiled. "And maybe find a clue?" he asked.

Mary planted a kiss on his cheek. "I may not be an official Ivy Bay police detective," she said, "but I figure the more people who are looking for Amanda, the better."

Jack nodded as she went to the door. "You've always been a good detective, Mom," he said. "I could never put anything over on you when I was a kid."

"You see," she said, "that's how I went to detective school. Making sure you didn't drop all your vitamins down the heating vent."

"I got out of a day's worth that way," Jack said with a grin.

"But only one day!" Mary reminded him. She planted a quick kiss on his cheek as she went out the door. "I'll be back soon," she promised.

Jack squeezed her arm. "Can't wait," he said.

———

A few minutes later, Mary pulled up outside Amanda's house, just a few blocks away from Betty's, in a neighborhood of slightly smaller homes. Mary had visited it before, when she dropped Amanda off after an afternoon shift, so she quickly recognized the classic Cape Cod, with trim yellow shingles and blue shutters.

She was slightly surprised not to see a police car outside, but, she told herself as she walked up the front walk between neat rows of sea grass planted on either side, it didn't make sense for any available officers to be at Amanda's home, since it was the one place they could be sure she wasn't. There was a good chance they'd already been here to collect any clues they could find and then taken off to continue the search for Amanda.

It took Heather so long to answer the door after Mary knocked that Mary started to wonder if Heather was there either. But just as Mary began to shuffle on the porch, wondering if she should knock again, or just head for home, the door opened.

Mary remembered Heather as a vibrant, outgoing woman with a pretty face and a cloud of blonde curls. But she barely recognized the person who answered the door. She was dressed, despite the early hour, but with a closer look, Mary guessed that might be because she had slept in her clothes. Her once-crisp pink collared shirt was creased, and her jeans were rumpled. Her curls were tousled and unkempt. But her face showed the most strain of all. Her skin was grayish with fatigue and worry, and her eyes were red.

When she saw Mary, she didn't even say anything, just caught her in a tight hug. For what seemed like minutes, she held on without letting go. When she finally released Mary, Heather's eyes were full of tears.

"Mary," she said, "thank you so much for coming. I had friends with me till late last night, but I finally sent them home to get some sleep."

"You don't look like you got much yourself," Mary commented.

"You're a mom too, aren't you?" Heather asked.

Silently, Mary nodded.

"Could you sleep if one of your kids was missing?" Heather said.

Mary knew she didn't really need to answer that. Of course she couldn't. She pressed Heather's hand.

"Is there anything I can do?" she asked.

Heather took a deep breath and led Mary over to the living room couch. A stack of misplaced cushions told the story of where Heather had spent the wee hours of the night. "I just wish I knew what to ask," she said. "I've already been in touch with the police this morning. They're doing everything they can."

"Anything?" Mary began, then trailed off.

Heather shook her head. "I think they were hoping I'd tell them she'd come home." A tear slid down her cheek. She didn't bother to wipe it off. "I wish she had," she said.

Mary put her arm around Heather's shoulder as she cried, then pulled herself together.

"I'm sorry," she said. "I keep thinking I've got myself under control, but I don't think you ever really can in a situation like this. I don't know how to explain it. Nobody else could understand how it feels."

Mary patted Heather's arm gently, thinking back on Jack, and how he'd insisted that a father would be just as upset over a missing child as a mother. "What about Amanda's father?" she asked. Things might not have worked out between him and Heather, she thought. But at a time like this, he would be the only other person in the world who understood the depth of Heather's worry over Amanda. And maybe he'd even have some clues.

She was surprised by the violence of Heather's reaction. "*Him*," Heather almost hissed. "He gave up any right to call himself Amanda's father seventeen years ago."

Mary's hand slipped off Heather's arm as Heather twisted to look at her, her puffy eyes bright with anger. "I'm sorry," Mary said. "I didn't know."

Heather's shoulders slumped and she shook her head. "No, no," she said. "You're right to ask. The police did too."

"So they've been in touch with him?" Mary asked.

Heather shrugged. "I wouldn't know," she said. "I haven't talked with him since Amanda was only two months old. That's when he left us. Me with a baby and nothing more than a few years' experience waiting tables at the fish fry down on the docks." These words seemed to come to her a lot easier than the few things she'd been able to stammer out about Amanda's disappearance. Mary had the sense that this was a story that had been told, and told again. "Just up and left," Heather went on. "No note or anything. No explanation. And he never showed a lick of interest in her after that. Not even a phone call on her birthday. He didn't even pay us child support until she was three, when the courts got involved. But I told them I never wanted to hear his voice again. Not after what he did to me—and especially Amanda. He was never a good man, not even while he was here. I never felt"—she paused—"safe with him. So that's all handled by lawyers. That's whose number I gave to the police. They'll have to find him through the court, I guess. If they can find him at all."

Mary patted Heather's shoulder again. "That's hard," she said.

"Not for me," Heather said. "I always say that Hank walking out on me was the best thing that ever happened to me. I should have known he was trouble from the beginning. I was just too young and too in love. But him walking out on Amanda: Well, that just shows you what kind of man he was."

Mary took a deep breath. "I knew he didn't live in town," she said. "But I didn't realize the situation."

"I don't talk about it much," Heather said. "Me and Amanda, we have a good life together. Just the two of us, against the world. That's what we like to say. I don't like to dwell on the bad things. Just on everything we've got. That's how I was, even back then. I put my waitress apron back on, and I went back to the restaurant, and I worked to take care of my baby. And then one day, they asked me to be manager, instead of a waitress. And a few years later, someone asked me to manage another restaurant, where I didn't have to work those evening hours. I managed to make a life for us, even without him. What doesn't kill us just makes us stronger. That's what I always tell Amanda."

When she said her daughter's name, tears filled her eyes. "There I go again," she said. "I just don't get used to it. I can't believe she's still missing."

"A missing child isn't something you're supposed to get used to," Mary told her, squeezing her hand. "And you're not going to, because we're going to find her, wherever she is, and we're going to bring her back."

As she spoke, she looked around the room, taking in anything she could about Amanda and her life with her mother. The living room wasn't remarkable: just a small amount of inexpensive but tasteful furniture, with a few pictures scattered here or there, all of Amanda, or Amanda and her mother. It was clear that the two of them were very close. But there weren't many personal signs of Amanda in the main room. Mary felt for Heather in her distress, but she also itched to get a look at anything else that might help her to find Amanda.

"Have the police already looked around for any clues?" Mary asked.

Heather nodded. "But they didn't stay for very long. They tried to keep it under wraps in front of me, but I heard them talking in the hall outside her room. They took her computer as standard practice, but the deputy said they didn't expect to find much on it. They don't think she walked away on her own. They think someone took her. So they didn't think the clues they needed would be here. They thought they were somewhere"—she gestured into the bright sunshine outside her front window as her voice broke—"out there."

Mary held Heather's hand until the spell of tears passed, but she couldn't help remembering the figure she'd taken for Amanda, slipping into the shadows of the docks.

"What do you think?" she said.

"About what?" Heather sniffled.

"Well," Mary said, treading carefully, since Heather was obviously volatile, "can you think of any reason Amanda might have had for wanting to get away? Anyplace she might have wanted to go?"

Heather looked at her as if she had just started speaking in another language, and she couldn't understand a word Mary was saying.

"Why?"

Mary held her tongue for a minute, considering her answer. "You know Amanda so much better than I do," she said finally. "That's why I thought you might have some idea."

Heather seemed genuinely shocked. "What could make her want to do this?" she asked. "Leave without telling me where she was going? Stay away all night? Why would she do something like that? We're so close. She knows doing anything like that would kill me. She would never do something like that."

Mary nodded. It was hard to argue with Heather. Mary had trouble imagining Amanda doing anything like this of her own will too. Still, she didn't have an explanation for the Amanda look-alike she'd seen the night before. And as Jack had been saying, teenage girls were complicated. They were still figuring out who they were. And sometimes, their experiments didn't work exactly the way they'd planned.

Mary glanced at the door to the hall where Amanda's room must be. Heather caught her glance.

"Do you think there's anything the police might have missed?" she asked. "Any clue to whoever might have done this?"

Mary shook her head. "I don't know," she said.

"I wanted to look, but I just couldn't," Heather said. "When the police came, I took them down there, but I just couldn't go in. I stood in the door and looked at all her things, and I just started crying and crying. One of the deputies had to bring me back out here to the couch. I was crying so hard I couldn't even put one foot in front of the other."

Mary gave her hand another comforting squeeze. "Well," she said, "I'd be glad to take a look. If you didn't mind, that is."

"Do you think?" Heather said. "I just keep thinking…, maybe there's something there that could tell us something else. Someone she knows who might have done something like this?" Her voice dissolved into tears. "Amanda did say you were a bit of a local mystery solver," she managed after a minute. "And I just couldn't go through her things. Not right now. But I'd feel so much better if I knew nothing was missed."

"Well," Mary said, rising from the couch and trying not to seem too eager, "it never hurts to look."

SEVEN

———◆◆◆———

A manda's room seemed just like Amanda did: clean, light, orderly. Her bed was neatly made, and her clothes hung by color in her closet. She'd made a collage of magazine pages, drawings, and mementos on one wall, and Mary was touched to see that she'd included several book covers from the promotional materials that had come to Mary's bookshop while Amanda had worked there. Mary hadn't known that the week they'd spent together had affected Amanda so much, but it felt good to know that the time Mary had invested in her meant something to Amanda as well.

The only thing that was out of place was the large blank spot on Amanda's desk—where an Ethernet cord and a power cord both ran up to the space where Amanda's computer had been before the police took it.

For a minute, Mary hesitated in the doorway. Jack was right that she'd been a bit of a detective in keeping up with her own children's lives. As far as she was concerned, it was a mom's job to keep up to date on what her kids were doing— who their friends were, what kinds of books and music and TV shows they were interested in. But she'd never been the kind of mother who snooped through her children's things, went into their rooms without their permission, or read their diaries. That had never felt right to her, and the idea of going through Amanda's room felt strange for the same reasons.

But these weren't normal circumstances, she had to remind herself. This wasn't prying. Amanda was missing, maybe in danger, and Amanda's mother had asked Mary to find anything that might help.

She took a deep breath and stepped into the room.

It was small, just like the rest of the house, and Amanda kept it so neat that there didn't seem to be many places to hide anything. Gingerly, Mary pulled out the drawers of her dresser and pushed the sweaters and T-shirts this way and that. She found a few sachets and a small stuffed rabbit, but nothing that would explain Amanda's disappearance. Amanda's closet held nothing but clothes, and the shoe boxes stacked neatly below her skirts and dresses contained nothing but shoes. Her jewelry hung on a series of colorful novelty doorknobs that she might have installed herself beside her mirror. The necklaces and bracelets were beautifully organized, one per knob, and not one seemed to be out of place. In the shallow drawer of Amanda's vanity, Mary found a small cache of letters tied with ribbon. When she undid them, she found a handful of notes, all signed by Amanda's boyfriend, Jared. Mary scanned through them quickly, with the sense that she was trespassing, but she quickly discovered that Jared wasn't one of the world's most innovative correspondents. All the letters seemed to follow about the same pattern: He'd tell her he was bored in this class or that, that he missed her, and couldn't wait until he saw her again. Sometimes he'd add a compliment at the end, but he always signed, "Love, Jared."

Carefully, Mary retied the letters and replaced them. Amanda's bed and desk took up the rest of the room. Mary flipped the bedcovers up so she could see anything hidden under the mattress and found a collection of seasonal clothes in matching plastic tubs, but even a quick search through each of the tubs didn't turn up anything out of the ordinary. The only unusual thing was Amanda's talent for organization relative to the other teenage girls of Mary's acquaintance. With her own daughter Lizzie, she'd had to fight numerous battles over the question of whether the huge mess Lizzie liked to cultivate in her room during her teen years did or did not constitute her freedom of expression as guaranteed by the United States Constitution.

After Mary recovered from her foray under the bed, she clambered to her feet and confronted the desk. It was small, but even a small desk could entail weeks' worth of sorting, as she'd learned during her skirmishes with Lizzie years ago and continued to be reminded of by the piles of paper that she continually did battle with in order to keep her own front counter at the shop neat.

As she looked it over, she realized something. Even though the room was tiny, she hadn't seen the keepsake album that Amanda had purchased through her shop. Had the police taken it?

She slipped back out into the living room where Heather still sat.

"Heather?" she asked. "Do you remember the police taking an album with them?"

"An album?" Heather said, then shook her head. "No," she said. "No, they didn't."

"*Hmm*," Mary said.

"That's not a surprise, really," Heather told her. "Amanda's never been a big one for albums. Neither of us is, actually. We like to live in the present, not in the past."

Mary didn't contradict Heather. "Well, thank you," she said, and started back toward Amanda's room.

"Did you find anything?" Heather asked.

"Not yet," Mary said.

When she went back into Amanda's room, she confronted the desk again. It was the only thing big enough to hide an album of the size Amanda had ordered from her shop.

She pulled open one of the deep drawers on the left-hand side. It took her a moment to understand what she was looking at, but when she did, she laughed out loud. The drawer was hung with file folders, neatly labeled by subject: British Literature, Geometry, World History, Spanish, Chemistry. A quick flip through their contents revealed that the labels were as accurate as they were neat, and that Amanda seemed to organize her assignments, both past and current, by date, with the materials she needed to complete the current assignment filed at the front of the file.

No wonder she had such a good GPA, Mary thought, with a mixture of disbelief and admiration.

The other drawers were the same way. Mary found pencils, pens, tape, scissors, a stapler, and a candy box full of paper clips in the center drawer of the desk, all neatly placed and easy to reach. The drawer on the right-hand side wasn't rigged with files, but it was just as neatly organized into what seemed to be an archive of materials from Amanda's previous projects and classes. Mary found materials for a science project about the distances between stars and note cards for a presentation on Don Juan, all labeled in cardboard boxes. Amanda had even allowed herself one box labeled "junk," but even this one was a carefully chosen treasure of memories: movie tickets, theater programs, and a few dried roses. Mary sorted through the ticket stubs and programs, but most of them were years old, and none of them seemed out of the ordinary.

It was as she was replacing that box in its spot at the back of the drawer that Mary noticed it didn't fit in quite as easily as it had come out. She turned the box slightly, to see if it was just a matter of orientation, but it still didn't fit.

The back of the drawer was hidden in the darkness of the desk. She slipped her hand in to see if there was anything she'd missed.

Her heart leapt a little when her hand closed on another cardboard box, slimmer than the rest. But when she pulled it out, her face fell at the sight of one of Amanda's now-familiar labels: US History.

Still, she'd looked through everything else. Automatically, she lifted the brown kraft cover from the box. When she did, her heart jumped in earnest.

Inside was the album Amanda had ordered from Mary's shop, on top of a whole jumble of other items. Instead of the neat lines of Amanda's handwriting, or the carefully typed and stapled reports and papers, the album and box were full of scraps of newspaper, photocopies, and notes scrawled on whatever paper must had been at hand: a half sheet noting library hours, an advertisement for heirloom seeds. The first item Mary read didn't seem to mean much of anything. It was simply an address in Ivy Bay, on the other side of town. But the next one made her skin tingle. It was a newspaper article from almost twenty years ago, covering a home football game, where a "Hank Branson" had scored the winning touchdown. Was this Amanda's father? Under his name in the article were two faint dots, as if someone had rested their pen under each word for just a moment as they read it. The boy's handsome face, square-jawed, with laughing eyes, stared out from the senior picture one of his parents had likely provided to the local paper to accompany the article. The next item was a sheaf of copies of academic records with Hank's name on them: grades for his sophomore, junior, and senior years. Under that was a printout that seemed to be from a genealogy site for the Branson family. Beside some of the names of family members who were still living, Amanda had written local addresses or phone numbers. The box also contained several pages that had been copied from decades-old yearbooks, all containing shots of Hank. Under a whole collection of items like this, all containing some piece of information or connection to a man Mary could only assume was Amanda's father, Mary found a scrap of newspaper in the bottom of the box.

Although it was at the bottom, it was actually the most recent piece of information about Hank Branson in the stack. It was a simple news item, little more than a mention, about a business he had opened up in Boston several years ago: Branson Seafood Company. No phone number or address was listed.

Mary stared down at the article. Was this how Amanda's apparent search for her father had begun? she wondered. Had she run across this mention of her father in a paper and set off on this investigation, which she had obviously hidden from her mother?

She also felt a chill as she looked down into the eyes of the young man in photograph after photograph. He looked friendly enough, mugging with his friends or posing in his football uniform.

But he also looked big. Powerful enough to threaten someone into doing something. Or to simply have the strength to carry them off. Especially a young girl. Heather's words echoed in her head: *"He was never a good man . . . I never felt safe with him."*

Had Heather warned her daughter about her father? Or had she kept the problems she'd had with him secret, so that when Amanda went looking for him, she had no idea what she was getting into?

Whatever the case, the fact that Amanda had been researching her father in the months before she disappeared was key. Mary replaced the lid on the box, and carried it back out to the living room, where Heather was sitting on the couch, staring dully at a photograph of her and Amanda from several years ago, when Amanda looked to be about ten or eleven years old. Her hair was in pigtails, but she already had the unmistakable smile that Mary knew so well.

"Heather," Mary said, wondering how to phrase this. She decided to introduce the idea slowly. "I think I may have found something."

Maybe the best way, she thought, was to let Heather see for herself. She sat down beside Heather on the couch and handed her the box.

"What is this?" Heather said. "One of Amanda's school projects?"

"Not exactly," Mary said.

Heather lifted the box and looked blankly at the album and the stack of papers. "What is it?" she said.

Mary had expected the sight of her ex-husband's name, or even one of his pictures, to spark some insight for Heather, but she just sifted through the papers, almost unseeing. "I don't understand," she said.

Mary sighed quietly. After all, Heather was under the huge stress of a missing child and hadn't slept much. Mary couldn't be sure how observant she'd be under those circumstances either. She pulled out the old news article with Hank's picture and laid it on top.

"Hank?" Heather said.

Mary nodded.

"What is this doing here?" Heather asked, her voice turning ugly. "Where did this come from? How did this get in my house?"

She looked at Mary accusingly, as if Mary might have brought it in just to torment her.

"I found this in Amanda's room," Mary said gently. "It looks to me like she was trying to learn about her father."

"What?" Heather cried.

"There are all kinds of details here," Mary said gently. "She was looking up family members on the Branson side. She apparently looked up his academic records while she was working in the school office."

"But why would she *do* that?" Heather exclaimed.

Mary had seen Heather teary before, but now she was working herself up to a whole other level. Her voice rose and her eyes widened.

In response, Mary dropped her own voice. "Well, it's natural that a girl might be interested in knowing her father," she said. "Especially if he hasn't been around for her to get to know." Before Heather could interrupt, she rushed on to the central question. "There's information here that might have helped her find his current whereabouts. I heard you say that you didn't feel safe around him. Listen, if Amanda did find him and reached out to him, do you think she could be in any danger?"

"She would never do that!" Heather said, her voice high and her eyes now full of tears. "She knows what that man did to me! To us! She wouldn't ever want anything to do with him. She told me so herself! She—"

Heather's tirade was broken off by the sound of the doorbell. Mary twisted in her seat. Through the glass of the front door, she could see two women on the front porch, waving. Mary nodded and stood.

Heather's silence didn't last for long. When Mary got up to answer the door, Heather broke into sobs.

"Oh, honey!" one of the women said when Mary answered the door. She was petite and plump, with short, shiny dark hair, and she rushed over to Heather on the couch. "Honey, I'm so sorry. We should have gotten here sooner."

Heather wrapped her arms around the woman and buried her face in her shoulder.

Mary quickly recognized the other woman as Julia Martin, who attended Grace Church. They'd gotten to know each other, although not well, when they'd both volunteered at various church food drives and meal services for the poor. But somehow small talk about the next soup kitchen didn't seem appropriate now. "How is she doing?" Julia said, her voice low. "I didn't realize you were friends with Heather too."

Mary nodded. "I'm a friend of Amanda's," she said. "She did an independent study at my store. I just thought I'd come by to check on Heather."

"Thanks," Julia said. "We were here until after midnight. I wanted to stay, but she wouldn't let us."

"I'm sure she's glad you're here," Mary said.

"If you can be glad," Julia answered. "Under the circumstances."

Mary went back to the couch. The box full of scraps and copies had fallen to the side of Heather's lap as she embraced her friend. Quickly, Mary retrieved it.

"Heather," she said, "I think this might be something good to share with the police. Do you mind if I just take this with me?"

Heather waved her hand without looking up.

Julia looked at Mary quizzically. "What is it?" she asked.

"It's some research it looks like Amanda might have been doing," Mary told her. "On her father."

Julia's face soured. "Hank?" she said. "He never cared about Amanda enough to be mixed up in anything like this."

"Well," Mary said, tucking the box under her arm, "it's nice to see you. Heather's lucky to have such good friends."

"Well, we'd all want a friend, wouldn't we?" Julia said. "At a time like this."

Back in her car, Mary quickly dialed Chief McArthur's number at the police station. A clerk she didn't recognize answered. "I'm sorry, he's not available right now," she said.

"I've got information that I think might help him on the Branson disappearance," Mary said. "Are you able to get in touch with him?"

"Please hold," the woman said.

A few moments later, the chief's voice crackled over the line, obviously patched in from some kind of cell-forwarding system. "Yes?" he said. "Go ahead."

"Chief," Mary said. "It's Mary."

She heard a pause on the other end of the line. Obviously, this information hadn't been communicated to him yet. "Hello, Mary," he said. "What can I do for you?"

"I've just come from Amanda's house," Mary said. "And I found something there. A box full of research Amanda had been doing on her father. Her mother didn't know about it. And she says her father might be dangerous. I'm just worried that—"

"Well, thanks, Mary," Chief McArthur interrupted. "On a case like this, we want to run down every lead. But I'm afraid we're a step ahead of you here. I spoke with Amanda's father last night and had the Boston PD pay him a visit this morning. He's just as worried as we are."

"I see," Mary said. The visions she'd had, of an older and more sinister version of the young man in the photographs, fleeing across the country with an unwilling Amanda in tow, mercifully vanished.

"Is there anything else?" Chief McArthur asked.

"Yes. I think you will find this interesting. She has this whole box. It was hidden in her desk, and it's very thorough. She was researching her relatives on her father's side. Digging up his grades from high school and old yearbook photos. It's clear she has a lot of curiosity about him."

"That is interesting," Chief McArthur said.

Mary thought for a moment. "So Amanda hasn't reached out to her father, then?"

"Uh-uh," he said. "But if she does, we'll be the first ones he calls. He is as anxious as we are."

"Is he coming to Ivy Bay? For the investigation?" Mary asked.

"I told him to stay put in Boston," Chief McArthur said. "In case she comes looking for him. With this box you found, sounds to me like that's even better advice than I thought it was."

Mary could hear another voice begin speaking in the background.

"What's that?" Chief McArthur said to the person on the other end. Then he came back to her. "Mary, sorry," he said. "We've got another lead on this fellow down by the bank. I've got to go."

EIGHT

Mary sat for a long moment with the box in one hand and her phone in the other. Every clue she'd found in this case had seemed so promising until she'd taken them to the chief. But every time she'd brought him something, she'd wound up feeling like a kid digging in the sand: all excited about the shell she found, until she realized that every other kid on the beach had found one too.

Still, she thought, as she set the box on the seat beside her, even though the clues she'd found had seemed small, she trusted her gut that they must add up to something. She began to think through the events of the past several hours. Who had the girl down by the docks been? Even if it wasn't Amanda, why had she hidden from Mary? Whose was that strand of hair between the fishing shanties? When had Amanda developed her interest in her father? And did it have anything to do with her disappearance? Her clues might not have answered the chief's questions, but he hadn't been able to explain her clues away either.

She sighed, buckled her seat belt, and started to tuck her phone into her purse for the drive home.

As she did, she noticed a text message waiting for her. It was from Henry. "Just wanted to thank you for the talk last night," it said. "Glad to have a friend like you. And glad to know you're on Amanda's trail. I'm praying for you, and her."

Mary smiled. The message was just the encouragement she'd needed, when she'd been tempted to doubt herself. She started again to put the phone in her bag.

Then it rang.

It took Mary a minute to place the voice, although the woman on the other line spoke with all the warmth and familiarity someone might lavish on their oldest friend.

"*Mary,*" she said somewhat breathlessly. "How are you *doing?*"

"Fine," Mary said, her mind working to identify the speaker.

"I'm so glad I caught you," the woman said. "I tried over at the store first, but Rebecca said you hadn't been in yet. I've just organized a little gathering of our prayer group, and I wanted to make sure you knew about it."

Now Mary knew exactly who she was talking to: Dorothy Johnson. When her pastor had invited Mary to start up a women's prayer group at church, he'd also suggested that Mary invite Dorothy to join. Dorothy was used to leading things at the church: She was in charge of the altar flowers, the spaghetti suppers, and the wedding planning. And sometimes Dorothy's constant suggestions and hints of disapproval were so frustrating to deal with that Mary just felt like giving in to her. But Dorothy had never gone and outright scheduled a meeting that Mary didn't even know about before. Mary gave her head a slight shake before she answered. Jack and Christa and Daisy were waiting for her at home, and she wanted to get back as quickly as possible to spend time with them.

"A meeting?" she said. "Today? But we already have one scheduled for Wednesday, and that's only a few days away."

"Well, yes," Dorothy said. "But this is an emergency meeting. For Amanda. I just couldn't sleep last night, thinking about that poor girl. And I was so frustrated that there was nothing I could do for her. But then I realized there was something: We could pray. So I just called up a few of the girls, and we're all going to meet over at the church in a few minutes, before the day gets too busy. We'd love it if you could come."

Mary stifled a sigh. Of course, Dorothy was right— instead of running all over town, it did make sense to stop and pray for Amanda.

Mary hadn't meant it this way, but her long silence seemed to make Dorothy nervous. "I hope it's all right that I planned this meeting," she said. "I didn't mean to overstep anything."

"No," Mary hurried to say. "It's a good idea. I'm glad you want to pray for Amanda. You say you're meeting in a few minutes?"

"At the church," Dorothy said. "In the prayer chapel."

"I'll try to make it," Mary said, and hung up.

A moment later, she dialed Jack's cell phone. After a few rings, he answered, his voice cheerful. "Mom!" he said. "You on your way home? Your timing's perfect. Daisy just got up, and we're making plans for the day."

Mary wondered briefly whether Daisy's face would be as cheerful if she could see her. "Well," she said, "that's why

I'm calling. They're holding a prayer meeting for Amanda up at the church. I hate to miss any time with you, but I—"

As she hesitated, Jack broke in. "Don't even think twice about it, Mom," he said. "We're very well situated here. After all, Aunt Betty's is the best hotel in town."

Mary smiled.

"And I know you've been working to find Amanda, but it sounds to me like this is every bit as important as everything else you've been doing. We can take care of ourselves for a little while longer."

"Are you sure about that?" Mary said.

Jack laughed. This was a standard joke between the two of them. No matter how old Jack got, Mary never stopped reminding him to bring a coat if it was cold or to drive carefully if it was dark. Jack loved to ask her how she thought he'd managed all these years by himself, when she wasn't around to take care of him. Now she was making the joke for him. "Pretty sure," he said. "Don't worry about it. You'll be home before we know it."

"Thanks for understanding," Mary said.

"Well," Jack said, "maybe we'll add some of our prayers to yours right here at the breakfast table."

"That sounds good," Mary told him. "See you soon."

"Love you," Jack said, signing off.

It was a smaller group than usual when she reached the church, just Bernice, Dorothy, and Jill, who was dressed in a soccer league T-shirt, with her blonde hair pulled back into a loose ponytail. Bernice's friendly face crinkled into a smile when Mary walked in.

"I think that's everyone," Dorothy said, as Mary settled into the small circle of comfortable stuffed chairs in the back of the sanctuary. Mary felt another flash of annoyance at the suggestion that she was the latecomer to a meeting she'd just heard about five minutes before, but she stifled it as Jill started to speak, her eyes wide.

"I'm so glad we're having this meeting," she said. "As a mother, this has just been a terrible day for me. I can't imagine what Heather's going through. But it also makes me worry about my own kids. You just never know what's out there. And you can't protect them from everything, no matter how hard you try. I was even nervous about leaving them at the soccer game to come here. If their dad hadn't been at the field too, I don't know if I would have. Not today, anyway."

Bernice patted her hand. "When we think like that, worry wins," she said, her voice sweet as ever, but firm. "It's hard, but we have to learn to trust God with our kids."

"Well, He gave them to us to take care of them," Jill said.

Bernice nodded. "Yes," she said. She shook her head solemnly. "Poor Heather. This is not the kind of 'letting go' parents prepare for when we raise our children. The kind where we realize our kids are going to grow up and move off to New York City, or—"

"Arizona?" Jill said, with a smile. That was where Bernice's own daughter lived, and the prayer group did a fair amount of praying for her life out west, even though she was a mother herself now.

Bernice nodded. "Right," she said. "If we do our jobs right, someday they'll probably wind up someplace where we *can't* take care of them. Because we'll have taught them how to take care of themselves. And if we don't practice that right now, while they're still under our roofs…well, it can be a hard road, when parents can't let go. Not just for the parents, but for the kids too."

Jill nodded. "I know what you're saying," she said. "I've seen it too. But it's just so hard, sometimes, especially with something like this happening in town. And that girl who vanished up north a few weeks ago.…It just makes you wonder if something else is going on. If there's some stranger among us on the Cape, after our kids."

Mary's mind flashed back to the description of the suspicious-seeming stranger people remembered seeing by the bank. Until now, she'd dismissed him. But she hadn't heard any other stories of kids disappearing from the area before. "I didn't hear about that," she said.

Jill turned to her. "It's probably nothing," she said. "It's just, there was another girl who disappeared from a town a lot like ours. Late last month. Just a few miles up the coast."

"Well, people do go missing," Dorothy said. She probably meant to sound comforting, but it came out more like a teacher scolding a slow child. "But they're not always connected. And sometimes they don't want to be found."

"But these are *kids*," Jill insisted. "And I talked to a woman up there when our travel team played them in soccer. She said people saw a strange man in town right before the girl went missing. And when she vanished, so did he."

"But they found that girl, didn't they?" Bernice asked. "I thought I read something about her coming home."

Jill looked a little abashed. "I don't know," she said. "The soccer game was a few weeks ago. I hadn't heard anything since."

"I think that girl was all right in the end," Bernice said.

"Are you sure?" Mary asked.

"Not positive," Bernice said. "Why do you ask?"

Mary shrugged. She had only gotten her information about the stranger by the bank because she'd been in the area of a police investigation, and she didn't want to turn what could be an important clue to an item of town gossip.

Jill shook her head. "It just shows how a mother's mind can go crazy with these things, if you let it."

Mary gave Jill's shoulders a little squeeze. "That's just a sign of how much you care for your kids," she said. "It's a good thing. But maybe we should pray now, since God's the only One who knows the answers to all these questions."

"That sounds good," Jill said gratefully.

Together, the four women bowed their heads. As each of them prayed, Mary felt the anxiety and pressure she'd felt since she'd heard about Amanda's disappearance lift from her shoulders. She didn't have any new answers, but she wasn't carrying the weight of the world anymore either. The worry she'd heard in Jill's voice vanished too, as Jill prayed for Amanda, someone else's child, to be safe wherever she was and to return home soon. And as Dorothy took her turn to lift the situation up to God, Mary's annoyance at her melted away. Dorothy might seem condescending and controlling sometimes, but there was no missing the sincerity of her prayers. She almost seemed like a different person when she prayed. Instead of the polite posturing she seemed to do with everyone else, when she spoke to God, she was humble and direct. And she talked to Him as if He were a real person, just sitting there with them, waiting to hear what they had to say. Most people were comfortable talking with each other, but when it was time to pray, they slipped into all kinds of strange, pious, or formal religious language: not what they really meant, but whatever they imagined God might like to hear. Dorothy was almost the opposite. She could be relentlessly formal with other people, but when she addressed God, all her defenses and poses came down. She talked to Him just the way He'd said to, Mary reflected: as if she were His daughter, and He were her Father. It was enough for Mary to overlook a lot of her frustrations with Dorothy. After all, who knew? Mary might be doing all kinds of things that Dorothy found incredibly frustrating too. But when it came right down to it, both of them were just trying to follow the same God.

After their time of prayer, Mary and Dorothy walked out together. "Thanks for organizing this," Mary told Dorothy.

"I'm glad to," Dorothy said. "In fact, I needed it just as much as anyone. You do a lot of things around town too, so maybe you understand. But there are some times when you know, no matter how much you do, it won't be enough. That's how I learned how much I need to pray. Because the more you think about it, the more you realize you can't *do* anything. Not about the things that really matter."

Mary nodded. "I understand," she said.

On the way home, she stopped at Jimmy's Hardware. She'd been meaning to get an extra set of keys for Jack and Christa, but in all the activity surrounding Amanda's disappearance, she hadn't gotten to it yet.

When the bell overhead chimed as she came through the door, Jimmy looked up and smiled, although his smile was tinged with fatigue.

"Mary," he said, "good to see you. What can I do for you? Need a key?"

Mary nodded and held out her key ring. "Yes," she said. "I just need two of each. My son and his wife are in town, along with my granddaughter Daisy."

"That's right," Jimmy said, nodding as he took the keys from her and peered at them. "I met Daisy last night."

"Of course," Mary said as he turned back to choose the appropriate blanks from the large collection of keys by the register. "You really do have a beautiful collection," she said.

"I'm sure I've told you how much I love keys," Jimmy said. He had, but Mary liked hearing Jimmy talk about something he was so passionate about, so she gave him an encouraging smile. "I've loved keys ever since I was a kid. I used to save up my lunch money to buy the strangest ones I could find. It's what first got me interested in owning a hardware store. My key rep tells me I've got the best collection south of Boston."

Mary smiled and glanced at the rows of keys she'd seen many times before. He had the standard aluminum and brass, but also plastic, checkerboard, and, near the register, a suite of novelty keys stamped in the shape of auto brands or Disney characters. But the most elaborate one she had never noticed before. It was a beautifully wrought key in the shape of a ship at full sail. But it was so much bigger than the others that Mary couldn't quite imagine it fitting on a standard key ring, or even turning under most knobs. "Do you get much call for that one?" she asked, pointing.

Jimmy laughed ruefully and shook his head. "Nope," he said. "I've actually never sold one. I made one for myself, for the shed in my backyard. And I gave one to a friend. That's about it."

Mary nodded and smiled as he fitted one of the blanks he'd pulled into the machine and began to cut her a new key.

"You look a little tired," she said.

Jimmy nodded as the metal whined. "It was quite a night," he said.

"I've just come from Amanda's," Mary told him.

Instead of leaning closer to share information like the women at the prayer group had, Jimmy glanced away from her. He gave his head a slight shake. "She's not back," he said.

"No," Mary said. Did he know that already? she wondered. But then she realized that might just be his way of phrasing the question. "It must be so hard for you," she said. "I'd be going over everything in my head, just wondering if there was anything I missed."

Jimmy's friendly expression vanished. "I've already told the police everything I can think of," he said in a clipped tone. "Several times."

"Oh," Mary said, caught off guard. "Well, I just thought—"

Jimmy shook his head, cutting her off again. "I really don't think I should talk to anyone but the police about this," he said.

"Well, yes," Mary said. "I can understand that. I understand it must be hard to deal with. Especially since this was your first year with a July Queen float. And to have this happen..."

"We've always had floats," Jimmy said. "Every year."

"Yes," Mary said. "But not usually with a queen."

Jimmy shrugged, his expression still guarded as he pulled a new key ring from the wall and threaded the new keys through it. "Amanda just came into the store one day, looking for a sponsor. She seemed like a nice enough girl. We were already doing a float. So I said, sure, she could ride on it."

"Did she help you and Betty with the float design?" Mary asked. "I don't remember Betty talking much about her."

Jimmy glanced out of the shop, over Mary's shoulder. He shrugged again. "Not much," he said. "She didn't seem real interested in that part of it."

"I just keep thinking, if there are any clues, they'd be on the float," Mary said, rubbing her temples. "Or maybe in it. Is it around here still?"

"Well, you and the police think alike, I'll give you that," Jimmy said. "They took it into evidence last night. As far as I know, it's still there. I don't think either of us is going to get near it anytime soon."

This time, the set of Jimmy's jaw was unmistakable. "I'm sorry," he said. "I'm just not comfortable talking anymore about an ongoing investigation, Mary. It just doesn't seem to be my right."

"Of course," Mary said, trying to smooth the waters. "I'm sorry to bother you. I just want to do anything I can to help."

Jimmy's expression softened as he rang up the cost of the keys. "I know," he said. He met her eyes when Mary handed him the cash. "I guess we all do."

This time, when he glanced away, Mary got the strong sense that there was something he wasn't telling her. Suddenly, she realized that if anybody in town would have been in a position to know about the disappearance, either before or after it happened, it was Jimmy. He'd helped build the float Amanda disappeared from, and he'd been driving the trailer when she disappeared. But if Jimmy had something to do with Amanda's disappearance, what was he doing here at work in his shop the next morning?

In any case, the distant expression on Jimmy's face told Mary that she wasn't going to get any further with him in this conversation. Politely, she thanked him again, then walked back to her car with the uneasy feeling that he knew more than he was telling her—or the police.

NINE

"Hi, Grandma," Daisy said from her place at the kitchen table.

"Hi, Mom," her mother, Christa, echoed.

"Hi, sweetheart," Mary said, kissing the top of Daisy's head. She looked around at Jack and Christa apologetically. "Sorry it took me so long to get home."

Jack, who had been standing at the sink, doing the dishes left over from breakfast, looked back over his shoulder and nodded. Betty, who stood beside him, wiping the dishes with a cloth before she replaced them on the shelves, raised her eyebrows at Mary. Mary had been able to tell by the false notes in Daisy's and Christa's voices that something was wrong, and Betty's look confirmed it.

Mary set her purse down on an empty chair and gave Christa's shoulder a squeeze, for solidarity. It was obvious that she had interrupted a tense conversation. Christa looked up at Mary gratefully. Then she looked back at Daisy.

"Well, it hardly makes sense to come all the way out to the Cape if you're never going to leave the house," Christa said to her daughter, her voice equal parts of pleading and exasperation.

"There's nothing to do out there anyway," Daisy said and folded her arms.

"Oh, pumpkin, come on," Jack said in a teasing voice, clearly trying to keep things light. "That's not what you used to say. We never used to be able to get you to come in off the beach. You'd play in those waves until your fingers and toes were purple from the cold."

"I'm not four years old anymore," Daisy said, with quite a bit of attitude. "In case you hadn't noticed."

"You don't have to be a four-year-old to enjoy the ocean," Christa said, her patience wearing thin.

"What about the whales?" Jack said. "The last time we went whale watching, you talked about it for months. Do you remember watching all the different tails, trying to tell which one was which? You had a favorite, remember? The one who had a nick taken out of his tail in a fight? And you gave him a name. What was it?"

"I don't remember," Daisy muttered.

Mary wasn't sure if she wanted to laugh or give Daisy a good talking to. Her granddaughter was in full pouty teenager mode, and she didn't seem the least bit embarrassed to be talking to her parents this way, even in front of her grandmother.

"Come on," Jack persisted. Mary had to admire the way he was reaching out to his daughter. A lot of fathers would have given up by now. "It was something hilarious, if I remember correctly. I think you named him after one of the generals you were studying in world history. Did you call him Napoleon?"

"I don't know," Daisy muttered again. Then her voice rose in challenge. "And I don't care."

Jack was a patient dad, but he did have his limits. He turned back from the sink, his hands still shiny with dishwater. "You know, Daisy," he said, "there are a lot of kids who would feel really lucky to get to spend this time on the Cape this weekend."

"Or to have a dad as nice as yours," Christa pointed out.

Betty raised her eyebrows at Mary again, giving her a look that said, "What's going to happen now?"

Daisy tightened her arms across her chest. Her face clouded even more. A moment later, she dissolved into actual tears. "I don't get to have any say over what I get to do!" she cried. "That's fine! You can make me come out here. There's nothing I can do about that. *But you can't make me like it!*"

With that, she pushed her chair back, stumbled a bit as she twirled around, looking for the door, and then barged out through it, her footsteps fading toward the special room Betty and Mary had made up for her upstairs, with the best view of Betty's beautiful gardens.

Jack stood with his back to the sink, shaking his head.

"Was I this bad as a kid?" he asked Mary.

"Sometimes you were worse," Mary said. "Daisy hasn't driven a car through the garage door yet, has she?"

"She doesn't have her license yet," Jack reminded her. "So we have that to look forward to."

Mary crossed the kitchen to give her son a hug. "Well," she said, "I can tell you one thing. Everything I ever had to put up with from you, it was all worth it. I wouldn't trade a second of it."

"I'm not sure if I could say that," Jack said, hugging his mother back.

"Yes, you could," Mary said. "You might feel like trading her in now, but when you think about what it would feel like if she were really gone—"

"Like this girl Amanda," Christa said.

Mary nodded. "Yes," she said. "Like that."

"You're right," Jack said, releasing Mary. "I'd take all the temper tantrums in the world before that."

"Well," Christa said, "she does need to learn to stop throwing tantrums whenever she doesn't get her way."

"Oh, don't worry," Jack said. "She's going to learn that lesson, loud and clear."

"You're right," Mary said. "But think about it from her side once in a while too. She's growing up into a young woman. And she's feeling like she doesn't get to make many of her own decisions."

"Well, we couldn't leave her in Chicago to go to a party while we were out of town," Jack said. "And I wasn't going to miss the Fourth of July with my own mom."

Mary patted his arm. "I'm glad about that," she said. "And I don't think you did the wrong thing. I'm just saying, while you do what you need to do, it might not hurt to try to look at things now and then from Daisy's point of view."

"See," Jack said, putting his arm around his mom's shoulders, "this is why we had to come to Ivy Bay this weekend, instead of stay in Chicago."

Mary smiled up at him.

"Jack said you went to visit Amanda's mother," Christa said. "Is there any more news about her?"

Mary shook her head. "No," she said. "But I did find out a few interesting things." Quickly, she brought everyone up to date on her conversation with Amanda's mother, the discovery of the box of Amanda's father's things, the reports from the women at the prayer meeting of another missing girl farther up the coast, and Jimmy's strange evasiveness.

"What worries me the most," she said when she was done, "is the fact that Amanda was clearly looking for her father. And Hank Branson didn't just leave his family behind when Amanda was still a baby. You should have seen how strongly Heather reacted when his name came up. She could barely talk about him. She seems to think he might actually be dangerous, although Chief McArthur says that Hank is in touch and concerned about Amanda. And I don't want to be paranoid, but if Amanda reached out to him, he could easily be lying to the police. There's no telling what part he played in all of this. And even if he isn't lying, Amanda may still be trying to find him. And if she does, I'm not sure she'll like what she finds."

"Well," Betty said, "I'm not so sure about that."

Everyone in the room swiveled to look at her.

"What do you mean?" Mary said.

Betty left her drying rag on the dish drainer and took the seat that Daisy had abandoned when she fled the kitchen. "I've been friends with Hester Peters for the past twenty years," she began.

"Hester Peters?" Mary interrupted.

"Hester Branson," Betty said, with a significant look. "Before she was married. She's Hank's big sister."

"Have you talked with her?" Mary asked. "About this?"

"Not in so many words," Betty said. "She's pretty private about what happened with Heather and Hank. But I know

Hester. Even knew her mom and dad, before they passed away. I've never met Hank, but there's nothing about that family that would make me think they'd raised a dangerous man. And a few times when it has come up, Hester's said things to suggest that the story Heather's been telling around town for the past seventeen years may only be one side of it."

"Like what?" Mary said. "What kinds of things has she said?"

"I couldn't tell you word for word," Betty told her.

When Mary looked at her, slightly exasperated herself now, Betty shrugged. "I'm sorry," she said. "I had no idea at the time that Amanda would be missing, or that this might matter. But I know what she was trying to tell me. And that's that Heather wasn't telling the whole story."

"You said she didn't seem like she wanted to share the details," Mary said. "Do you think she might now? If we let her know it might help us find Amanda?"

Betty shrugged. "It'd be easy enough to find out," she said. "Hester started growing heirloom tomatoes a few year ago. Got so many of them, now she's got her own booth down at the farmers' market on Friday mornings." She glanced at the clock. "You've still got a few hours before it closes. If you go down there now, you shouldn't have any trouble at all finding her. Then you can ask her anything you want."

"And," Christa said, "it sounds like a great excuse to visit the market."

Mary looked at her for a moment in surprise. Then she smiled. This was a perfect opportunity to spend some time with the family, even while she kept up her search for Amanda. Maybe even one of God's little gifts in the day. *Thank You*, she prayed briefly. "Would you like to come along?" she asked Christa.

Christa smiled, her eyes eager. "I never turn down a chance to visit a farmers' market. There's not much I like better than freshly picked produce."

"Unless there's someone there selling kettle corn," Jack teased. "Or handmade soap."

Christa gave him a playful nudge. "But I save so much money getting them at the farmers' market," she said. "Instead of some fancy Chicago shop."

She gave Jack's arm a quick squeeze. "You want to come down to the market with us?"

Jack shook his head. Then he smiled ruefully. "I've never been crazy about the farmers' market."

"You want us to bring you anything?" Christa asked. "Kettle corn? Handmade soap?"

Jack shook his head. "But you two have a good time," he said.

TEN

〜◆◆◆〜

I love this market," Mary told Christa as they trailed between the card tables and booths where Ivy Bay's farmers and craftspeople displayed their produce and wares. "I just wish I got over here more often. Friday is such a busy time at the store."

"It's a beautiful market," Christa said, looking over the makeshift booths where farmers displayed cucumbers and berries and bunches of hand-picked wildflowers on card tables, and folding chairs, and from the backs of their pickup trucks. Since Ivy Bay had a strong local fishing industry, it had something a lot of other farmers' markets didn't: several booths where the catch of the day was displayed on piles of ice so people could choose for themselves exactly which cut they wanted to take home—and even one booth where a few dozen captured lobsters knocked their dark claws against the sides of plastic buckets.

Christa stopped almost immediately at a table offering small baskets of freshly dug potatoes, beside a stand selling hunks of artisan cheese. "I feel like we could make a delicious dinner out of these," she said, investigating the fresh spuds. She turned a box of Yukon Gold from side to side. Then she pulled out a box of Red Bliss. "Which do you like better?" she asked.

"I guess it depends," Mary said. "The Gold are so smooth. But the Red look beautiful."

"*Hmm*," Christa said, deep in thought.

Beside her, Mary shifted impatiently. Normally, she would have loved nothing better than to browse with her daughter-in-law, but today, she was on a mission.

Christa, always sensitive, looked up quickly. "Oh," she said, "I forgot. We're not just here to buy vegetables, are we?"

Mary shook her head. "But you should look at everything you want," she told Christa. "I just need to spend a few minutes speaking with Hester."

Christa glanced down the row, which also included several craft booths where local artists sold beeswax candles and hand-embroidered linens.

"I think I can amuse myself," she said.

"You don't mind?" Mary asked.

"Mind?" Christa said. "I couldn't be happier!"

Mary left Christa lingering over the potatoes and pressed on through the market.

She thought she remembered having seen heirloom tomatoes there, in the far corner, with the beautiful green- and yellow- and red-striped fruits arranged in neat pints or quarts. And when she scanned the busy market scene, looking for Hester's booth again, she found it just where she'd thought and made a beeline for it.

As Mary walked up, the woman who stood behind the antique card table that displayed the array of heirloom tomatoes smiled. She was trim-looking, in a tasteful collared shirt with a muted floral pattern. Her salt-and-pepper hair was trimmed in a pixie cut, and her blue eyes were bright. "I'm Hester," she said. "Just let me know if you have any questions. All these tomatoes are grown from heirloom seeds. Some of them are from my great-grandmother's garden," she said, pointing to a rough basket of pink tomatoes shot through with green stripes. "But I've also collected my favorite varieties from around the country."

"Wonderful," Mary said. "Thank you." She looked down at the tomatoes for a few seconds to collect her thoughts. Then she looked up.

"I was so sorry to hear about Amanda," she said.

Hester's face showed a real flash of pain. Then it turned suspicious. "Do I know you?" she asked.

Mary smiled. "I'm so sorry," she said. "I should have introduced myself. I'm Mary Fisher. Betty Emerson's sister. We were just talking about Amanda this morning, and Betty mentioned you were related to her, when she told me you also grow these wonderful tomatoes. I was just thinking this must be such a hard time for your family."

Hester's face didn't soften much at Mary's explanation. "I've been worried sick about Amanda," she said. "But I can't tell you I know much more than anyone else about what's going on. We haven't really been"—she paused, clearly choosing her words—"close. Amanda's mom never really wanted to have much to do with the family. And after she and Hank split up, she got her way."

"Amanda worked in my bookshop this year," Mary said. Hester nodded again, still wary.

"I got to know Heather a bit while I was working with Amanda," Mary said. "I just went over there earlier this morning."

"Have they heard anything?" Hester said, her eyes eager. "I was hoping it was all some kind of mistake, and that she'd just come back."

Mary shook her head. "I'm sorry," she said. "As far as I know, she hasn't."

Hester's face fell. Mary hesitated. Hester's eyes met hers again. Mary felt an instinctive connection with her, but she barely knew her. Then again, she told herself, Betty trusted Hester. And Betty was a good judge of character.

"But I did find something interesting while I was there," Mary finally said. "I understand Amanda and her father haven't been in touch since Amanda was small."

"No," Hester said, with strong emotion. "They haven't."

Mary nodded. "Well," she said, "there was a box in Amanda's bedroom. It was full of things Amanda had collected about her father. All kinds of things, from newspaper articles to some of his old report cards, copied from the school office. It seems that Amanda may have been looking for him."

The suspicion in Hester's eyes had changed. Now she seemed gratified. She almost had to resist a smile. "I guess a girl gets curious about her father, no matter what anyone might tell her about him."

"That's what I was concerned about," Mary said. "Would you know anything about whether Amanda did make contact with your brother or not?"

Hester shook her head, guarded again. "I haven't heard anything like that from Hank," she said. "But I don't talk with him all that much since he left town. And like I said, Heather hasn't exactly encouraged Amanda to get to know her Branson relatives."

"Heather seemed to think that Hank wasn't very interested in getting to know Amanda," Mary began.

Hester's eyes flashed at this. "That wasn't for lack of trying," she said. "All Hank ever wanted in this life was to be a good husband and a father. He just picked the wrong girl to marry, I guess. He may not have had a part in Amanda's life, but it wasn't by his choice, I can tell you that."

Mary could see what Betty had been talking about. The story Heather told and the one Hester was telling didn't match up at all. The question was, who was telling the truth about Hank? His ex-wife, who clearly still had strong feelings about him? Or his sister, who couldn't exactly be expected to be unbiased either? Or did the real truth lay somewhere in between the versions each of the women gave?

Mary knew one thing: Hester's insistence that Hank had wanted to be in touch with Amanda didn't set her mind at ease. Many children who disappeared, Mary knew, were actually taken by parents who weren't able to get custody of them for one reason or another. If Hester was right, and Hank had wanted to be a part of Amanda's life, that only made the situation more worrisome in Mary's mind.

"So you say Hank did want to be part of Amanda's life?" Mary asked.

Cautiously, Hester nodded.

"I hate to ask this," Mary said. "But...do you think there's any chance that Hank might have any idea where Amanda is now?"

"What are you saying?" Hester snapped. "Are you asking me if my brother kidnapped his daughter?"

Mary shook her head. "I'm just trying to be any help I can to the authorities, so they can bring Amanda home safe," she said.

"Hank would never do something like that," Hester said. "No matter what Heather ever did to him, he'd never do anything to hurt her. Or to hurt Amanda. He'd die himself, first. His problem is that he's too nice a guy. Always was."

"Well, I've heard Heather's side of the story," Mary said. "And thanks for telling me yours. I'd love to hear Hank's."

Hester's face closed up again. "That's not for me to tell. Bransons don't spread our business all over town. Unlike some other people I could mention," she said pointedly. "If you want to know his story, you'd have to talk with him."

"Do you know a good way to reach him?" Mary asked.

"I'm not sure I'm comfortable handing out my brother's personal information to a stranger," Hester said.

"Well, you know Betty," Mary said, even though she knew she sounded a bit desperate. "And I'm not going to just disappear with his information," Mary said. "You know where the bookshop is. You can always find me there, if you ever have any reason to look for me."

Hester still seemed unconvinced.

"The whole town knows the story Heather's been telling," Mary reminded her. "This might help to even the balance."

That seemed to decide Hester. "I can give you his number at work. He has a business in Boston."

"I saw that," Mary said. "Amanda had an article about it in her research."

"It's still pretty new," Hester said. "So he's always there. You can try him here." She rattled off a number, which Mary hurried to scrawl down on a scrap of paper from her purse.

As Hester finished reeling off the number, a woman in a wide straw hat ambled up, her arms full of fresh celery, carrots, and radishes. "I know I want some of your beautiful tomatoes," she said. "I'm just not sure how I'm going to carry them and all of this."

Suddenly, Hester's serious expression was replaced by her saleswoman's smile. She pulled a paper bag out from under the table and rattled it open. "Well," she said, "I can help you with that."

"Oh, thank you," the woman said, as vegetables began to drop from her arms into the bag. Once her hands were free, just as Hester had planned, she began to reach into the various baskets of beautiful heirloom tomatoes.

"Thank you," Mary told Hester, more quietly.

Hester barely nodded at her as Mary slipped back into the crowd, clutching the scrap of paper.

ELEVEN

◆◆◆

Mary sighed as she stepped into the bookstore. A feeling of calm stole over her as she looked around the orderly shelves and the neat stacks of books on the main tables. She'd dropped Christa off at the house after their visit to the market, where Christa had loaded up on Yukon Gold potatoes, striped red-and-white beets, ripe peaches, and, to Jack's delight, a paper bag of fresh kettle corn. But despite her desire to spend more time with her family, she'd promised Rebecca that she'd drop into the shop, and she didn't feel comfortable leaving her alone there all day on the busy holiday weekend.

She'd thought it might just be another hurried errand, but Mary was surprised by how much comfort she took just from stepping inside the door of the little business she'd built. The world outside might be an impossible snarl of worries and unanswered questions, but in here, there were answers to all the mysteries, right where they belonged: at the end of each book. She took a deep breath, drawing in the familiar scent of Susan working her morning magic at Sweet Susan's Bakery next door, and rolled her shoulders back. It felt good to take refuge in a place where everything was just where it belonged, even if it was only for a moment.

Rebecca, who had been reshelving books in the children's section, waved from behind the bathtub where children loved to curl up with books from the hundreds of kids' titles that lined the surrounding nook. "Mary," she said, "it's good to see you. You've caught us at a quiet moment. We've been busy this morning."

"That's great," Mary said, circling behind the counter. She had hoped that the extra traffic of vacationers for the Fourth of July weekend would provide a nice bump in business. The store was doing just fine, but there were a few improvements she wanted to make, if she could get just a little more cash on hand. She had seen a beautiful lamp at Gems and Antiques, made from shells that glowed pink and white and purple when the bulb inside was switched on. It would give a perfect air of hominess, mystery, and beauty to the tables of books at the front of the shop—if the receipts added up satisfactorily at the end of the month.

Ashley, who was manning the register, looked up. "We've sold twenty-one titles already today," she announced.

Rebecca and Mary shared a quick glance of amusement. If either of them had been running the register, there was a good chance neither of them would have been able to so quickly cite the number of the titles that had passed through their hands that morning. But Ashley took her duties around the shop incredibly seriously and had a grasp of details that sometimes verged on the frightening.

"Twenty-one?" Mary said. "That's a lot of customers."

Ashley shook her head. "It wasn't that many customers," she said. "One woman bought eleven of them all by herself."

Rebecca laughed as she came over from the kids' section. "She bought a whole series of cozy mysteries set on the English coast," she said. "She said she doesn't know why she bothers to come on vacation anymore, because all she does is sit on the porch and read books about being someplace else. I asked her if she reads like that when she's at home. She said no. She guessed that must be why she comes on vacation."

"Well, that's a good sale," Mary said, smiling at Ashley. "Thanks for taking care of it for me."

"Ashley didn't just ring it up," Rebecca reported proudly. "She's actually the one who introduced her to the series. The woman came in saying she was looking for something with a coastal feel. I'd just started reading one of the stories to Ashley at home, so she remembered the detective lives in a house on a bluff overlooking the English cliffs. Ashley walked her right over to the section, and ten minutes later, she walked up to the register with a whole armful of them."

"I'm going to have to start putting her on commissions next," Mary said.

"What's a commission?" Ashley asked.

Rebecca rumpled Ashley's hair. "You know how sometimes I take you down for ice cream if we've had a good day together here at work?" she said. "That's a commission."

"I like commissions!" Ashley said. "Can I have one now?"

"After we're all done here," Rebecca said. "That's how commissions work."

Mary gave her a grateful smile. "It looks like you've got everything under control here," she said.

"Well, I hope so," Rebecca told her.

"Wonderful," Mary said. "I know I told you I'd planned to be here earlier this morning, but I've been trying to do what I can to help locate Amanda. Not to mention, my family's in town." She gave Rebecca a knowing smile, fully aware that she was far too busy for someone who was supposedly living a relaxed life on the Cape.

Rebecca smiled, but then her face turned serious. She'd worked with Amanda too, during the week Amanda had spent at the shop, and the two of them had developed a friendly bond. "I wondered if you might have something to do with that," Rebecca said. "I haven't been able to stop thinking about her. Have you heard anything at all?"

Mary gave her head a little shake. "Not yet," she said. "I've talked to her mother Heather and Amanda's aunt. And Chief McArthur. As far as I'm aware, nobody has come up with anything solid."

"It's so scary to think about," Rebecca said, keeping her voice low. "It's hard to believe someone would take her. But knowing Amanda, it's hard to believe she would just run away. I can't even imagine her doing that, actually. But do you really think that a child could just disappear from Ivy Bay?"

Mary took a deep breath. "I don't know what to think right now," she said. "Ivy Bay's a safe place. But on a holiday like this, all kinds of strangers pass through town. We have no idea who they are, or what kind of people they might be." She thought back to the stranger the chief's deputies had described to him the night before.

"Is there anything I can do?" Rebecca asked.

Mary nodded. "Just exactly what you are doing," she said. "Holding down the fort. Do you think you can manage for the rest of the day on your own?"

Behind the register, Ashley shifted and gave both Mary and her mother a pointed stare.

"Well, I'm hardly on my own, am I?" Rebecca said broadly. "Not with Ashley here."

"Of course not," Mary said. She raised her voice for Ashley's benefit. "Ashley, what do you think? Can the two of you handle the shop for me today while I work on some other things?"

Ashley considered this for a moment, like a businessperson adding up columns of figures in her head before giving an answer. Then, with a grave expression, she gave a calm nod.

"There," Rebecca said. "See? We'll be fine."

"Wonderful," Mary said. "Thank you."

"But you'll let us know?" Rebecca said. "If you hear anything."

"Absolutely," Mary said. As she spoke, she turned toward the computer behind the counter. "If you'll excuse me, I'm just going to make a few quick calls."

"Ashley," Rebecca said, gesturing to her daughter, "why don't you come with me? I've still got some books to file in the children's nook."

Obediently, Ashley hopped down from her stool and followed her mother to the far side of the store.

Mary sat down in front of the computer. *Lord,* she prayed, *I don't know if I'm even helping at this point, or if I'm just getting in Chief McArthur's way. But I just want to do anything I can to bring Amanda home. Even if that's something small. Please show me the way to go. Please use me, if I can be useful.*

Then she clicked open her search engine and typed in "Hank Branson" and "Boston."

Immediately, a personal listing came up, with not just an address but a phone number. Mary pulled the scrap of paper where she'd scrawled the business number that Hester had given her out of her purse to compare them. They didn't match. Was this Hank Branson's home number she had just discovered?

An instant later, she had the phone in one hand and was tapping away at the dial pad with the other.

She waited, staring at the address on the computer screen, while the connection was made.

Then there was a familiar set of three tones, and a recorded announcement came on. "We're sorry," it said. "The number you have dialed has been changed or disconnected. If you'd like to try again, please hang up and dial again."

Mary tried the number one more time, to be sure she hadn't misdialed it in her excitement. The same message came up a second time. She replaced the phone in its cradle.

Next she typed in "Branson Seafood Company." She found a few search hits, including a White Pages listing with a number that matched the one Hester had given her. But the business didn't seem to have any kind of Web page or presence other than mentions on other pages. That wasn't completely surprising. From her friendships with other fishermen in Ivy Bay, Mary knew they still tended to be hands-on people who liked to do their business in person, by handshake, rather than through a computer screen. It looked like the only way to find out more was to call the number Hester had given her directly.

She picked up the phone and dialed again.

This time, instead of the disconnect tones, the phone rang. Mary's shoulders relaxed in relief for an instant. Then they tightened again as she realized she didn't know what she was going to say.

"H'lo?" The voice of the man who answered was gruff, with a thick Boston accent—not the lilt of the Cape fishing families that Hank had come from. So it sounded like before Mary even had to figure out what to say to Hank, she still needed to get him on the line.

"Hello," she said, using her most businesslike voice. "I'm trying to reach Hank Branson."

"Hank ain't here," the man told her.

Mary waited for a moment, expecting him to offer some explanation or at least to take a message. After another moment, she realized he wasn't going to.

"Oh," she said. "Well, can you tell me when he might be back?"

"Honestly, lady," the guy said, "I got no idea. Can I put you on hold?"

"Of course," Mary said. "Thank—"

There was a loud beep, and Mary expected to hear silence or Muzak, but instead the guy's voice came across the line, just as loud. Except it no longer seemed that he was talking to her.

"Yeah, yeah, yeah," he said. "I got some woman here wants to talk with Hank; you believe it? He's been in and out all week, no rhyme or reason that I can see. Not that there's any rhyme or reason to anything else that's been going on around here either. Last night we had a big delivery truck come in, middle of the night. With nothing in it."

A garbled voice answered off the line.

"You're telling me," the guy on the other end of the line said. "The driver doesn't ring up or anything. Just sits out there in front of the shop, with his rig rattling and shaking for so long that I finally get up to see what's going on. I figure, okay, you know, fish. It's an unpredictable business. You got to take what you get when it comes, all right. And maybe this order comes in the middle of the night. Two AM. And Hank, of course, is nowhere to be found. That's what he hired me for. So I throw some clothes on and go down, you know, to let them in. But when I get there, I'm looking at an empty truck. And this guy I never saw before, not one of our regular delivery guys, he takes one look at me, then he hops in the cab and drives off. I talk with Hank about it this morning, and he says he's got no idea what it was. He didn't have any orders coming in. Not at that time, anyway. But he still ain't been in this morning. I'd like to have some idea when things are going to happen around here too, believe me. But your guess is as good as mine, these days. Anyway, you seen Hank? You know when he's coming back?"

The garbled voice spoke something unintelligible again. Then there was another loud beep, and the man came back on the line.

"Hello?" he said. "You still there?"

"I'm here," Mary said.

"Yeah, Hank's gone," he said. "We don't know when he'll be back. You could try again pretty much anytime. Your guess is as good as mine."

"Well," Mary said, "thank you so much for your help."

"Hey," the guy said, as if he'd just had a major brainstorm. "You want me to leave a message for him? The next time he comes in?"

"Oh," Mary said, her mind racing again. Hank's man at the business had been so distracted that she hadn't had to invent her own cover story after all, and now that he'd asked for one, she couldn't think of anything. "That's okay. I'll just try back later."

"All right," the guy said, as if she was making a decision he didn't quite approve of but didn't feel like arguing with. "Talk later, then."

"Thank you," Mary said.

When she hung up the phone, she quickly began to scrawl times on a scrap of paper. Amanda had vanished from the parade at sunset. From Ivy Bay, it took about two hours to drive to Boston—or more, on nights like last night when tourist traffic clogged the main arteries that led between the Cape and the mainland. But even with heavy traffic, Amanda, or someone traveling with Amanda, could easily have made it to Boston by 2:00 AM—which is what time the empty truck showed up at Hank's business—with the right transportation. Of course, there would have been challenges to face. For one thing, Chief McArthur had had his police force crawling all over town looking for Amanda less than an hour after she disappeared. And as far as Mary knew, there were no immediate reports of missing cars from the night before, which made it unlikely that Amanda had driven off under her own power.

Still, the timing of the empty truck's arrival at Hank's business seemed to match too closely with the timing of Amanda's disappearance to be coincidence. What if the weird delivery Hank's employee had described to her wasn't from a fish company at all? What if it had something to do with Amanda's disappearance? The man didn't seem to think he'd seen anything, but he'd been looking for a delivery of fish, not a missing girl. Maybe, if she questioned him again, she could jog his memory, come up with another clue that might help point her in the right direction, or even tell them all where Amanda was.

Mary picked up the phone again and dialed, formulating questions as she did. What had the driver of the truck looked like? Had he noticed any name on it or any identifying marks at all? Had there been any other vehicles parked in the area, or idling? Had he seen anybody else nearby? A young brunette? Or, Mary realized, remembering the girl she'd seen disappear among the docks, a blonde?

The phone rang and rang, but now there was no answer.

TWELVE

A ny luck?" Rebecca asked, as Mary slung her purse over her shoulder.

"Possibly," Mary said.

"But still no answers," Rebecca said.

Mary shook her head. "Thanks for holding down the fort," she said as she reached the door.

"Glad to," Rebecca said, waving as Mary went out.

Mary sat behind the wheel of her car for a moment before she started it up, thinking. She still couldn't be sure that Hank Branson had had anything to do with his daughter's disappearance, but she was sure of one thing: Nobody had yet told her the whole story of what really happened between Heather and Hank all those years ago. And Mary wasn't the only person who was interested, she knew. Amanda, it appeared, had been trying to solve the same mystery herself. And with all the strange activity that Hank's employee had described up in Boston, the same night of Amanda's disappearance, she still couldn't shake the idea that Hank might have something to do with it.

She thought briefly about trying to call Chief McArthur to give him this new clue she'd discovered. But she'd had enough conversations with him in the past few days, trying to share the other clues she'd discovered, to know how this one would go. Chief McArthur would quickly dismantle the strange events that seemed so tantalizing to her. He'd ask her what she thought an odd delivery time in Boston had to do with Amanda's disappearance, and she'd have to tell him again that she didn't really know, even though it happened outside Amanda's father's business. When she mentioned Amanda's father, Chief McArthur would probably tell her that he'd just talked with Hank again, and Hank had given him some completely plausible explanation that made all of Mary's suspicions seem just as silly as Chief McArthur had made all her other ideas about the case seem.

No, she thought. She couldn't go to Chief McArthur again until she had something that really constituted proof. Otherwise, maybe he was right: She really was just getting in the way of an investigation that Chief McArthur could do better on his own.

The question was, she realized, what kind of man was Hank? Mary wanted to believe that he was the good man his sister had described. But the fact of the matter was that his daughter was missing. A police force was looking for her, and an entire town was on edge. That was a frightening situation. It lined up a lot better with the frightening description Heather gave of him. And Heather, Mary realized, was the only person in town who really knew what kind of a husband and father Hank had been. It might not be easy to get her to talk, given her state this morning, but it was worth another try, especially with the new information Mary had gotten from Betty and Hester.

When she arrived at Amanda's house, there was a new vehicle at the curb, along with the little convertible Heather's friends had arrived in as Mary was leaving earlier in the day. This one wasn't a car. It was a motorcycle. Mary guessed the owner immediately: Amanda had told her more than one story about how much she enjoyed riding along the Cape roads that overlooked the Atlantic, on the back of her boyfriend Jared's bike. Mary remembered thinking wryly to herself that she wasn't sure which one Amanda was more enthusiastic about: the motorcycle, or Jared himself. But from Amanda's loving description, Mary would have recognized the bike instantly: a vintage Indian that Jared's father had ridden when he was Jared's age. According to Amanda, Jared had spent a year begging his father for permission to restore it, and once he'd won permission, he'd spent two years painstakingly bringing the classic machine back to its original perfection. He'd started before he was even old enough to drive, but he finished it the same summer he got his license, and at the end of his very first ride, he'd stopped by Amanda's house to pick her up and take her out on it.

Mary's guess was confirmed when she knocked on Amanda's door, and Jared answered. He was big, at least six feet tall, with the broad shoulders of a linebacker, and a ready smile under sandy blond hair.

"Hi, Jared," Mary said. "I'm not sure if you remember me. Amanda worked in my shop for a week this year. I'm Mary Fisher."

Jared's familiar smile was weak today. His eyes were red from exhaustion, and Mary wondered if Heather hadn't been the only one in town who didn't sleep the night before, wondering where Amanda had gone. Jared's demeanor, though, was as polite as ever.

"Sure, sure, Mrs. Fisher," Jared said. "I remember you. Amanda loved working in your shop. She still talks about it all the time." As quickly as his smile had lit up, it winked out at the mention of Amanda, replaced by a strange uncertainty.

Mary's heart went out to him. Jared wasn't married to Amanda, but feelings could still run strong, even at their age. After all, that was when she and John had first fallen in love. And their marriage had lasted for decades. She patted Jared on the arm.

"I just came over to talk with Heather a bit," she said softly. "About Amanda."

Jared stepped back to let her into the narrow entryway that led to the living room, but he looked dubious. "She's not feeling very well today," he said. "I don't know how much she'll want to talk."

Mary nodded, but went by him anyway, giving him a measured smile. "It can't hurt to try," she said.

Jared watched her go by with an expression that said he wasn't sure of that at all.

Mary found Heather just where she'd left her, on the couch in the living room. But now the woman who had been hugging Heather when Mary left sat beside Heather, and Julia sat across from her in a love seat. From a glass of soda on the table between them, Mary could see that Jared had risen to answer the door from the empty seat beside Julia.

Heather looked up at Mary when she came in, her eyes wide. "Mary!" she said. "Have you heard anything?"

Mary shook her head. "I'm afraid not," she said. "But don't worry. If I hear anything about Amanda, you'll be the first to know."

"When you hear," Heather said. "You seem so sure."

"Heather," Julia reprimanded her gently, "don't start thinking like that."

"I know, I know," Heather said.

Mary nodded at Julia and extended her hand toward the woman on the couch. "Please, don't get up," she said. "I'm Mary."

"Clarissa," the dark-haired woman said, with an attempt at a smile.

"Amanda worked at my shop this year," Mary said by way of explanation.

"Heather said you've been doing some detective work of your own," Clarissa said.

"Oh, I'm not a detective," Mary said. "I think we all just want to do anything we can to help find Amanda."

Jared had trailed her back into the room. Now he hesitated beside the love seat and gestured to it. "Would you like to sit down?" he asked.

"No, please, keep your seat," Mary said, sinking into a nearby chair that completed the little group of furniture. "Thank you."

Jared took his seat again. Heather looked at Mary warily.

Mary offered what she hoped was a reassuring smile. From Heather's reaction to her questions earlier that morning, she suspected her new line of questioning wouldn't be popular. But every minute she waited was another minute that they hadn't found Amanda.

"Heather," Mary began, "could I ask you a few questions about Hank? I'm curious about a few things."

Immediately, Heather's face hardened. "I'm the last person in the world who would know anything about Hank Branson," she said. "I thought I knew him, once. But it turned out I didn't. I was too young and foolish to see the truth about him. And now it's been seventeen years. I haven't spoken to him since he walked out that door and left me and my baby girl behind."

Mary nodded. She had heard the details of this story before, and she was starting to get the feeling that Heather got some kind of satisfaction from repeating them again and again. "I understand," she said. "And that's what I want to ask about. I'm wondering if you can tell me a bit of what happened back then."

"Those weren't good times for me," Heather said. "I don't like to think about them."

"What does this have to do with finding Amanda?" Clarissa straightened up to defend her friend as Heather grew more and more visibly upset.

"Well, as far as I can tell, Amanda has become interested in learning more about her father," Mary told her, and glanced at Heather to make sure that this fact sunk in with her as well. "I'm not sure that's connected with her disappearance, but at this point, I think it's good to think about anything that might help the police find her. They have been in touch with Hank, and he says she hasn't made contact with him. But I'm trying to understand his story, in case she's out there and she does try to reach out to him. Do you have any reason to believe she'd be in any danger if that were the case?"

Heather's brows drew together in anger. She nodded. "Hank Branson couldn't be trusted," she said. "Not when I knew him. And I've got no reason to believe he's any different now."

Mary took a deep breath. "Can you help me to understand what that means?" she said.

"I don't know how I can be clearer than that," Heather said. "If you can't trust a man, there's no going back."

Mary nodded. "Yes," she said. "And I know some people say nobody can really judge what happens in a relationship. Just the people who were there. In this case, you're the only one who was. I'm just trying to understand.... Did he ever give you any reason to be afraid of him?"

Heather blinked at her. "I don't know how to answer that," she said. Both of her friends watched Mary with growing suspicion. Jared's eyes were wide and somewhat more sympathetic.

"What was he like when you were together?" Mary asked.

"I told you, it was years ago," Heather said, tears starting to creep into her voice. "And he was never the man I thought he was."

"I talked with Hester Peters today as well," Mary told her. "She seemed to think that Hank loved Amanda very much."

"Love," Heather scoffed. "He could talk about it all day long, but when it came to showing any..." She let her words trail off.

"Has he been paying child support all these years?" Mary said.

"He didn't start that until she was five years old!" Heather insisted.

"I thought you said this morning that he didn't start paying until she was three," Mary pointed out gently. She'd suspected from the way that Heather kept avoiding her questions that there was something Heather wasn't telling her. This contradiction seemed like a scrap of proof, but Mary had to remember, she told herself, that Heather was also under incredible pressure with her daughter missing. No one could blame her for getting a fact wrong here or there. Without more information, Mary couldn't be sure what anything proved.

But more information, it looked like, would be hard to get. When Mary pointed out the contradiction in what Heather said, Heather's face began to crumple up with tears. Before Mary could collect herself to ask another question, Heather was snuffling loudly. "I'm sorry," she said. "I just don't see how this is helping. It's already such a hard time. I don't know why we have to go back there." She glanced at Julia and Clarissa appealingly. Both of them turned toward Mary, their glances hardening.

"Of course," Mary said. "I understand. I'm so sorry to have to ask. I just thought maybe it would help us understand where Amanda might have gone."

"She would never *go* anywhere!" Heather said, her voice rising into a wail. "That's what makes this so awful. If my baby were able to come home on her own, nothing would keep her away from me. She'd never let anything keep us apart. So somebody must have her. Somebody who won't let her go where she wants. I just..." At this point, words failed her, and she let her head drop onto Clarissa's waiting shoulder while she sobbed. Clarissa patted her friend's arm gently, but the look she gave Mary was by no means gentle.

"Jared," Clarissa said, "maybe you can show Mrs. Fisher out."

Jared jumped awkwardly to his feet. "Sure, sure," he said.

Mary hesitated for a moment. She felt a twinge of remorse over Heather's emotional distress, but by now, she could also see that it served in part to mask a story Heather didn't want to tell. Mary wasn't about to be put off by a few tears, under these circumstances, but she also recognized that she wasn't likely to get any more useful facts out of Heather in this state.

She stood, then leaned over and squeezed Heather's arm. "I'm so sorry to upset you," she said. "I just thought if you could help me understand a bit more about the research Amanda was doing, it might be helpful."

In answer, Heather snuffled into the tissue Clarissa handed her. "I understand," she said. "I can't blame you for wanting to help. I just want my little girl back."

"I know." Mary smiled at her and followed Jared into the little entryway by the front door.

"Phew," he said, and pushed his hair back. "I guess everyone's nerves are a little on edge."

A thought occurred to Mary as she looked at him. "Jared," she said, "did Amanda ever tell you about the research she was doing on her father?"

For a minute, Jared looked just as wary as Heather had. But then he nodded, slowly. "I didn't know how much she'd done," he said. "Mrs. Branson said you found a whole box and everything."

Mary nodded. "She'd collected quite a bit of information," she said.

"She told me some of the things she found out," Jared said. "She knew he had a business in Boston. Before that, her mother had told her she didn't even know where he was."

"How did Amanda seem to feel about him?" Mary asked. "Was she afraid at all? With the kinds of stories her mother told her?"

"That was the thing that actually got her looking for him," Jared said. "Before she found out anything at all, she still had her own memories. Her mother would tell her what a bad guy her dad was. How he couldn't be trusted. How he left them. But Amanda had all these memories. From when she was really little. So little you wouldn't really expect her to remember them. She thought maybe she only did because they were her only memories of her dad."

"What were those memories like?" Mary asked.

Jared stuck his hands in his pockets. He looked a little sad. "Good," he said. "She said they were all good. Him laughing or playing or picking her up. Tucking her in at night. Giving her hugs. She couldn't understand how that fit with the stories her mom told her. I guess that's what she was trying to figure out, with that collection in her secret box."

Mary thought back to Heather's emotional outbursts. She doubted that she was the first one to experience them. She suspected that Amanda was familiar with them as well. And if that was the case, as much as Amanda loved her mother, there was a good chance that she had had to find other people, like Jared, to confide in.

Her glance drifted over the group of pictures displayed in the front hall, and caught on another familiar face: Amanda laughing, with her arm around one of the girls Mary had seen on the float with her—Paige Bailey. Mary knew her well. She was Tess Bailey's daughter, and Mary had spent plenty of time with both of them as she created new flavors for Bailey's Ice Cream Shop each month.

"Amanda's good friends with Paige too, isn't she?" Mary asked.

Jared nodded. "Great friends," he said.

"Do you think she might have told her anything about her father?"

"I'd be surprised if she hadn't," Jared said. Mary made a quick mental note to stop by Bailey's and talk with Paige. But thinking back on Paige at the float made her remember something else as well—how Betty had said that Jared and Amanda seemed to be arguing before the parade.

"What about you and Amanda?" she asked. "Was everything all right between you two?"

Mary couldn't be sure, but it seemed to her that she saw a trace of fear on Jared's face before he wiped it away with a friendly smile. "Oh, sure, Mrs. Fisher," he said. "They were great. Amanda's great. I'm the luckiest guy in town. Everyone knows that."

"Jared?" someone called from the next room. "Is everything all right?"

"Okay," Jared said, glancing back over his shoulder. "I guess I'd better go."

Mary smiled at him as he turned away. Then she stepped out, heading for the ice-cream shop, to find out what Paige knew about the secrets Amanda had been collecting about her own past—or her disappearance.

THIRTEEN

◆◆◆

The crowd was thin at Bailey's Ice Cream Shop when Mary entered, but just as she'd hoped, Paige was behind the counter, a fresh-faced girl around Amanda's age with her dark-haired pixie cut and a striped blue-and-white fisherman's shirt. She was working by herself, but she had learned all of Tess's good work habits and worked her way quickly through the small crowd ahead of Mary, giving each of her customers such a dazzling smile that Mary thought she could easily have taken Amanda's place as the July Queen.

"Sorry for the wait, Mrs. Fisher," Paige said when Mary reached the counter. "What can I get for you?"

"Actually," Mary said, "I came in to talk with you."

"Oh?" Paige said. She was obviously surprised by this answer, but she maintained her poise, like a pageant contestant waiting for the next question.

"I was hoping we could talk about Amanda for a sec?"

Paige's expression fell. She looked behind Mary to see that no one was behind her and gestured to a table in the parlor, where they both sat. "I'm so worried about her."

"I know," Mary said. "We all are. That's why I'm trying to do my part in looking for her." Mary scooted in her chair a bit. "I don't know if you remember, but Amanda worked at my bookshop earlier this year."

Paige smiled. "Of course I remember. She loved that."

Mary nodded. The poise with which Paige held herself reminded Mary that Paige wasn't just a source of information about Amanda's history. She had been there right on the float during the window of time when Amanda vanished. She was one of the only witnesses to Amanda's disappearance.

"I've just been trying to understand what might have happened to Amanda," Mary said. "Would you be willing to tell me the story? What you saw from where you were?"

Paige paused for a beat. Mary didn't feel quite sure she really knew what was going on behind Paige's cheerful smile. But then Paige nodded.

"I already told this all to the police," she said. "But I don't see how it can hurt to talk with you. I was actually the first one to realize Amanda was gone."

"You were?" Mary said. This detail had never been clear to her, even with all the information Betty had given her and she had watched Chief McArthur grapple with the past night.

Paige nodded. "Yes," she said. "I've been thinking about it, and I think it must have been when the supporters of that congresswoman all crowded into the parade route. She was walking ahead of us all the way, but right before we got to the end, a bunch of supporters came out of the audience to shake her hand. Jimmy actually stopped the truck completely for a couple of minutes. I was pretty frustrated, because I'd been smiling and waving and breathing dry ice at that point for almost an hour, and all I wanted was to get off that thing, put my swimsuit on, and dive in the ocean. My dad's been taking us swimming down by the shore during the fireworks for years. I was going to have to rush to get there, but there's nothing like it."

"So the float stopped," Mary prompted, hoping to lead her back to the main topic, Amanda's disappearance.

"Right," Paige said. "But that wasn't the only thing that was going wrong. The dais Amanda was sitting on had gone into the tree just like it was supposed to a couple of minutes before. I kept waiting and waiting for her to come out, because I had all these stupid jokes I wanted to make about how we were stuck behind the congresswoman. You know, all her people were wearing T-shirts that talked about progress toward the future and everything, but I didn't see them making much progress themselves. But she never came out."

"When did you realize she was gone?" Mary asked.

"At first, I figured she was just stuck," Paige said. "Something was wrong with the smoke machine, too, by then. Suddenly it was letting off like ten times as much smoke as it had been. We could barely see anything. Cindy was actually pretty upset, it seemed like. I think she thought this was going to be her big moment, you know. Getting to ride on the July Queen float and everything.

"I just figured," she went on, "we were practically at the end of the parade. Nobody could really even see us with all the smoke. We could hear Amanda in there when we talked to her. We'd just get her out when it was all over. But then we got back, and she wasn't there." Her eyes widened as she said this, with all the flair of a kid telling another kid a ghost story. She seemed to know that she had a good yarn to tell. But she didn't, Mary noticed, seem worried about her friend, despite what she had said. It was hard to tell with teenagers, though. As Jack had observed about Daisy, they lived moment to moment, happy one minute and worried the next.

"I also had some questions about Amanda's father," Mary said. "I found some things at Amanda's house this morning that made it seem as if she might have been trying to find him. Would you know anything about that?"

Suddenly, both the smiling July Queen attendant and the enthusiastic storyteller vanished, and Mary found herself face-to-face with a sullen and suspicious teenager. "Why would you think I'd know anything about that?" Paige asked.

"Well, I understand you're very good friends with Amanda," Mary said, adjusting her glasses. But that didn't bring back the sweet girl she'd just been talking to.

Paige raised her chin in defiance. "I don't know if I'd say *that*," she said.

"I saw a picture of you and Amanda at her house today, in fact," Mary said. "Right in the front hall. And Jared mentioned that you and Amanda were close."

At the mention of Jared's name, Paige's face darkened even more. "Did he?" she said, her eyebrow arched.

Mary studied her. Why this sudden change of attitude? And why in the world would Paige deny her friendship with Amanda when it was so evident? Her mind flashed back to the young woman on the docks who she thought she'd recognized as Amanda and the questions that had followed. She couldn't imagine what would have possessed Amanda to leave the parade. And why in the world hadn't she come back, when she knew her mother must be worried sick?

But a new thought occurred to her too: If Paige was right there on the float with her, could she have had anything to do with it?

Instead of responding to Paige's change in demeanor, Mary kept her own voice friendly and even. "I didn't mean to pry," she said. "I just thought, if you were friendly with Amanda, that maybe you might know something that would help."

"Like what?" Paige said, still wary.

Mary shrugged. "I'm not sure," she said. "That's why I thought I'd ask you. Everybody seems to have seen something different that day."

At this, Paige's expression softened. Sensing an advantage, Mary carefully pressed on. "Can you think of any reason Amanda might have for wanting to disappear?" she asked.

She saw a flicker in Paige's eyes that made her think for a moment that her question had struck a chord. But Paige just shook her head. She glanced past Mary, out the front window, as if she was trying to decide something.

Then she looked back. "Well," she said, in the same poised, welcoming tone she had used when Mary first arrived, "I don't want to get anyone in trouble...."

"This isn't about getting anybody in trouble," Mary said. "Like all of us, I just care about bringing Amanda back, safe and sound. Nothing else matters but that."

Paige seemed to struggle a little bit with herself. But then she took a deep breath and crossed her arms. "It's Cindy," she said. "I can't prove anything, but—"

Mary waited a second, so that she didn't seem too prying. Then she offered a prompt. "But...?"

Paige let the breath out and leaned in across the table. "The way they chose the court this year," she said. "They didn't just have Amanda pick her friends. I guess the vote was really close this year. Cindy almost won it. So the class officers thought it would be good to at least let her ride in the parade. Usually the queen gets to pick two people to ride with her as her court. But because the class chose Cindy for her, Amanda only got to pick one person for her court, instead of both of them."

"She picked you," Mary said.

Paige nodded.

Since Paige seemed to be willing to talk now, Mary refrained from pointing out to Paige that Amanda choosing her as her only friend for the July Queen court seemed to indicate that the two of them must be closer than Paige claimed. But the contradiction in Paige's stories did give her a moment of pause as she listened. Mary could tell clearly that there was a contradiction here. But were there other contradictions in Paige's story? Ones Mary didn't yet have enough information to see?

"Yes," Paige said. "And Amanda didn't complain about it at all. You'd never know from her that she didn't choose both of us. We all went shopping together for our dresses, and she brought us both our corsages for the parade day and everything."

"So what do you think all this might have to do with Amanda's disappearance?" Mary asked.

"It wasn't Amanda," Paige said. "It was Cindy. I just got the feeling that she was"—she looked out the window again, as if afraid of being overheard, then met Mary's eyes—"jealous."

"What gave you that idea?" Mary asked.

Paige shrugged, still with a somewhat furtive air. "I don't know," she said. "It wasn't any particular thing. More like the way she looked at her. Sometimes if Amanda wasn't sure quite what to do, or how to climb up on the float, or wave, or something, Cindy would get this look in her eyes."

"Like what?" Mary asked.

"Like she thought she could do a better job," Paige said, "if she were the July Queen."

Mary tried to call up any memory of Cindy, the other girl who had ridden on the float, but she couldn't bring much to mind. Amanda had done such a beautiful job of keeping her cool and waving to the crowd in the midst of the crazy contraption of the float that the other girls had faded completely into the background. The fact that she couldn't remember Cindy's face well wouldn't help Mary with her investigation, but it did lend credence to Paige's claim that Cindy might be jealous. Mary could see how it might sting to see another girl take all the attention on the float, especially if Cindy had known that she was only a few votes away from sitting on that same throne herself. But still, there was a long way from being a little jealous of a high school rival, to being mixed up in the disappearance of a girl who had now been missing for almost twenty-four hours.

"I can see how she might be jealous," Mary said. "But how jealous do you think she was? Enough to be mixed up in Amanda's disappearance?"

Paige shrugged. "I'm not saying she would have wanted to really hurt Amanda," she said. "But there were definitely times when I felt like if she had been able to just make Amanda disappear, she would have. Like I said, it was more of a feeling than anything I can prove."

Mary nodded.

"I'm not saying she *did* anything," Paige said. "Or at least, that she meant to. But you know how things go sometimes. You mean something for a prank, but something goes wrong, and suddenly it's a whole lot more serious."

"Do you think that's what happened to Amanda?" Mary asked. "A prank gone wrong?"

"I'm not sure about anything," Paige said. "But you were asking about anything else I saw. That's something I saw. Cindy was jealous of Amanda. If I were looking for Amanda, Cindy would be somebody I'd ask. At least a few questions. Maybe there's nothing there," she said. "But maybe there is."

"And where would you go," Mary asked, "if you wanted to talk with her?"

Paige answered this with a model salesgirl's slightly too-bright smile. "That's easy," she said. "She took a summer job at the Black & White Diner."

"Well," Mary said, "maybe I'll just walk over there now."

Paige started to nod, then glanced up at the clock on the wall behind Mary. Paige's face fell. "Not today," she said. "She only works breakfast and lunch. And we're coming up on dinnertime now."

Mary glanced back over her shoulder. Paige was right. She'd spent so much of the day searching for Amanda that she hadn't realized how late it had gotten. She'd barely seen Jack and Christa and Daisy at all. Thinking of them gave her a sudden pang. With difficulty, she brought her attention back to the question of Amanda's disappearance.

"Do you think Cindy would be working tomorrow?" Mary asked.

Paige nodded. "Every weekend," she said. "They're the busiest times of the week. With all the summer people coming in for a break before the week begins again."

Mary nodded. She knew this phenomenon well from the way traffic changed at her own shop between the lazy weekdays and the hectic weekends. "Well," she said, "thanks so much for making the time to talk with me."

Paige flashed her a brilliant smile. Mary was struck with the strong impression that Amanda and Cindy weren't the only ones on that float who could have pulled off the role of July Queen. "Oh, I'm glad to, Mrs. Fisher," Paige said. "I'd do anything to have Amanda back. We all would."

Mary smiled at her as she went out. But as she went, she realized that only one part of Paige's parting words rang true to her. She really believed that Paige, with her bright smile and easy poise, was a girl who could do anything. But she wasn't totally convinced that bringing Amanda back was the first thing on Paige's mind.

FOURTEEN

———◆◆◆———

"Hello?" Mary called as she set her purse down on the kitchen chair. She had hoped to be greeted by the big band of family she'd left there this afternoon. Even despite the friction with Daisy, she was never happier than when she had as many of the people she loved in one place as possible, and getting to share a few moments with Jack and Christa and Betty and Daisy, all in the same place, was wonderful, under any circumstances. Thinking of that gave her a jolt of longing for Lizzie. And the thought of having Lizzie and Jack in the same place made her miss John as well. But how could she have selfishly enjoyed her family when Amanda was missing and perhaps in danger?

And she'd been out investigating Amanda's disappearance for hours, she told herself. She couldn't very well expect her family to sit around the house, just waiting for her to come home. Especially not on a sunny July day on the Cape, with all the beauty of the rugged coast beckoning them to come outdoors and enjoy it. She'd actually been glad when Jack had called her earlier to let her know they were going out to explore Ivy Bay. And she could easily call them now to find out where they were and join up with them for their evening plans. First, though, it might be good to have a few moments to herself, just to think things over.

But as she walked through the house, she heard a strange rattle and shuffle deeper in the house.

Instantly, she froze. Under normal circumstances, she would have just explained the sound away as Gus exploring a new nook or a poorly balanced book slipping off a stack. But with Amanda gone, and reports of other missing girls on the Cape, and Daisy here to visit, Mary's nerves were on edge. Still, she managed to calm herself enough to test her first sensible explanation for the sound.

"Gus?" she called.

Instantly, Gus leapt up from a nearby chair, where he'd been half hidden in a pile of throw pillows, and probably dozing, which was why he'd missed her entrance. He blinked up at her somewhat balefully, as if waiting for her to tell him what exactly had been so important it had required interrupting his sleep. Then he seemed to remember that he was actually glad to see her come home and began to thread through her ankles, purring loudly.

The sound hadn't come from Gus, Mary realized as she nudged him gently out of the way with her toe.

So what had made it? Or who?

She padded carefully across the carpet, until she reached the door of the room where she'd heard the sound. When she did, she caught a flash of motion by the window seat, where no motion belonged. As her heart rose in her throat, the figure in the window started and whirled around.

Daisy, wearing headphones that were leaking some kind of loud music, wrapped in a blanket, with a computer in her lap, stared at her grandmother, wide-eyed, then began to laugh. "Grandma!" she said. "What are you doing, sneaking up on people! You almost scared me to death!"

Mary was so relieved to find Daisy safe and sound, instead of whatever else she had been afraid to find lurking in her back room, that she didn't even bother to scold her for having the headphones turned up so loud that she hadn't answered when Mary first called. Instead, she leaned over to gather her granddaughter in an awkward hug, then straightened up to take a look at what Daisy was working on, on the computer. To Mary's surprise, the screen was full of pictures of the parade.

"Where did you find those?" Mary asked.

"I took them," Daisy said. "I'm just posting them to Facebook right now. So people in Chicago can see what a real Cape Cod Fourth of July parade looks like."

"Oh, Facebook," Mary said teasingly. She wasn't much of a fan of social networking. But secretly, she was pleased to hear that Daisy had found something in Ivy Bay that she thought was interesting enough to merit the attention of her sophisticated city friends back home. But she knew better than to say anything. Daisy had made it clear that she didn't want to be pushed into enjoying this vacation. And if she was starting to enjoy her visit all on her own, Mary didn't want to spoil it by pointing it out too soon. "I'd love to take a look at those," she said instead.

"Sure!" Daisy told her. "It's easy. They're all just on my Facebook account, so you can go look at them anytime."

"Can I do that even though I don't have a Facebook account?" Mary asked, sitting down beside Daisy.

Daisy looked at her with disbelief. "You *still* don't have a Facebook account?" she repeated, as if Mary had just told her that she was born without thumbs.

Mary shook her head good-naturedly. "I'm afraid not," she said. "There just hasn't seemed to be much use for it. Or much time," she added. "To tell the truth, I've enjoyed my life this long without it. I'm just not sure why I would need it now."

"Well," Daisy said after a minute, with an expression of relief at having solved a knotty problem, "we can just make you one."

Mary almost objected. It wasn't just that she hadn't gotten around to making herself a Facebook account. It was that she preferred to live her life in real life and not over a computer connection, thank you very much. But, she realized, this must be how people got drawn into it all. Because real people, who they really loved, were also out on these social networks. And Daisy hadn't seemed as interested in doing anything since she got to Ivy Bay as she did in helping her grandmother set up an account. So Mary couldn't bring herself to refuse.

"All right," she said. "But what do we have to do? I don't really like to give out my personal information."

"You don't have to tell them anything you don't want to," Daisy said, clicking away at the keyboard.

The images of the parade vanished, and a screen full of blank fields came up.

Mary watched with bemusement as Daisy typed in Mary's name. Then Daisy glanced over at her grandmother. "Which e-mail address do you want me to use?"

Mary's brow furrowed. "I only have the one," she said.

"The one I write to you at?" Daisy said. "At the bookstore?"

"That's it," Mary said.

"Okay," Daisy said. "We won't even tell them anything else about you. You'll be like a ghost on the Internet. The government will think you're a spy or something."

"That sounds exciting," Mary said.

A moment later, a field of tiny photographs showed up on the screen. Daisy scrolled through them until she found one of herself. "There we are!" she said, and clicked on it. "I'm going to send myself a friend request from you," she said. "Then, once I accept it, you can look at any of those pictures you want."

"Wonderful," Mary said. "But I thought we were already friends."

Daisy looked like she had a quick retort to her grandmother's corny joke, but on second thought, she thought better of it. Instead, she continued to scroll through the pictures. "Here's Mom," she said. She clicked on Christa's picture, then hit a button on the page that came up next.

A little box came up, announcing "friend request sent."

"What are you doing there?" Mary asked.

"I'm sending out some friend requests for you," Daisy said. "So people know you're here."

"Well, you don't really need to ...," Mary began.

"It's no trouble," Daisy said. Then she added, "You want to be friends with Mom, don't you?"

Mary couldn't think of any answer for that but "Yes."

Daisy gave her an "I told you so" smile, and continued clicking. "And Dad," she said. "And here, I found connections to Grace Church." She clicked what seemed like a hundred times. "Oh, look! Here's Aunt Lizzie! Now you can look at all her pictures."

"*Hmm*," Mary said, and watched while Daisy clicked to make connections between her and half a dozen other relatives and friends who Daisy happened to recognize.

"All right," Mary said then. She had no intention of keeping this account, but she was thrilled to see her granddaughter so engaged. "Now show me how to take a look at your parade photos."

"Hang on a minute," Daisy said. With a new flurry of clicks, she logged out of Mary's new account, opened her own, and went up to a corner of the screen, where she clicked on a file of tiny faces, including a strange little cartoon icon. "This one's you," she said.

"It's not a very good picture, is it?" Mary said.

It took Daisy a minute to realize Mary wasn't serious. Then she smiled. "We'll have to choose a photo for you," she said. "Just as soon as we upload one. Or maybe I have one in here we can use."

"Who are these other people?" Mary asked, before Daisy could begin hunting for a profile picture for her.

"Oh, just some people I met last night in the warehouse," Daisy said. "Aunt Betty introduced me to them. They were all right. I'm going to meet up with them again tonight in a little while."

Again, Mary hid her smile. It sounded like Daisy might be enjoying the trip more than she even admitted.

"Actually," Daisy said and checked the time in the upper corner of her computer, "I'm supposed to be there pretty soon. I got distracted loading all these photos in. But they're all there now," she said. "And you can look at whatever you want now."

Quickly, she tapped a few more keys, closing out her own account and calling Mary's up again.

"Your password is 'lovesbooks,'" Daisy told her as she was typing it in. She gave her grandmother a mischievous smile.

Now the screen showed just one single photograph.

"See?" Daisy said. "I'm your only friend."

"Hardly," Mary protested.

Daisy gave her a playful eye roll. "Well, for now," she said. "Pretty soon other people will begin to respond to our requests, and you'll be friends with them too. But in the meantime"—she hit a few buttons, and the gallery of parade photos that had been on her screen when Mary came into the room flashed up again—"you can look as much as you like," she said, and handed her grandmother the laptop.

"Wonderful," Mary said. She looked down at the bottom of the screen. "Two hundred pictures?" she said. This was a far cry from the rolls she and John had taken of the parades back when Jack and Lizzie were young, when both film and developing were pricey enough to be luxuries for a family like theirs, just starting out.

"They're mostly from the end of the parade," Daisy said apologetically. "I didn't really think to take pictures until late." Mary noticed that Daisy didn't mention the argument she'd had with her father around the same time. Instead, Daisy hopped up from the couch. "Does it all make sense?" she said. "You just use these buttons to move forward and back."

"I've got it," Mary said. Then she teased, "It's not the first time I've used a computer. Thanks, sweetie."

"Okay," Daisy said. "Then I'd better go. I don't know how much time I've got. Dad says I have to meet him and Mom for dinner in a little while." Mary could tell from Daisy's face that she thought this was another of her father's unreasonable demands.

"Some girls might like to get to spend so much time with their dads," Mary said gently, thinking of Amanda and the box of artifacts she'd so painstakingly collected in an effort to get to know her own father.

But Daisy just shrugged breezily. "I guess," she said.

"Have a great time," Mary said.

As Daisy darted out, she flashed her grandmother a big smile that made Mary think maybe she'd forgotten her resolution not to enjoy her time in Ivy Bay after all.

Mary listened until she heard the front door thunk, indicating Daisy had made it out of the house. Then she started to click through the photos in the album, one by one.

They were clearly from the end of the parade, as Daisy had said. Everyone on the floats and marching on foot seemed to be wilting a bit, from the high school band to the July Queen and her court. Daisy had a good eye, though, and she'd done a great job capturing some lovely moments: a trombone player struggling to adjust his hat without losing his grip on the slide of his instrument, a July Queen court member leaning down from her float to put a Tootsie Roll directly into a toddler's hands. And besides the parade itself, Daisy had taken a lot of shots of the town and the crowd, probably because they seemed strange and exotic to her city-trained eye.

She'd even, Mary noticed, taken a series of shots of a little girl watching the parade from her father's shoulders near the bank. Mary's heart quickened when she saw this. The location was close to where Chief McArthur's deputies had reported the sightings of the strange man, and the timing was right. Was it possible that Daisy had captured an actual photograph of the stranger and his unwieldy package? And what had been in the package? Mary wondered.

But as she sifted through Daisy's pictures, scanning every face in the crowd by the bank, she didn't see anyone or anything that seemed out of place.

Disappointed, she moved on. More pictures of the parade, this time, the politician and her crew, who had swirled around the float at the same time it was breaking down. Again, Mary studied the pictures intently, looking for any trace of Amanda, or anyone who might have been involved in her disappearance. If there was a clue there, Mary didn't see it.

The next picture was another great example of Daisy's eye for street photography: a sweet, almost sentimental shot of a pair of teenagers surreptitiously holding hands as the parade went by. It was well after Amanda's float had gone by. You could see the shape of the tree she'd disappeared into, off in the distance. But Mary lingered over it even though it was no discernible help to her investigation, just because it was such a sweet image.

Then something caught her eye. Instantly, she zoomed in so she could get a better look at the faces of the couple. She peered at the image for a long moment. Then, when she was certain, she sank back in her seat.

The young man in the picture was Amanda's boyfriend, Jared. And the young woman whose hand he was holding was not Amanda.

As she clicked the photo to release the superzoom back to normal size, her phone rang.

"Mom!" Jack's voice came over the line. "I know you've been busy, but Christa and I are about to put in a reservation for lobster dinner at the Harbor View. Are you interested in coming with us?"

Mary glanced at the photograph again. She couldn't be sure what all this meant yet, but as she looked at it, she realized that if Daisy had posted this many pictures on the Internet, other people in town must have as well. What other evidence could she find of the scene Amanda had disappeared from, if she went looking?

"Mom?" Jack asked.

Even in the midst of this new discovery, her son's voice cut through all the confusion. Chief McArthur and all his force were on this case as well, Mary told herself. It wasn't up to her to solve it. Her son and his family had come all the way from Chicago to see her, and she was determined to spend some time with them.

"I'd love to," she told him.

"Great," Jack said. "They're saying about fifteen minutes."

Daisy wouldn't be excited about how soon Jack was planning dinner, Mary thought ruefully. She'd just be meeting up with her friends when Jack called her to join them.

"I'll be right down," Mary said.

But before she got up to go, she sat staring at the picture for another long moment, wondering what Jared was doing with another girl, but also what other images of the parade she might be able to find, not just on the Internet but anywhere else in town.

A short while later, Jack waved eagerly from a roomy table near one of the Harbor View's famous windows overlooking the water. Mary crossed the restaurant and sat down.

"We don't even need to look at the menus, right?" Jack said. "There's only one thing you could order in this place."

"Lobster," Daisy said from her seat next to him.

Jack nodded, and Daisy gave him a big grin.

Mary was grateful to see that there was at least one thing the two of them seemed to agree on.

Christa squeezed Jack's hand. "We had a great day in town," she said. "I found some wonderful things at the Tanaka Garden Center."

"It's a good thing they won't let us take plants on the plane," Jack joked.

"I'm actually not as interested in buying plants as I am in getting new ideas from what people do with them in different regions," Christa said.

"See, there's something for everyone in Ivy Bay," Jack said. "Christa likes the new ideas. I like the things that don't change. Lobster, for instance. That's the same, every year. And so is the Harbor View. For the most part," he said. He nodded at a small television that had been installed behind the counter, that was just visible from his angle. "I see they've got a new security system of some kind this year. But it mostly seems to be taking video of seagulls."

Christa laughed, but Mary's eyes suddenly grew wide. She'd been so busy sifting through still pictures of Amanda that she hadn't thought to look for video. And she knew just where one of the only other security cameras in town was placed: right along the parade route, only a block from where Amanda had disappeared, just outside the Ivy Bay Bank & Trust.

FIFTEEN

———◆◆◆———

Mary paused just inside the bank and looked around. The place had been built during the historical boom years by a fisherman-turned-banker who had hired a Boston architect to build an edifice imposing enough to convince Ivy Bay's somewhat suspicious-minded fishermen that their money would, in fact, be safe in his hands. Now officially owned by a New York bank, it was still run like a small-town establishment, helmed by Owen Cooper. The building itself wasn't big by Boston standards: just a high-ceilinged entrance with a handful of tellers' windows and offices to the side. But among the rest of Ivy Bay's clapboard storefronts and true Cape Cod architecture, it always felt to Mary like Boston, her girlhood hometown and the city where she'd spent the best years of her marriage with John.

Under normal circumstances, she often liked to stand there for a little while, drinking in the atmosphere, the ornate details in the old-fashioned ceiling and the brass of the teller windows. But this morning, she was one of the bank's first customers, and she crossed immediately past the seating area, where eight leather chairs surrounded a low square granite table, and knocked on the office door that belonged to Steve, her favorite banker.

Steve's face broke into a welcoming smile at the sight of her. "Mary," he said. "Good to see you! Come on in."

Mary smiled and sat down in one of the chairs for guests across from his desk.

Steve spread his hands. "What do you have for me today?"

"Actually," Mary said, "I was hoping you might have something for me."

Steve's eyebrows shot up. "Oh?" he said.

Mary's brow furrowed as she collected her thoughts. "You've heard about Amanda by now?" she said.

Steve's smile vanished. "Of course," he said. "It's terrible. I've been praying for that girl to come home. I can't stop thinking about her. I used to give her bank lollipops when she was only four or five. They'd come in together, just her and her mom. Her mom always seemed real worried, which I can understand, raising a girl like that on her own. But Amanda always had the biggest smile in the world. You couldn't resist smiling back when she smiled at you."

Mary nodded. "I was just looking through some pictures my granddaughter took of the parade," she said. "Looking for anything that might help us find Amanda. And then I realized, we don't have many security cameras on the streets in Ivy Bay, but—"

"I know where you're going with this," Steve said. "You'd like to look at the surveillance camera again."

Mary nodded. "Nobody saw what happened," she said. "But I realized last night, there were cameras everywhere. I've been looking at some pictures of the parade that people posted online. But then I also realized you might have video of the parade, even right here at the bank."

Steve nodded his head. "Smart thinking," he said, and smiled. "And you're not the only one in town who's thought of it."

Mary's eyebrows shot up. "Oh?" she said, startled.

Steve gave his head a brisk shake. "Nope," he said. "We had someone in from the police here yesterday morning, asking the same thing."

"Chief McArthur?" Mary asked.

Steve shook his head again. "Nope," he said. "Some woman from out of town. Part of some team the chief brought in. Specialists in missing children."

"Oh," Mary said, with a sinking feeling. She was glad for anything and anyone that might help bring Amanda back home safe and sound. She didn't care who it was. But it seemed like at every turn, Chief McArthur had been one step ahead of her. It made her feel like a foolish old lady, running around and sticking her nose into other people's business. And in this case, it seemed, she hadn't even gotten here until everyone else had been there and left.

But Steve didn't seem put out by the fact that she had turned up. "Do you want to see it?"

She'd come this far, Mary thought. She didn't know exactly what she might see that a professionally trained law enforcement agent would miss, but it couldn't hurt to look. "Yes, please," she said.

Steve turned the giant screen on his desk to face her. A video popped up on the screen. After a few more keystrokes, the video began to play. "I think this is the part they were interested in," Steve told her.

Mary could see immediately that he had started the video in the right place. The normally spacious sidewalk outside the bank was crowded with parade goers.

Now Mary could see at what point they were in the parade. The middle school band was just marching by, playing the Darth Vader theme from *Star Wars*. That meant that Amanda's float was just a few minutes behind, near the end of the parade. The faces of the surrounding crowd confirmed this: They were still happy, but they had lost some of the initial excitement of the beginning of the celebration, and had begun to show some fatigue, or even boredom.

Then, on the narrow strip of empty sidewalk not completely overtaken by the watching crowd, Mary caught sight of a strange figure. Unlike the rest of the crowd, he was staring down the street toward the oncoming parade, not watching the band that passed directly in front of him. And he was carrying a large, unwieldy package, wrapped in some kind of brown paper.

Mary's heart skipped a beat. Was this the stranger who people had reported seeing outside the bank around the time of Amanda's disappearance?

Steve noticed her agitation. "The police seemed to be real interested in this guy too," he said.

Mary could see why. The man was obviously not there as a parade goer. He wasn't dressed for it, for one thing. Everybody else around him was wearing beach gear or casual clothes, but he stuck out like a sore thumb in a light summer suit, glaringly out of place in an informal seaside town like Ivy Bay. But even if he'd been dressed just like anyone else in the crowd, his demeanor was so strange that he would have stuck out anyway.

The man was obviously under some kind of profound stress. His eyes darted up and down the street, scanned the crowd, then stared up the street again. From time to time, he paced back and forth, clutching the weird package. Then he'd stop and stare up the parade route, to where Amanda's float moved slowly down the street. Even in the video, Mary could see people taking quick glances at him over their shoulders—probably some of the same people who had mentioned him in their reports to the police.

"Real strange guy, huh?" Steve said as Mary watched.

She glanced away from the video feed to nod.

"Now, watch this," Steve said.

Mary had no intention of watching anything else. As she did, the strange man, who had been dithering back and forth in front of the bank for several minutes, seemed to catch sight of something off camera, on the parade route. Whatever it was, it obviously created some strong emotion in him. Even more agitated than before, he suddenly broke from the spot of sidewalk where the camera had captured him and headed off into the crowd. Just before he reached the limit of what the bank cameras were able to encompass, he actually ducked into the path of the parade, crossing through it on Main Street to the other side of Meeting House Road. Then he disappeared.

Mary's mind raced, fitting this new fact with all the others she had collected. Why would the strange man cut *through* the parade? What could be so important that he couldn't wait for the traffic to clear? But before she could put these new questions into place, something else happened on-screen: Amanda's float rolled into the frame, with Amanda still clearly in view, waving to the crowd from between the boughs of the giant papier-mâché tree. The bank was only a few blocks away from the spot where the parade would later grind to a halt, and Amanda would slip inside the tree—and disappear.

While the float, and Amanda, slid by on the screen, Mary glanced again in the direction the man had disappeared, trying to figure out what he could possibly have been doing, dragging the big package down Meeting House Road.

"Pretty interesting, huh?" Steve asked.

Again, Mary had an impulse to call Chief McArthur up and insist that the blonde girl she'd seen must have had something to do with Amanda's disappearance. But he had all the information she did, she realized. She'd told him everything she knew. And he had a copy of this recording. She couldn't run his investigation for him. And it sounded to her like he was ahead of her in the game anyway.

She sighed.

"Yep," Steve said. "There's not much excitement after that. Especially if you already watched the parade in real life."

He hit a few keys, and the tail end of the parade froze on the screen. "I assume you would like a copy?" he said, knowing well Mary's frequent involvement in mysteries around town.

"Of course," Mary said with a rueful smile. "Thank you."

Steve hit a few more keys, inserted a disk with the bank logo on it into a port, and the drives on his desk began to whir, copying data.

A moment later, he pulled the disk free and handed it to her. "There you go," he said.

"Thank you," Mary told him.

Steve shook his head. "It's nothing," he said. The temporary pride he'd shown in his security gadget faded from his face as the seriousness of the situation set in again. "If this provides even the tiniest clue to bring Amanda home, it'll be worth every penny we invested in it. I hope you and Chief McArthur find something in it."

"I hope so too," Mary said, then rose and went out.

She made her way out to the lobby and stepped outside into the bright morning. She couldn't shake the image of the man disappearing into the crowd, or the other image that had haunted her for the past few days, of the strange blonde girl disappearing into the shadows.

She glanced up at the video camera mounted over the door behind her, silently recording all the morning's activity in Ivy Bay, including hers. A moment later, she had left it behind, heading down the street to retrace the steps of the man in the video.

SIXTEEN

❖◆❖

"Jack?" Mary said when she heard the click of the receiver from Jack's cell phone.

But instead of Jack's familiar baritone, she heard a girlish giggle. Then Daisy's voice came across the line, dropped unnaturally low, in imitation of her father's. "Yes, this is Jack Fisher," she said. "How can I help you?"

Mary could hear Jack's futile protests in the background, but at least the freeze between them seemed to have thawed for the moment.

"Hi, sweetie," Mary said. "How is everything going over there?"

"Grandma," Daisy said, "you're almost as bad as Dad. How do you think any of us survive in Chicago when you're not there to check on us every minute?"

Mary smiled wryly. Once again, Daisy sounded more like her father than Daisy would like to admit. "Honey," she said, "I'm not calling because I want to check up on you. I'm calling because I love to hear your voice. If it weren't so important to find Amanda, I'd be spending every minute of this weekend with you. I'm just trying to spend all the time with my family I can, even if it's by cell phone."

"That's sweet," Daisy said, slightly chastened.

"And I want to check in on you," Mary teased. "How are you all doing? Is everyone okay?"

"Grandma!" Daisy moaned.

Mary heard a slight scuffle at the other end of the line. Then Jack's voice came on the phone.

"Mom," he said, a joking tone in his voice. "I don't know what I'm doing wrong. I'm sure I was a perfectly obedient child, but for some reason, Daisy can't be convinced just to do everything I tell her."

"That is strange," Mary said, joking along with him. "How are you doing over there?"

"Great," Jack said. "We're just finishing up breakfast, and then I think we're going to head into town and see what kind of adventures we can rustle up. You have any news on Amanda?"

"I'm not sure," Mary said. "I have a few things I'd like to check out. But I'm missing spending time with you and Christa and Daisy."

"Don't worry about that," Jack said. "If Daisy were missing, we'd want everyone we know looking for her. And there's nobody I'd rather have on the trail than you. We understand. We can fend for ourselves. You're our favorite attraction in Ivy Bay, but there are a few other ways we can find to amuse ourselves."

"Well, I don't want you to get too used to not having me around," Mary said.

"Don't worry about that either," Jack said. "We miss you plenty."

"Thanks, Jack," Mary said. "I'll catch up with you just as soon as I can."

"That sounds great," Jack told her.

Mary ended the call and surveyed the corner between her store and Ivy Bay Bank & Trust. For a few steps, she retraced the path where the strange man had followed the parade. Then, at about the same place he had, she stopped. She waited for the light to change, then crossed where he had crossed, heading through the intersection toward the wide yard of Grace Church.

Once she reached it, she was out of range of what the bank's cameras had recorded. Now she stepped along uncertainly, looking for anything that might give her some clue as to what had lured the strange man over to the other side of the street in the middle of the parade.

Well, if nothing else, he hadn't seemed to be in any mood to dawdle on the street. With this in mind, Mary continued down the block, past the grocers, and then to the high school, still not sure what she was looking for. Then, just past the high school, she came to a dead stop.

She was standing across from the entrance to Kemper's Alley. The alley was hardly a secret in town. It was well known because it was the quickest route from Ivy Bay's commercial district to the shore. It began by the high school, but a series of well-worn footpaths also led to it from behind the Main Street stores. Ivy Bay kids were always darting between the gaps between stores to wind their way out to Kemper's Alley and down to the shore.

Mary crossed the street to the alley entrance. Like everything else in Ivy Bay, it was meticulously well kept. Stacks of cardboard boxes for deliveries were piled neatly by the back doors of several businesses, and a few business owners had even planted sweet window boxes of shade-loving plants in their back windows, a kind of inside joke between them and the longtime residents of Ivy Bay who knew the back way, since few of Ivy Bay's visitors would ever find the narrow shortcut. The alley didn't follow the normal grid of Ivy Bay, but instead, it jutted and jogged in a series of blind alleys and weird turns, cutting through empty lots and back ways until it spilled out onto Shore Drive.

As Mary's mind completed the route the stranger might have taken after the alley crossed 6A, she drew in a sharp breath. The shortcut emptied onto Shore Drive almost exactly where Mary had seen the blonde girl slip into the shadows when she called out to her, just after Amanda had disappeared.

But had the stranger ever even been here?

Mary looked around.

The entrance to the alley was guarded by a set of industrial bins that served the needs of the high school. Other than that, the school maintenance crew had done a beautiful job. The alley was remarkably free of litter. This length of the alley had even been recently paved, probably with some additional funds from the school.

With a sigh, Mary started past.

But just as she reached the other side of the next set of bins, something caught her eye.

A scrap of brown paper peeked from the otherwise pristine bins.

Wrinkling her nose slightly, Mary approached them. It was probably just a grocery bag, she told herself. After all, they'd be common in the high school, for all kinds of things: material for projects, low-cost lunch sacks, even makeshift luggage. But her mind couldn't help thinking back to the brown paper she'd just seen, wrapping the package the strange man had been carrying in the bank's surveillance video.

Gingerly, she lifted the light plastic top of the bin.

To her surprise, it was empty except for a large wad of brown paper that seemed to have been so hastily bunched and discarded that it had been caught in the lip of the bin as it was abandoned.

Mary's skin tingled. This wasn't solid proof, she knew. But it certainly felt like a clue. Had the strange man unwrapped his package for some reason in the alley? And where had he gone then?

Quickly, Mary followed the familiar path through the back alleys of Ivy Bay and out to Shore Drive.

She knew the back way shaved time off travel between the business district and the docks, but she was surprised, when she actually counted it off, how much more quickly she arrived at Shore Drive. It took her just a few minutes to reach the road, while it would have been a good five minutes, at least, if she'd followed Main Street down, then turned at the corner where Amanda disappeared.

But it was where Kemper's Alley emptied out that took her breath away. She'd guessed it was near the spot where she'd seen her mystery blonde. But when she stepped out of the alley, she found herself immediately across from the now-familiar cut between the two fishermen's shanties, where she'd seen the girl vanish and discovered what she believed was a telltale blonde hair. And that spot couldn't have been more perfect, she realized, for someone to hide while waiting for another person to emerge from Kemper's Alley.

Her mind roiled with questions. Who was the mystery man, and what had brought him to Ivy Bay? Had the blonde woman she'd seen been Amanda, as she first assumed? Or was she someone else entirely? Mary doubted that, at this point, but it was still possible that she was on the completely wrong track.

She continued to think about the mystery man. If he had anything to do with Amanda's disappearance, had she left with him voluntarily? Or had he taken her away against her will—perhaps with the use of something in the large package he had been carrying throughout the video?

As she wondered, she scoured the area again, looking for anything that might shed any more light on the situation: a scrap of cloth, a footprint, another scrap of brown paper like the one that had concealed the mystery man's parcel from the prying eyes of the security camera. But she faced the same problem now that she had the night of the parade: thousands of people had passed that night. The ocean wind had blown ever since. And hundreds more people had passed through since then. If the out-of-town experts, with their specialized techniques, hadn't been able to find anything here, what could she expect to find? Mary thought.

Lord, she prayed, *I don't seem to be doing anybody much good these days. But You see how much we all care for Amanda. Even if what I'm doing doesn't help Chief McArthur's investigation at all, please take everything I'm doing as a prayer, to bring her home.*

She wandered down by the docks, glancing here and there, wondering what direction the man had gone after he left the alley—back down toward the parade? Into the darkness, toward the fireworks?

By the time she reached Sam's Seafood, nestled in among the docks, she was both discouraged and hungry. She only hesitated for a moment outside the familiar door to his friendly establishment. Then she pushed it open and went in.

Sam's face lit up as it always did when she arrived.

"Mary," he said. "Well, this is a lovely surprise. Here for an early lunch?"

Mary nodded and settled down at the long counter that Sam ruled the restaurant from. "Sure," she said. "What have you got today?"

"Got a great catch of lobster last night," Sam said with a wink. "How about a famous Cape lobster roll?"

"On your sourdough?" Mary asked.

Sam nodded. "Only the best."

"That sounds perfect," Mary said.

"Anything to drink?"

"You have iced tea this early?" Mary asked.

"For you?" Sam asked. "Always."

He set a tall glass of sweet tea on the counter in front of her and typed her order into the console. Through the swinging door behind the counter, Mary could hear someone spring to life back in the kitchen, probably starting to make her sandwich.

"So what brings you down to the docks today?" Sam said. "I would have thought you'd be up at your own shop, at least till lunch."

Mary nodded. "You're right," she said. "And normally I would be. I was just—" She hesitated, not sure exactly what she'd been doing. "Looking for Amanda," she finished after a minute.

Sam's face clouded. "Ah," he said. His eyes fastened on hers. "Any luck?" he asked.

Mary shook her head. "There's not much left to find," she said. "At least not that I can see. Not after the crowds came through. It wasn't exactly a slow night in town."

Sam nodded vigorously. "You're telling me," he said. "The Fourth of July crowd is one of the biggest we ever have in here. We spend the whole parade chopping lemons, cutting bread, reserving ice, because so many people come in, the machine can't keep up. One of my servers said this year it was like battening down for a hurricane. And that's what it feels like, when they all hit. But I love it," he admitted. "I didn't open this place to look out at the water by myself. I always imagined it packed to the gills."

Mary smiled at the image of lemons and bread piled up on his counter. But then her smile disappeared as her mind connected something. She'd thought the docks were deserted when she slipped down to look for Henry during the parade. But she hadn't been the only one down there. Sam had been there too.

"Sam," she said, "did you see anything that night?"

"Besides whitefish and crab legs?" Sam said. "Not much."

"What about before the dinner rush?" Mary asked. Sam was famous for standing out on the dock, clapping strangers on the shoulders and bellowing at them that they ought to come into his restaurant and try the best seafood on the Eastern Seaboard. "Were you out on your welcome mat?"

Sam shook his head. "There wasn't time," he said. "It was an all-hands-on-deck situation in the kitchen." Then he turned his head to the side. "Wait," he said. "I did get out for a minute. Just after the fireworks began. We had a good crowd in here, but I always like to slip out and get a little glimpse. Otherwise I feel like I missed the Fourth of July."

Mary's heart beat a little faster. "Did you see anything?" she said.

Sam's brow furrowed, but he shook his head no.

Mary pressed on. "Did you see a blonde girl at all? Long blonde hair? Maybe seventeen?"

Sam shook his head again. "Not that I remember," he said.

"What about a man in a suit?" Mary said. "He would have been carrying a big package."

"No . . . ," Sam said, drawing out the word as he thought. Then he shook his head again, decisively this time. "I would have remembered that. Guy in a suit in that crowd would have stuck out like a sore thumb. There was really a guy in town in a suit that night?" he asked, somewhat incredulous.

Mary nodded. "A couple of people reported seeing him. And the bank video caught some footage of him."

Sam shook his head. "Well, if he came down this way, I missed him," he said.

A bell dinged from the kitchen. "I think you're up!" Sam said, and disappeared through the swinging doors.

A moment later, he emerged again, with a white plate decorated with a simple navy stripe, piled high with his famous sea-salt french fries and a generous helping of sweet lobster in a creamy dill mayonnaise, with a bright green sprig of lettuce, on a toasted sourdough bun. The plate was finished with a spike of Sam's own dill spears, a recipe he made himself, starting with genuine Atlantic salt water.

"First one of the day," he said. "You'll have to tell me how it is."

"Thank you," Mary said, settling her napkin in her lap. The first bite, as always, was heavenly: a delicious mix of delicate meat, tangy sauce, and toasty bread. "It's perfect," she told him.

"That's what I like to hear!" Sam said.

As she enjoyed the sandwich, he puttered around behind the counter, putting things in order for the coming day.

"You know," he said, as she tried a crispy wedge of fried potato dusted with sea salt, "we do have our own mystery here down on the docks this morning."

"You do?" Mary said, curious.

Sam nodded, suddenly sheepish. "It almost seems a shame to mention it, because it doesn't matter much compared to finding Amanda. But a boat was discovered missing this morning at the marina."

"Missing?" Mary repeated.

Sam nodded. "Yep," he said. "Just gone from the slip."

"You're sure they're not just out for an early sail?" Mary asked, thinking of Henry's habit of taking his own boat out into the misty solitude of first light.

Sam shook his head. "Nope," he said. "It was gone yesterday too. Never came in, last night or this morning."

"I hope everyone's okay," Mary said.

"Oh yes," Sam said. "Everyone present and accounted for. That's the first thing they check at the marina when something goes missing."

"Then do they think it might have been ... taken?" Mary said.

Sam shrugged. "They might not know for a while," he said. "They don't usually call in a missing boat for a few days. It's not like you have to file a flight plan with the FAA before you go out for a sail. And you don't want to put out an APB on your buddy if he's just a little late coming in one night ... "

"Do you know whose boat it is?" Mary asked, polishing off the last bite of her sandwich.

"I sure don't," Sam said. "But I have to walk by the empty slip to get to work. It's just a few spots down. Real pretty windsock on the end of the dock. Shaped like a jellyfish, with all its tentacles blowing out."

"This was delicious," Mary said. She pushed her plate across the counter, and laid a bill down beside it.

"Let me get you some change for that," Sam said.

Mary smiled at him. "I'm all set," she told him and headed for the door. A few slips down the way, just like Sam said, she saw the flash of open water between two boats that bobbed gently against the docks that ran out on either side of Sam's restaurant. A quick check of the area showed the windsock he'd been talking about too, a gray slip of fabric with pale pink and gray streamers blowing out behind it like the limbs of a man o' war.

Gingerly, Mary made her way down the dock, looking for any clue to the vanished boat. But looking into the waves made looking for clues to Amanda's disappearance seem easy. The ocean was even more mysterious. If the person or people who had taken the missing boat had dropped anything into the water, it was long buried at the bottom of the bay or carried far out to sea. And the silvery wood of the dock wasn't telling any tales.

She sighed and looked out to sea.

"Are you here about the boat?" The voice came from below Mary, so close to the surface of the bay that, for a moment, she had the eerie feeling that the water she had just been gazing into was talking back to her.

Then she caught a glimpse of motion to her side, and her glance fastened on a pert, middle-aged woman who was energetically unwinding ropes and tying off knots on one of the nearby vessels, preparing her boat for a sail.

"Oh," Mary said. "I just came down from Sam's. He mentioned a boat was missing, and I thought I'd take a look."

"It's funny," the woman said. "I thought it came in late yesterday, but when I came back this morning and it still wasn't here, I thought, something must be wrong."

"Do you know whose boat it is?" Mary asked.

The woman nodded. "I've only been sharing this slip with them for ten years," she said. "It's Craig and Ellie. The Wilsons. I actually tried to give them a call last night to make sure everything was okay, but no one answered."

Wilson. The name echoed in Mary's head for a minute until she made the connection. "Do they have a son?" she asked. "Jared?"

The woman smiled and nodded. "They sure do," she said. "Real nice kid. That's why I decided not to worry last night. I figure if they'd gone missing, he'd have raised an alarm by now. Or if he'd gone out, they'd be looking for him."

"That sounds right," Mary said. "But I hope they find the boat."

"Me too," the woman said. "It's nice to have some breathing room, but they've been good neighbors."

Mary smiled and then turned to go.

As soon as she reached the end of the docks, she dialed information. "Wilson," she said. "Ivy Bay." She confirmed the street the operator gave her, and the operator made the connection for her.

A moment later, a young man answered the phone. "Wilson residence," he said. "This is Jared."

"Hello," Mary said. She didn't give Jared her name so that she wouldn't tip him off to who was calling. "I'm calling for Ellie. Is she available?"

"Ah, no, I'm sorry," Jared said. "Mom and Dad went to visit friends in Michigan for the holiday weekend. Can I take a message for her?"

Mary's heart thudded in her chest. She already had good reason to believe that Jared wasn't absolutely trustworthy, and she wasn't sure what his dalliance with the other teenage girl had to do with Amanda—if anything at all. But if Jared had anything to do with the disappearance of Amanda, or of his parents' boat, there was no point in tipping him off to the fact that she'd heard about it until she understood more.

"No, thanks," she said. "I'll just call back."

When the connection broke, she hit a few strokes on her phone, dialing again. This time Jack's voice came across the line.

"Mom," he said, "how's it going? Any news on Amanda?"

"Nothing solid," Mary said. "What are you and the family up to?"

"We're doing some very serious business," Jack said. "Let me see. This morning I made pancakes with Mickey Mouse ears. We got those all cleaned up. And now we're downtown, making a very important decision between midmorning pie at the Black & White Diner or a visit to Cape Cod Togs."

"That sounds like a serious decision," Mary agreed. "What are the arguments on either side?"

"Well," Jack said, "Christa has pointed out that anything we get at Cape Cod Togs could serve as a great reminder of this wonderful weekend."

"That's true," Mary said. "And on the other side."

"Well," Jack said, "pie."

"Didn't you say you already made pancakes this morning?" Mary asked.

"Yes," Jack said. "But we ate those with our regular stomachs. We have separate stomachs, just for the pie."

Mary heard laughter, and then a jumble of syllables in Christa's voice in the background. "Okay, Christa says she doesn't," Jack amended. "But Daisy and I do."

"It must be genetic," Mary said. "I think you get that from your father."

"Just like I got my mother's brains," Jack said. "So, what do you think? Want to play tiebreaker?"

"You have a tie between the three of you?" Mary said.

Jack laughed. "It's the pie," he said. "We start trying to count votes, and then we get distracted. But really, what do you think? We'd love some advice from our favorite local."

Mary thought back quickly to her conversation with Paige Bailey, when Paige had suggested she talk with Cindy Adams, who was working at the Black & White Diner for the summer. "Pie always sounds great to me," she said. "In fact, what if I meet you there?"

SEVENTEEN

◆◈◆

As always, Nicole Hancock greeted Mary with a bright smile when Mary stepped into the Black & White Diner. Her blonde hair was swept up in a messy knot, and a pair of rhinestone flags sparkled on either ear.

"So patriotic," Mary said, glancing at them.

Nicole's smile widened. "I know we're past the Fourth now," she said. "But I figured I could wear them through the weekend, at least."

"Absolutely," Mary agreed.

"And you're probably looking for your family," Nicole said. "I just seated them."

Mary glanced around the diner and quickly caught sight of Christa, Daisy, and Jack in a corner booth. "I see them," she said. "Thanks so much."

"Oh," said Nicole, "we're always glad to have you. And we love having your family too."

Mary trailed quickly through the scattered tables between her and her family, while keeping an eye out for Cindy Adams. The Black & White Diner wasn't a five-star tourist destination like the Chadwick Inn, and it didn't have a beautiful view of the water like the tables at the Harbor View, but it was a favorite with locals for breakfast and lunch. It was exactly the kind of establishment that thrived by hiring talented teenagers who were eager and presentable, but hadn't yet gained the kind of experience in the restaurant business that a place like the Chadwick Inn or the Harbor View might demand.

Although Mary hadn't been able to call her face to memory, when she saw Cindy, Mary recognized her immediately from the float, even though her pink gown had been replaced by a neat navy-blue polo shirt and sensible khakis, and her brunette hair was tied back, instead of free around her face.

But it didn't look like she'd get a chance to talk to her anytime soon. The lunch rush had just begun, and Cindy seemed to have her hands full, juggling the orders for several tables.

Mary slipped into the seat Jack patted for her in the booth. "Well," she said, "I'm glad getting together with me got your vote."

Jack smiled, but Daisy scowled. Mary had hoped that the light conversations she'd had with them earlier indicated a thaw in relations, but that didn't seem to be the case.

"You call this a democracy?" Daisy said.

"I'm just curious," Jack said. "When was the last time you paid taxes?"

Daisy crossed her arms and sank back in the corner.

Jack shook his head and forced a smile for Mary.

"How's it going, Mom?" he asked. "Any word?"

Mary shook her head and took another glance at Cindy. She didn't want to talk about the ongoing investigation where anyone might hear. And she didn't want to tip off Cindy about why she had come to the diner before she got a chance to talk with her.

The family lapsed into an uncomfortable silence.

"But enough about that," Mary said. "What are your plans for the afternoon?"

Christa smiled and took Jack's hand. "Jack's chartered us a boat for the afternoon," she said. "It's going to take us quite a ways up the coast."

"That sounds lovely," Mary said enthusiastically. She glanced at Daisy to see her granddaughter's reaction.

"I'm not going," Daisy said.

"She was invited," Christa said. "But she decided she'd rather not come. So it's going to be a nice date for me and Jack."

Jack looked at Daisy unhappily. "We were actually wondering if you'd be willing to keep an eye on Daisy while we're gone."

"I'm sixteen years old," Daisy said. "I don't need a babysitter. People actually hire *me* to babysit."

"Do you remember when I babysat you when you were little?" Mary asked, quickly changing the subject. "What did we used to do then?"

"We made chocolate-chip cookies," Daisy said. "That were mostly chocolate chips." Seemingly against her will, a smile played on her lips.

"We could always do that again," Mary suggested.

Daisy shook her head.

A waitress approached and laid big slices of pie down before each of them. "We ordered for you," Jack said. "Blueberry. But if you want to, I'll trade you for my cherry."

"Blueberry's perfect," Mary said, digging in.

For the rest of the meal, the family chatted idly, comparing the various pies and speculating about what Jack and Christa might see on their afternoon charter. Then Jack got the check, and they rose to leave.

"We need to be down at the docks in about half an hour," he said. "I guess we'd better head home."

Mary glanced around the diner. The lunch crowd had thinned while they'd been eating, and now Cindy looked as if she might actually have a minute to talk. She stayed in her seat in the booth. "You go ahead," she said. "I'll be home before you need to go."

"Okay," Jack said, kissing his mom's cheek. "See you at home."

After Jack and Christa left, with Daisy trailing reluctantly behind them, Mary turned her attention back to the diner. It didn't take her long to get Cindy's attention. When Cindy came over, she gave Mary the same smile she'd given all the other customers she'd greeted. Like Paige, she was confident and friendly, but her smile wasn't quite as dazzling, which somehow made her seem more approachable.

"Can I help you?" she asked.

"Actually," Mary said, "I was hoping to talk with you a bit. About Amanda."

Cindy's smile vanished. "Oh," she said, her eyes wide. "I'd be really glad to." She looked over her shoulder at the restaurant. "But we're finishing our rush," she said. "I don't want to get in trouble."

"It won't take long," Mary promised her.

"Tell you what," Cindy said, "could you wait just a little while? I could be with you in just a minute."

"That sounds good," Mary said.

With a smile, Cindy went off to finish serving her last customers. When Mary's own server came, Mary ordered a cup of mint tea. As she sipped the tea, she watched Cindy move around the restaurant. Her smile was unfailing, and she didn't even seem to mind holding a baby a mother passed her as she struggled to work the mechanics of a high chair for the child to sit in. After a few minutes, the rush seemed to die down. Cindy came over and slid into the seat across from Mary.

"Phew," she said. "I'm sorry about that. But I've got a few minutes now, I think. How can I help you? Are you working with the police?"

"I'm a friend of Amanda's," Mary said. "I'm just trying to understand a little better everything that happened."

"I wish I knew," Cindy said. "I mean, I was right there, and I still don't. It's so hard. I just keep going back over and over it. But I already told the police everything I know."

"Would you mind going back over it with me?" Mary asked. "Maybe we'll come up with something you didn't remember before."

Cindy glanced over her shoulder to make sure her section was still free. Nobody stood waiting for a seat. "Sorry," she said. "I just have to keep checking. But, yeah, I'm glad to go back over it. The biggest thing, I guess, is that I did see Amanda go back into the tree that last time. I'd been wondering how it worked, because she'd been joking around the whole time about how she felt like a doll on top of a music box, just spinning around and around, but I kept waving to the crowd and getting distracted every time she actually went in. The kids are ridiculously cute," she added. "You wouldn't believe it. And they're all jumping up and down and shouting, 'Princess!' Or, 'Candy!' It's kind of irresistible."

"But you did catch her going into the tree?" Mary prompted. "That last time?"

Cindy nodded. "I did," she said.

"Tell me what was happening at that moment," Mary said. "I understand that the float had stopped because of a slowdown with the parade."

Cindy nodded. "Yep," she said. "There was a snag with all these politicians marching around us. And then Jimmy got out to check that everything was all right under the chassis."

"He did?" Mary said. She'd talked to both Jimmy and Paige, and neither of them had mentioned anything about this detail. Paige had complained about Jimmy's long stops, but not about him getting out of the truck. Were they keeping something from her? Or was Cindy embellishing the story?

"Did it take him long?"

Cindy shook her head. "Not very. I guess he decided whatever it was he could just figure it out at the end of the parade. By that time, the dry-ice machine had gone crazy too, so we were pretty much covered in smoke. It looked more like a forest fire than an enchanted forest. Jimmy was back in the cab in just a couple of minutes. The politicians weren't even out of the way when he got back in. So nobody was really where they were supposed to be for a couple of minutes."

"Nobody?" Mary asked.

Cindy shook her head. "No," she said. "I mean, Amanda wasn't supposed to be stuck in the tree for very long. It was kind of a magic trick, you know. The July Queen goes in.

The July Queen comes out. Nobody really wants to see a float with the July Queen stuck inside a tree. Usually, she was only in there for a minute or two. Long enough for the crowd to ooh and aah, and then the dais would turn and she'd pop back out. So we knew pretty much right away that something was wrong. And when the truck got stopped by that crowd of politicians, Paige got up and tried to see what was wrong. She was messing around with the mechanism for a little while."

This was another detail that Paige hadn't mentioned. Mary tried to search Cindy's eyes, but she seemed totally open. Which one of them was telling the truth? Or did they just remember different details?

Cindy went on. "But when she saw Jimmy heading back to the cab," she said, "Paige got back in her seat before he started the truck up. It's actually kind of hard to keep your footing on those things while they're moving. It's kind of like trying to stand up on a train when you visit Boston. You want to be sitting down on the float while it's moving. Because you don't have anything to grab onto, like on the train."

Since Mary couldn't be certain whether Cindy or Paige was telling the truth, she gave Cindy a subtle test. "Paige didn't mention that," she said. "When I talked to her."

Cindy looked slightly surprised. Then she shrugged. "Well," she said, "there was a lot going on. It'd be easy to forget. And it doesn't seem that important, even at the time. Not compared to Amanda going missing. I could have forgotten it myself, if you didn't come in here. I'm not sure I even told it to the police."

"Did you like riding on the float?" Mary asked. "It seems like it'd be a lot of fun. But I understand you were almost the

July Queen yourself." She tried to put some extra sympathy in her voice, in hopes that Cindy might open up to her about any resentments she had, but Cindy just laughed.

"Oh my gosh!" she said. "I'm so glad they didn't pick me! Do you know what you have to do if you're July Queen? It's not just riding on the float. You have to go to walkathons and cut ribbons at grocery store openings and hand out prizes for the biggest fish, all year long. I was never happier than when they finished that count and it turned out to be Amanda, not me. I even told them I didn't need to be on the float. But when I went home and told my mom that, it practically broke her heart. So finally I went back and told them, sure, I'd do it. She was so happy. And picking out the dress was fun. I think we tried out about a hundred of them before we picked that one."

"Normally, Amanda would have picked two of her own friends, is that right?" Mary said.

Cindy looked like she hadn't thought of this before. She was quiet for a minute, mulling it over. "Sure," she said. "I guess."

"Are you two friends?" Mary asked.

"I'd say we're friend-*ly*," Cindy said, with an emphasis on the "ly." "We get along fine. It was fun to help make the float with her."

"You must both have a lot of friends," Mary said, still probing to see if Cindy was just putting on a good show, hiding the jealousy of Amanda that Paige had told her about. "If you were so close in the running to be the July Queen."

Cindy shrugged again. "I think we both kind of do a lot of stuff. I don't know if we have a lot of friends, or if people just know our names. Either way, I guess. It's fine." She gave Mary another one of her bright smiles.

"Of course," Mary said, trying another angle to see what else Cindy knew. "Amanda's always seemed special to me, don't you think? She's such a pretty girl. And obviously well liked by her classmates. And Jared seems like such a nice young man. She must be very lucky."

For the first time, Cindy's expression clouded. She sat back against the booth opposite Mary, a slight frown crossing her face. "Huh," she said.

It was so obvious to Mary that Cindy was biting her tongue about something that she pressed on. "What's on your mind?" she asked.

Cindy's frown deepened as she struggled to find an answer. She was obviously laboring under some kind of deep emotion, but Mary couldn't tell whether it was the jealousy that Paige had mentioned or something else.

"Um," Cindy said, "Amanda's great. But I can't say I'd ever want to trade places with her."

"Why do you say that?" Mary asked.

Cindy twisted back to look over her shoulder. When she saw Nicole seating a new customer in her section, her relief was palpable. "I'm so sorry," she said, in a voice that sounded anything but. "But I've got to go take care of these people. You understand?"

Mary nodded and watched as Cindy crossed the restaurant and gave the new customers a bright smile.

After a moment, Mary checked her watch. It was close to the time she'd promised to be home so that Jack and Christa could go out on their afternoon date. She needed to get home to Daisy. She seemed to have enjoyed her time with the local Ivy Bay young people the night before, but relations between her and her parents were obviously still frosty. Mary was hoping that, if the two of them spent a bit of one-on-one time, just grandma and granddaughter, she might be able to help broker a peace between them. But before any of that happened, she had to make sure she got home in time for Jack and Christa to get to the boat Jack had chartered.

Mary laid a few bills on the table to cover her tea. Then she glanced up at Cindy again. Cindy's smile was so bright as she greeted the next guests that it made the shadow that had crossed her face when Mary pressed her about Amanda even more disturbing. Mary nodded at Cindy, who was leading the couple to a table as Mary stood to go. Then she stepped back out onto bustling Main Street.

She had hoped to clear things up by coming here, she thought. But if anything, she was even more confused than before. Now she had two different stories about what had happened that day on the float where Amanda disappeared, and no idea which one was true. But even more disturbing to her was the shadow that had passed over Cindy's normally cheerful face when Mary mentioned all the ways that Amanda might seem to have the perfect life. Clearly, she knew something she hadn't told Mary. But what did she know? And what made her so afraid to tell?

EIGHTEEN

———◆◆◆———

A burst of laughter echoed from the back room of the house. At the kitchen table, where she had retreated with her computer, Mary smiled. She'd been hoping to spend a bit of time with just her and Daisy, but when she'd returned home from the diner, Jack and Christa had been ready to walk out the door again, and Daisy was firmly ensconced in the back room with several local kids her age from Ivy Bay. Mary had kissed Jack and Christa good-bye, promised to keep a good eye on Daisy, then poked her head in the back room to say hi. But Daisy was in the middle of a group of four or five kids, smiling and laughing, so Mary had made herself scarce. It was bittersweet to have her granddaughter in the next room but not be spending time with her. But at the same time, Mary told herself, Daisy was growing up and finding her own way in the world. And Mary was glad to see her laughing and smiling. There hadn't been a lot of that since she'd arrived on this trip.

In the meantime, Mary had adjusted her glasses and returned to the Facebook account Daisy had set up for her. To her surprise, a number of people had responded to her friend requests, and she now had a good group of a few dozen tiny photographs in one corner of her screen, representing her "friends." Her screen itself had started to fill up too, with snippets of news and groups of photographs. It didn't take Mary long to realize that Daisy wasn't the only person who had posted photographs of the parade. Her news feed contained several images from the day Amanda disappeared, taken by various friends. And when Mary clicked on them, she discovered that they led her quickly to larger collections of pictures. Some people had posted a few dozen. Some people had posted as many as a hundred.

Soon, Mary was absorbed in combing through photograph after photograph of the parade: kids in self-applied face paint; retirees marching with the rest-home float; small dogs riding in the baskets of slow-moving bicycles; classic convertibles with cardboard signs attached to their gleaming sides, advertising local politicians, the Kiwanis Club, the Preservation Society of Ivy Bay, and the Library Guild. The downtown stores were in full display as well: rubies and turquoise with the historical items in the window of Gems and Antiques, a special street display of watermelons and sweet corn outside Meeting House Grocers, and a giant swag of bunting drooping from the window of Sweet Susan's Bakery.

At first, she scanned every photograph, eagle-eyed, looking for anything that might be out of place, anything she or the police or the person who took the picture might not have noticed. In particular, she searched the crowds for another glimpse of Jared or the mysterious man in the suit, with his strange package. If she could just get a different angle, maybe she could gather something from the expression on Jared's face, or figure out the identity of the girl he was with, or make a better guess about who the mystery man was or what he was carrying with him.

But it seemed that, although people remembered seeing the mystery man, no one in Ivy Bay had actually trained their cameras on him, which made sense, since he was walking behind the crowd, not through the parade, where the attention of the town was focused. And despite the close look Mary gave each picture, she didn't turn up any further pictures of Jared or the girl he had been holding hands with while Amanda rode down Main Street on her float. That also added up—Jared must have some skills in deception, she reflected, to be juggling two girls at a time. Maybe the real surprise, she thought, was that Daisy had caught any evidence of his dalliance with the other girl on camera at all.

The person who she was able to find photographs of, again and again, was Amanda. It seemed like everyone who had posted pictures had snapped at least one of Amanda as she went by: waving, or smiling, or leaning down to throw some candy to the children running beside the float, their arms extended. Some people took close-ups just of her, while others panned out to take in the whole scope of the gorgeous float that Betty and Jimmy had helped design. In all of them, Amanda offered the same dazzling smile. It was hard to believe that, just a few minutes later, she would vanish.

As Mary looked at picture after picture of Amanda, her heart tugged. This wasn't just a case of her satisfying her curiosity. There was a wonderful young girl out there who needed to come home. *Lord*, she prayed, *please be with Amanda, wherever she is. Please bless Chief McArthur's efforts. And please bring her home.*

She clicked past the most recent picture of Amanda she'd found, raising her hand in an airy way, to the next one. This one wasn't as great a shot. In fact, in the era before digital photography, when more people waited for the perfect picture before snapping the shutter, it might not have been taken at all. And Mary was actually a little surprised that it hadn't been edited out before uploading.

It was a close-up shot of Amanda, taken from the side, probably snapped in the few seconds after the last great close-up of her face, as the float was moving away. But it showed a view of Amanda that Mary hadn't seen yet: the way her hair swooped up away from her face and the neck of her dress. And something else: Peeking out the neck of Amanda's red gown, Mary saw a flash of some other fabric.

Quickly, she zoomed in on the picture. It got blurrier as she did, but not so blurry that she couldn't make a good guess about what she was seeing. It looked like the strap of a tank top, peeking out of the neck of Amanda's dress. A tank top, Mary realized, very much like the one she had seen on the girl she had mistaken for Amanda only minutes after this picture had been taken.

Mary let the picture snap back to its original size, and leaned back in her chair. As she did, she realized that the happy hum that had been issuing from the back room had dropped down to almost nothing.

Her ears pricked up. People liked to shush children when they got loud, but in her experience, when you really needed to watch out for them was when they got quiet. She waited for a moment, to see if it had just been a temporary lull in the conversation. But when she continued to hear nothing but whispers and low voices from the back room, she got up and headed in that direction. She couldn't be sure, but as she came around the corner, she thought she heard one of the kids say, "Amanda."

When she arrived in the room, however, they all looked up, blinking and silent.

Mary gave them all a bright smile. "I just thought I'd check in and see what you're up to," she said, glancing down. The kids were crowded together, some on the couch and some on the floor. They all seemed to be looking at one boy's cell phone. "Anything interesting?" she said.

The boy with the phone, who was dressed in a green-and-white-striped polo shirt, snapped his phone shut and started to put it back in his pocket.

"No!" Daisy protested. "I still think we should tell someone."

"It's no big deal," the boy said. "People have arguments all the time."

"But they don't *disappear* after them," Daisy insisted.

That was enough for Mary. "Is this about Amanda?" she asked.

The kids' mouths all snapped shut again. A few of them looked up at her. A few of them looked at each other. The boy in the green-and-white shirt looked at Daisy reproachfully, as if to say, "Now look what you've done."

After a moment, Daisy lifted her chin. "Amanda and Jared had a huge fight, right before the parade," Daisy said. "Brian has a video of it."

The kids glanced at each other. Then their eyes fastened on Mary again, as if waiting for her to tell them how they should react to this. Mary's mind flashed back to what Betty had told her the night of Amanda's disappearance: that she and Jared seemed to have had some kind of falling out.

"Well," Mary said, "that sounds like it might be important."

"It's awful," one of the girls said. "They're both really mad."

Mary didn't like to see the kids so shaken, but part of her was relieved. They hadn't been back here enjoying the video as a piece of gossip. They could tell something was at stake here. And they'd been struggling to know what to do about it.

The kid in the green-and-white shirt, who she guessed must be Brian, studied Mary's face along with the rest of them. Then he pulled his phone out of his pocket again. "I don't want Jared to get into trouble," he said. "But we wanted to help find Amanda, if we can. Do you want to look at it?"

"Sure," Mary said, and nodded.

Brian punched a few buttons on his phone, and a tiny video flashed up on the screen. "I was at the head of the parade route with them," he said. "My sister's on the girls' swimming team. I was just trying to shoot some video of the crepe paper flowers my mom made for the hood of the cab of the truck they were riding in. She designed them to move in a really cool way in the breeze."

In the corner of the frame that was mostly filled by the crepe paper flowers Brian had mentioned, Mary recognized the figures in the video right away as Amanda and Jared. They were standing behind the trailer Amanda's float had been built on, in the shadow of the tree. Jared gestured angrily. Amanda crossed her arms and shook her head. Then she uncrossed her arms and shook her finger at him accusingly.

"What are they saying?" Mary asked.

Brian hit a button, and the sound came up on the phone. It was all the voices of teenage girls, jumbled together. "I didn't get the sound," he said. "I was pretty far away. And I was just taking video of the float until I saw them. Then I got curious, so I kind of zoomed in." He looked a little embarrassed as he switched the sound off and the voices of the teenage girls cut out.

On the screen, Jared reached his hand out to Amanda. She turned her back on him and disappeared around the float. Jared made a frustrated gesture and stalked out of the scene himself.

"Have you shown this to anyone?" Mary asked.

Brian shook his head. "Just my friends. I didn't want to get Jared in trouble. And I figured at first that it was all some mix-up. Amanda would come back, and then it wouldn't matter what happened with them."

"But she hasn't come back," one of the girls said.

Brian looked down. "Right," he said.

Mary thought back to the image she'd seen the day before, of Jared holding hands with a girl who wasn't Amanda. And to Jared's family's empty boat slip that she'd just visited that morning. She didn't want to believe that Jared could have had anything to do with Amanda's disappearance. But then again, a few days earlier, she wouldn't have expected that Jared would have betrayed Amanda with another girl.

Still, he was only a teenage boy. And before anyone took something like this to the police and embroiled him in a full-out criminal investigation, she wanted to give him a chance to explain himself first.

"Are you able to send that video from your phone?" Mary asked, taking out her own.

Brian nodded. He looked relieved not to be the only one to have the information at last. "Sure," he said. "What's your number?"

Mary gave it to him. A moment later, her cell phone dinged with a message. Mary opened it and tested to make sure that the video worked. It did.

"Got it," Mary said. "Thanks."

"No problem," Brian said. "Do you think we should tell someone?"

"She's been working with the police chief to find Amanda," Daisy told him, with some pride in her voice. "She'll know what to do."

That was a great exaggeration, Mary thought to herself. Still, she appreciated her granddaughter's vote of confidence.

"Cool," Brian said, looking up at Mary.

"Are you friends with Jared?" Mary asked him.

Brian shrugged. "I see him at work," he said. "We're both over at the Chadwick Inn for the tourist season. He won't get in any trouble, will he?"

"Not if he didn't do anything," Mary said.

"Grandma," Daisy said, checking her own watch, "I'm sorry. We were just going to go meet some people for some ice cream. We should go."

Mary smiled and tousled Daisy's hair. She was glad to see anything that might make Daisy's visit more pleasant. But if the kids went to Bailey's for ice cream, she'd also be free to go over to the Chadwick Inn . . . and ask Jared for an explanation.

NINETEEN

———◆◈◆———

Jared Wilson?" the woman behind the tasteful desk at the Chadwick Inn repeated.

Mary nodded. "I'm told he works here," she said.

"I don't think he's in reception," the woman said. She frowned slightly, but her voice still had its professionally helpful tone. "Maybe in hospitality. He's probably one of our summer workers. Let me just check."

She picked up the phone and hit a few numbers. "Javi?" she said. "There's a woman here looking for Jared Wilson. Is he in your department? He is? Well, could she—" She paused to listen. "I see. I'll tell her."

She settled the phone back into its cradle and looked back up at Mary. "Yes," she said. "He's in our hospitality department. But I'm afraid they can't spare him right now. If you could leave a message, or come back…"

"Actually," Mary said, trying to sound official, "it's very important that I see him. I'd even be glad to go meet him, if it's too much trouble for him to come out."

The woman shook her head. "I just don't think—" she began.

"It's about Amanda Branson," Mary said, doing her best to feign authority. "I have some information, and I hope he might be able to help us find her."

At this, the woman's resistance left her. "Javi won't like this," she said. "But I guess if you go down there, you could talk to him while he's working."

Mary smiled gratefully. "Just tell me where to go," she said.

The woman pointed to a service door to the left of the reception desk. "Back there," she said. "It leads down to our laundry. They're doing all the linens this afternoon, after the room turns and before the banquets begin."

"Thank you," Mary said.

"Good luck," the woman called after her.

The door she'd pointed Mary to led to a sparse service staircase, very different from the lush appointments that the guests enjoyed on the public side of the inn. The stairs led down to a basement level, where Mary discovered a long hallway, painted with high-gloss gray paint. Doors led off of it on either side. Bins full of laundry and rolling carts stacked with cases of wine and water glasses littered the hall. She could hear the clink of dishes being washed and the hum of big machines—probably washing and drying laundry, judging by the warm smell of detergent and softener that hung in the air.

After surveying the area for a moment, she began to pick her way down the hall, glancing into each room for a glimpse of Jared. A pair of women blinked up at her in a room filled with mismatched clothes—probably the hotel's dry cleaners. Mary smiled at them, and they let her go on without comment. But they were the only people she saw until she came to a room about halfway down the hall, where a large man was shoving big stacks of linens and towels onto giant wire racks.

After a quick glance at him, Mary started on again, but the sound of her step in the hall made the man turn to see who was behind him. To her surprise, it was Jared.

She felt a quick flash of unease. She'd been thinking of him as a boy, but the fact was that he was a young man, and big for his age. And Amanda was energetic, but petite. If Jared had had anything to do with Amanda's disappearance, she would have been no match for him.

When Jared caught sight of Mary, he froze for a moment, clearly confused. Then he offered her a bewildered smile. "Mrs. Fisher!" he said. "You're about the last person I would have expected to see down here."

Mary smiled back, trying to put him at ease. "Actually," she said, "I'm looking for you."

"Oh," Jared said. His arms were full of the cream-colored tablecloths he'd been carrying when she stopped him. Now he stashed them on a rack and turned back to her. "What can I do for you?"

"I'm curious about a few things," Mary said. "About Amanda."

Jared gave a confident nod. "Shoot."

"When we talked about Amanda, you told me everything was going great between the two of you."

Jared gave an easy smile. "Yes," he said. "Sure. Absolutely."

"What about the argument the two of you had just before the parade?" Mary said. "Can you tell me about that?"

"Argument?" Jared said with a little cough, clearly stalling for time.

"Jared, why don't you take a look?" Mary pulled her phone out of her purse, and hit a button. Jared's and Amanda's angry gestures began to play across the screen. As they did, Mary noticed something she hadn't when she saw the video for the first time—another figure in the frame, watching the whole thing. Before she could make out who the figure was, the video ended, and Jared started talking.

"Oh," he said, "that was just nerves. We were over it before the parade even began."

"What was she upset about?" Mary said.

"I can't even remember," Jared told her. "We were both just nervous. It was just some little thing that didn't really matter."

Mary had to hand it to him. He was quite an accomplished liar. If she didn't have the evidence right there in her hands, she could have easily walked away believing him. "*Hmm,*" she said, and scrolled quickly to the incriminating reflection of him holding hands with another girl. She held the phone out. "Then can you tell me who the girl is in this picture?"

Now Jared blanched in earnest.

"I—I," he stammered. "She—" He broke off again. "Have you showed this to anyone else?" he said, a note of pleading in his voice.

Mary shook her head. "Not yet," she said. "I wanted to talk with you first."

Jared's shoulders slumped. "Okay," he said. "I don't know how to say this."

"I understand that not everything works out with high school romances," Mary told him. "That's not what I'm worried about. I'm worried about finding Amanda. And it sounds to me like you've been hiding some facts that might help us find her."

"No!" Jared said. His reaction was so strong that Mary had trouble believing he could fake it, even though he'd misled her so coolly about the other girl in his life. "I would never do that. I told you and the police everything I thought might help. Everything. I really did."

"Except the fact that you and she weren't getting along when she disappeared," Mary pointed out.

"I know," Jared said, looking abashed. "But I knew how it would look. I didn't want to get into any trouble. And I know I need to tell Amanda about Britt. I just didn't want her to find out from someone else. I wanted to tell her myself."

Mary's brow furrowed. "You seem more worried about Amanda finding that out than you do about whether Amanda ever comes back at all," she said. "You do understand that this is a serious situation, don't you? She's been gone for almost forty-eight hours now, with no contact. Not to the police, not to her mother. No one."

Jared nodded. "I know, I know," he said. "It's just... so confusing. I didn't know what to do. So I didn't do anything." Now he really did look like a boy, despite his big frame. His head hung and his hands clenched and unclenched by his sides. Then he looked up. "I love Amanda," he said. "I really do. But things haven't been easy with her recently. She's been so distracted. And then with the parade coming up, we never got any time together. Britt's always been around, you know. I've told her we were just friends. But she still wants more. And every now and then, it's nice to feel like someone wants to be with you. Especially when the person you want to be with doesn't seem to."

Mary shook her head. "So the argument you had at the float wasn't about Britt?" she asked.

Jared shook his head. His eyes looked wary. "No," he said. "Like I said, it wasn't really about anything. Just preparade stress." He glanced away as he said this, leaving Mary with the familiar feeling that he wasn't telling her the whole truth.

"What about your parents' boat?" she said, hoping to surprise him with a new tactic.

Jared's eyes locked on hers again, wide and surprised. "Our boat?" he repeated.

Mary nodded, her own eyes unflinching. "It's gone," she told him. "It's been missing for a few days. Maybe as long as Amanda has. Can you tell me anything about that?"

Jared seemed more agitated by Mary's revelation of the missing boat than he did over her discovery that he had cheated on Amanda. "No!" he said again. "Oh my gosh. Mom and Dad are going to think I had something to do with this. They're going to kill me. Have you told anyone about this?"

Mary shook her head. "But the marina will likely call it in sometime this afternoon. Some of the sailors in the neighboring slips noticed it was missing."

"Listen," Jared said. The note of pleading had returned to his voice. "You believe me, don't you? You can't tell my parents I had anything to do with this. I didn't. You have to believe me. I—"

"Jared?" An older man in a short-sleeved button-down shirt poked his head in the room. "What's going on here?"

"Ah," Jared said. "Javi, hello. This is Mrs. Fisher. Ah, a visitor."

"No visitors on the floor," Javi said, and glanced at Mary to let her know that went for her too.

Mary tried to charm him with one of her big smiles. "I'm sorry to interrupt his workday," she said. "We were just—"

Javi cut her off with a businesslike shake of his head. "I'm sorry, ma'am," he said. "It's not me; it's the regulations for hotels and restaurants. No visitors behind the house. For the safety of our guests. I'm sure you understand."

"But—" Mary tried.

"I'm afraid whatever it is will have to wait," Javi said. "You know where the exit is?"

Somewhat cowed, Mary nodded, half hoping that if she was agreeable, he'd leave and she'd have a chance to ask Jared a few more questions. But Javi was inexorable. "Jared," he said, "with me." He started off down the hall.

"Okay," Jared said, hurrying after him. He looked back and called over his shoulder as they disappeared down the hall. "Good-bye, Mrs. Fisher."

Mary sighed and started down the hall. The part of her that wasn't feverishly sifting through Jared's answers to her questions was bemused to find herself in the belly of the town's fanciest hotel. She'd never expected to wind up here during the course of her search for Amanda.

Which made her realize something: Why was Jared here, despite the fact that Amanda was still missing? Whether or not they'd hit a rough patch, Mary would have expected him to have dropped everything to try to find her. His family was well-off enough to afford a boat. They were hardly hurting for cash. It wasn't as if he couldn't afford to take a day off work to look for her or couldn't afford to lose his job if they didn't want to give him the day. Why didn't he seem more worried about finding his missing girlfriend? Why had Mary had to come to Jared's place of work, looking for clues on Amanda's disappearance? Shouldn't Jared be out there, somewhere, looking for Amanda himself?

TWENTY

———◆◆◆———

At the curb of the Chadwick Inn, Mary stopped in the shade of one of the Cape's famous whispering pines and took her phone out.

She pulled up the video of Jared and Amanda's argument at the back of the float and played it again. This time, as the mysterious figure she'd glimpsed when she played it last came on-screen, she paused the action and peered closer. Then she let it play a few seconds more and stopped it again.

The resemblance was unmistakable. The figure in the back of the scene was Paige Bailey. She'd been standing close enough to see the whole thing. And she hadn't mentioned the argument between Jared and Amanda to Mary—or to the police.

A few minutes later, Mary walked into Bailey's Ice Cream Shop again. Daisy, who was seated with a group of teenagers, looked up. At first, her smile brightened at the sight of her grandmother. Then she ducked her head in embarrassment. Mary just gave her a quick smile and went up to the counter, without doing anything else to exacerbate Daisy's discomfort. Just like before, Paige stood behind the counter. She greeted Mary with the same bright smile, as if she had no recollection of their conversation before and the tension between them when it ended. Or, Mary noted, of the fact that one of her close friends had been missing for days now and was still missing.

"Mrs. Fisher!" Paige said. "How are you doing today?"

"Fine," Mary said, matching her smile for smile. "Just fine."

"What can I do for you?" Paige said, her eyes wide and innocent. "I'm afraid I wasn't much help to you yesterday, but if there's anything at all I can do—"

"Actually, there is," Mary said, without giving Paige the time to complete her act. "I've just been looking at some images and video from the parade on Facebook, and I've found a few interesting things."

If this made Paige nervous, she didn't show it. "Really?" she said. "Like what?"

Mary searched Paige's face and decided to give her the benefit of the doubt. "Some interesting things around the beginning of the parade," she said. "Do you remember anything unusual happening as you were getting ready? At the staging ground, maybe?"

Paige appeared to consider this. Then she gave her head a decisive shake. "Not really," she said. "Nope. I don't think so. Unless you call getting dressed up in a fancy dress and riding around town with a bunch of papier-mâché trees unusual."

Paige's tone would have been appropriate at the July Queen crowning, Mary thought. But something about the light tone she took, given the fact that Amanda was still missing, rubbed Mary the wrong way.

"You're sure?" she asked.

Paige gave a pert nod. "Yep," she said.

Mary had had enough. She pulled her phone out of her purse, called up the video of Jared and Amanda's argument, and pressed Play. As Jared and Amanda began their angry gestures on the screen, Mary watched Paige's face. Her smile faded to an expression of faint confusion. Then she wiped it clean and blank. But when the image of Paige appeared on the screen, Mary paused the action.

"There," she said. "That figure in the back." It was obvious who she meant, but she pointed anyway. "To me, that looks like you," she said and met Paige's eyes.

Paige dropped her gaze to the counter between them.

"Paige?" Mary pressed. "Is this you in the video?"

Without looking up, Paige nodded.

Mary slipped her phone back in her purse.

"You didn't mention this argument to me when we talked," Mary said. She'd already known about the argument, but Paige had obviously withheld the information on purpose. "Did you mention it to the police?"

Paige shook her head. Then she looked up.

"Why not?" Mary asked.

"I knew how it would look to the police," Paige admitted. "A big fight with the boyfriend right before a girl disappears? How would you take that, if you were the police? Jared might not be perfect, but he's a good guy. I didn't want him to get in trouble. He didn't have anything to do with Amanda disappearing," Paige said. "He didn't."

A warning bell rang in Mary's head at Paige's confidence in this fact. "How do you know that?" Mary asked.

Paige fell silent again.

Behind them, Mary could hear the crowd of kids Daisy had come with get up and start to stream out the door. Paige glanced after them, as if hoping that the distraction would interrupt the conversation, but Mary wasn't about to be dissuaded.

"What was the argument about?" Mary tried.

Paige shook her head to indicate she wasn't going to answer.

"Was it about Britt?" Mary guessed.

She could see from the surprise in Paige's eyes that Paige hadn't expected her to know that name. "No," she said. "Britt isn't mixed up in this either. Amanda knew, but she hadn't told him she knew yet."

"Why not?" Mary asked.

"She had a lot of things going on," Paige said.

"Like what?" Mary said, trying to imagine what could possibly matter more to a teenage girl than the fact that her boyfriend hadn't been faithful to her.

Mary had startled Paige into revealing a few details, but now Paige was beginning to clam up again. She shrugged. "Just a lot," she said.

"So you knew things about Amanda that Jared didn't even know," Mary pointed out.

Paige shrugged again.

"I'd say that makes you very good friends," Mary said. She looked around the ice-cream shop. "Is it hard for you, having to work here, instead of being out there, looking for her?"

Paige gave Mary another sharp look. "The police are looking for Amanda," she said. "I don't know what I could do that they can't."

"So are you worried?" Mary asked. "About whether or not she'll come back?"

Paige pressed her lips together before she answered. "Of course I am," she said. Her words were right, but there was something mechanical about the way she said them. "It's terrible. I can't wait to see her again."

"You know," Mary said, "Jared's at work today too. I thought that was strange as well. I might have expected both of you to be out looking for your friend. That's what I'd be doing, if my friend disappeared."

"Yes," Paige said, her voice controlled. "I can see that."

"Do you know anything else that you haven't mentioned to me or the police?" Mary asked. "Like this fight between Jared and Amanda?"

"I told you," Paige said. "I've told you everything I know. No one wants to see Amanda come home more than I do."

This time, her words rang true. But Mary still felt uneasy about Paige's lack of anxiety. Her affection for her friend felt real. But she didn't seem like she was willing to do anything at all to help bring Amanda home. In fact, the closer Mary pressed about questions that might really help Amanda, the more tight-lipped Paige got.

"I just don't know if you kids realize how serious this is," Mary said.

Behind her, the familiar sound of the bell announcing a customer's arrival rang, and the door whined as someone walked in. Mary turned to see who it was. A small army of T-ball players, all about seven or eight years old, swarmed in, followed by a somewhat harried-looking coach. "Hello! Sorry!" he said.

Mary stepped to the side as the kids pressed up against the glass, staring down at the tubs of brightly colored ice cream. She shook her head at the coach to indicate that she didn't have any hard feelings.

"Excuse me," Paige said coolly, as she picked up an ice-cream scoop. "I need to take care of this."

Mary took another long look at Paige. She could wait out these customers, she knew, but she wasn't convinced that any amount of waiting would convince Paige to trust Mary with whatever it was she knew. She'd thought that Paige might tell her the truth if she confronted her with the video that proved she'd been keeping things from Mary before. But ironically, although Paige had given her an explanation for the argument Mary saw in the video, Mary felt even more certain than before that Paige knew even more that she wasn't telling. But Paige wouldn't be the one to tell her. She'd made that much clear.

So with a sigh and a smile, Mary turned and headed for the door.

As she did, her phone began to ring, deep in her bag.

TWENTY-ONE

⬩◆⬩

"M ary."

At the sound of Henry's voice, Mary felt the same feeling of happiness and comfort she felt every time he came into the shop or gave her a call.

"Henry!" Mary said. "How are you doing?"

"Well, I've been thinking of you. Specifically, I've been thinking of your new ice-cream flavor. It's the beginning of the month, right? So won't Tess have new barrels of your latest creation?"

"That's right," Mary said. "She does."

"Well," Henry said, in the tone that always let her know he was about to launch into a joke, "as a businesswoman and the creator of these flavors, I think it only makes sense for you to consume them yourself. As a sign of your confidence in the product."

"Of course," Mary said. "It's the only responsible thing to do, really. As a businesswoman."

"I agree," Henry said. "And as my mother always said, the sooner, the better. What are you doing right now?"

Mary thought. Jack and Christa were off on their date. Daisy and her friends were happily exploring the nooks and crannies of Ivy Bay. She'd been on the trail of Amanda for days now, and as of this morning, she didn't seem to run into anything but half-truths and dead ends. Maybe a little break was exactly what she needed. And she was already at the ice-cream store.

"Well," she said, "I was just thinking of meeting up with you for an ice-cream cone. How does that sound to you?"

"That's amazing!" Henry said. "I was just thinking the same thing."

"Great," Mary said. "Shall we say ten minutes?"

"I can make that," Henry said. "I'll just be coming up from the docks. Do you want to give me a preview of what flavor I'm about to enjoy?"

"Oh no," Mary said. "I wouldn't want to ruin the surprise."

"Ah," Henry said. "Well, I guess I'll find out soon enough."

A few minutes later, Henry and Mary stood side by side in front of Tess Bailey's crystal-clear glass cabinet of hand-created ice-cream flavors as the clean-shaven young high school student working with Paige behind the counter handed over a scoop of caramel-colored ice cream in a sugar cone wrapped in bright paper.

"Don't tell me!" Henry said, putting one hand over his eyes as he accepted the cone. "Let me guess."

After Mary had refused to tell him the flavor over the phone, he'd made a big production of not reading any of the signs before he ordered. "Just give me the new flavor," he'd told the kid behind the counter. "If Mary made it, I'm sure it'll be good."

Mary accepted her own cone from the young man and thanked him while Henry took his first bite. As he tasted it, his eyes popped open appreciatively.

"Wait, wait," he said as she smiled at him. "It's—"

He took another bite. "Peanut butter?" he said.

Mary nodded. "And?" she prompted.

"This is the best peanut butter flavor I've ever tasted in ice cream," Henry said. "And you're telling me there's more to it than that?"

"Go ahead," Mary said, taking a first bite of her cone. The flavor was peanut buttery, but still light, just the way she'd worked to make it in her own kitchen. Henry didn't need to have any worries about quality control with Tess, she knew. If anything, Tess probably followed Mary's recipes more closely than Mary did herself.

Henry's next bite revealed a thick stripe of gooey purple. His eyes widened as he swallowed. "And...," he started, thinking it through. "Jelly?" he asked. "Is that jelly I taste?"

Mary nodded. "Grape jelly," she said. "From Cape grapes. There's a farm stand about half an hour north that makes their own jelly every season."

"Peanut butter and jelly ice cream," Henry said. "Brilliant. Here I was thinking peanut butter and chocolate. Or peanut butter and...well, who knows what? But peanut butter and jelly. That's a classic. You can't argue with it. But I'd never think to put it in ice cream."

"Those are the best ideas, I think," Mary said. "The ones that seem so obvious you'd never think of them."

"Classic, yet full of surprises," Henry said. "This ice cream has something in common with the lady who invented it."

He took his wallet out to pay for the ice cream. Then he and Mary walked out of the shop and began to wander together along Main Street, then onto Shore Drive, in the direction of the docks.

As they went, she filled Henry in on the searching she'd done over the past couple of days, looking for Amanda. She nodded as they passed the little gap between the fishing shanties where Kemper's Alley must have led the mysterious man from the bank, and where she'd last seen the girl she'd thought might be Amanda.

"That's where I saw her last," she said.

"*Hmm*," Henry said, his mouth still full of one of the last bites of his cone. "But this is pretty far off the parade route," he observed after a moment.

Mary nodded.

"What brought you down here?" he asked.

Mary felt slightly shy all of a sudden, but she told herself there was no reason to be embarrassed. She'd just come looking for a friend, that's all. "I was actually looking for you," she said.

"For me?" Henry asked. He sounded surprised—and perhaps pleased.

Mary nodded. "I just knew the Fourth was always a special time for you and Misty. I thought it might be a time that you needed a friend."

Henry was silent for several steps as they walked along together. "Well, thank you," he said. "I was actually out on the *Misty Horizon*. Misty and I always used to watch the fireworks from the same spot on land. So I never got to see them from the water before. And I just thought, well, what's to stop me now? So I took her out past the fireworks barge, just outside the bay. Watched it from there, then brought her back in again."

"How was that?" Mary asked.

Henry fell quiet again. "It was real nice," he said after a minute. "The fireworks in the sky and all the light down on the water. And all you can see of the boats are the shadows passing through the light. But you were right."

"I was?" Mary said.

Henry nodded as they turned onto the pier where Sam's Seafood was situated. "I was a little lonely," he said. "Not too bad. But kind of wishing that I had a friend around. It's nice to know I had one, and I didn't even know it. And it was good to find you at the bookshop later."

Mary smiled at him as they crossed the weathered planks of the dock, passing the rows of boats in their slips, approaching the empty patch of water where Jared Wilson's parents' boat had been.

But just before they reached it, Mary drew up short, staring through the wide cracks in the lumber that composed the dock.

"What is it?" Henry asked. "Everything okay?"

"I don't know," Mary told him.

She'd caught a flash of something through the plank of the dock. That wasn't unusual. The sun cast all kinds of crazy light on the waves below the boats, and walking by the water on a sunny day always involved all kinds of stray reflections. But instead of the white of the July Cape Cod sun, this gleam was red.

Mary leaned over to get a better look. Then she crouched down. Then she scooched over to the edge of the dock and began to wave her hand around below it, hoping to catch hold of something.

"Whoa, whoa!" Henry said, catching her shoulder. "Careful, there. This isn't a swimming dock, you know."

"I know that," Mary said. "Here, give me a hand."

As she requested, Henry took her hand, thinking he was going to help her up. To his surprise, she used it to steady herself as she leaned all the way over to peer under the dock. There, stashed in one of the support beams that underpinned the whole network, was a plastic bag. Hanging out of the plastic bag was one corner of a red-sequined dress.

This time, thinking of the fact that the police had taken Amanda's float in as evidence, she didn't reach for it. Instead, she straightened up.

"That's Amanda's dress," she said.

"Where?" Henry asked.

"Just under the dock," she said. "Someone must have stashed it there the night she disappeared. Maybe just before they took off in the Wilsons' boat. It looks like it was easy to miss until the wind blew it open. Now you can see the sequins shining all the way through the planks in the dock." She stepped back. "Now, why would she leave that here?" she asked.

Henry squinted at the place she pointed at, through the wood. "Well, I'll be," he said.

"I need to call Chief McArthur," Mary said, pulling her phone out of her bag. "I'm sorry."

"Don't apologize to me," Henry told her. "I want to see that girl come home just as much as anyone."

As he was speaking, Mary dialed the Ivy Bay police station. A woman picked up the line and greeted her.

"This is Mary Fisher," Mary told her. "I'm trying to reach Chief McArthur."

"Chief McArthur is engaged in an ongoing investigation," the woman said. "Can I help you with something?"

"I'm calling about that investigation," Mary said. "I have a clue I think may be important."

"Hold, please," the woman said.

A moment later, Mary heard Chief McArthur's voice come across the line. "Chief McArthur," he said. "Go ahead."

"Chief McArthur," Mary said. "This is Mary. I think I have something."

She could hear the slightly skeptical pause before he answered. "Oh?" he said. "And what's that?"

"I'm at the docks," Mary told him. "And I've found Amanda's dress."

TWENTY-TWO

⸺ ◆◆ ⸺

Chief McArthur shook his head while an out-of-town forensics expert craned his neck over the edge of the dock, taking photographs to document the site where Mary had found the dress stashed in the dock support.

"Incredible," he said. "I've only had half a dozen people go over these docks half a dozen times. I don't know how we missed it."

"I don't know that anyone would have looked twice at it while the bag was closed," Mary said. "It would have just looked like another piece of trash blown up on the coast."

"I guess so," Chief McArthur said. "Still, I wish we'd found it sooner. This gives us a clear indicator of what direction the culprit took. And that they likely departed over water, rather than over land. We got the call about the missing Wilson boat this afternoon."

As he and Mary watched, the operative with the camera rose, and another law enforcement officer took his place. This one was a redheaded woman in a navy jacket, her hands carefully cased in plastic gloves. Gingerly, she knelt over the place where the dress had been stuffed, then leaned down and retrieved it. Probably very much, Mary thought, like the motion of whoever had stashed it there in the first place, on the night of the fireworks.

"But are you sure there was a culprit?" Mary asked.

Beside her, Henry raised his eyebrows, ready to listen. But Chief McArthur shook his head dismissively. "According to these experts," he said, "that's what we're likely looking at. Amanda just doesn't fit the profile of a runaway. She's involved with the community. Good friends. Strong ties. It doesn't add up."

"Still," Mary said, "I keep thinking about that girl who I saw heading to the docks the night of the fireworks. She just looked so much like Amanda. I can't help but wonder if she…"

When she trailed off, Chief McArthur raised his eyebrows. "You're right," he said. "It could have been her, Mary. But knowing that doesn't help us any more than suspecting she was taken does. We have the clues. And we're following them. That's the best chance we've got of getting her back, no matter what happened to her."

As Mary watched, the redheaded officer slipped Amanda's sequined dress, still half in and half out of the plastic bag it had been stored in, into another clear plastic bag. Then she scrawled something on the label on the bag. The woman looked up at Chief McArthur. "We need to get this back to the lab," she said. "There's not much more anyone can tell at this point by standing on the dock and looking at it."

"Sounds good," Chief McArthur said briskly. He nodded at Mary. "Thanks for the tip, Mary. We need all the help we can get on this."

"Have you had any luck with your other leads?" Mary asked. "The man at the bank? Do you know who he is?"

Chief McArthur pursed his lips. "I could tell you that's classified," he said. "But the fact is, we don't know much yet. They're running his face through a facial-recognition database, but it's a long process, and we aren't the first in line. Right now, we're just doing the best we can. And there's no substitute for good people who keep their eyes peeled. As you just proved."

The redhead was already clunking back down the dock, heading for the police cars they'd driven up in. Chief McArthur turned to follow her. "Thanks again," he said.

A few moments later, Henry and Mary stood alone again on the dock, as the police cars pulled away and headed back toward town.

"Never a dull moment," Henry said, and started to walk slowly down the dock again, in the direction they'd been headed before Mary spotted the dress.

Mary nodded, trailing along beside him. Her mind was still racing from all the details of finding and retrieving the dress and with all the other clues she'd collected over the past couple of days. They shifted this way and that in her mind, but she still couldn't see how all of them fit.

"...have you?" Henry asked.

He'd stopped walking a few steps behind her, Mary realized. And she'd been so lost in her own thoughts, she hadn't even noticed.

She turned back. "I'm sorry," she said. "What did you say?"

Henry laughed. "I said, you haven't heard a word I've been saying, have you?"

Mary sighed and shook her head. "I'm sorry," she said again. "It's just so hard to concentrate, when Amanda—"

Henry began to nod before she even found the words to finish. Even in the midst of all the questions and pressure surrounding Amanda's disappearance, it was good to feel that someone knew what she meant without having to be told.

"I understand," he said. "You're dying to get back to this mystery. And I don't want to keep you from it. It sounds like you've just given Chief McArthur one of the police force's first big breaks in the case. I wouldn't want to keep you from finding the next one."

"Are you sure you don't mind?" Mary asked.

Henry shook his head. "I'd mind if you didn't get back to the search again," he said, and turned back toward town. "Who knows what you'll turn up next?"

TWENTY-THREE

Gus circled around Mary's legs, purring like a motor to express both his desire for her to pet him and his displeasure that she hadn't given in to his entreaties yet.

She glanced down at him. "I know," she said. "But you're not the only one who's unhappy. I could be walking along the water with Henry right now."

Gus blinked up at her, unfazed by this revelation.

Mary leaned back in her chair by the bookstore computer, frustrated. On her computer screen, the video from the bank flickered, paused as the mystery man stepped out of the frame, just where she had stopped it.

"Well," a voice said, "what are you looking at so intently, Mary Fisher?"

Mary smiled at Bernice, who stood on the other side of the counter with a huge stack of books. She'd been browsing in the store for almost an hour, and it looked like she'd finally made her selections. Somehow, Bernice managed to get through a stack that size just about every week, and still came back for more. Although Mary wasn't sure how Bernice did everything else she did around town, and still did so much reading, Mary was glad for the business. And Bernice had taken to joking that since Mary opened her shop, her bookshelves were full to overflowing. "You'd better watch out," she'd started telling Mary. "I'm going to have enough books soon to open my own used bookstore, down the street from you."

"Let me know before you do that," Mary had told her. "We'll see if we can't open a 'gently used' nook right here in the shop, and let you manage it."

"What are you poring over there?" Bernice said, glancing at the computer, although she couldn't see the screen. "Orders for a new section of the shop?"

"It's not actually for the shop," Mary said.

"No?" Bernice said, raising her eyebrows.

"It's for something else I'm working on," Mary said. She didn't want to betray Steve's generosity in loaning her the DVD. Or interfere with Chief McArthur's investigation by talking about it too widely. And although she'd known that nothing she said to Henry would go any further than the two of them, Bernice loved to spread things around town—not because she was a gossip, but just because she always wanted to share her news with anyone who would listen.

"Amanda?" Bernice guessed quickly.

Reluctantly, Mary nodded. But to put Bernice off the subject, she started to rise. "Here," she said. "Let me ring those up for you."

Before she got to her feet, Rebecca came bustling around the counter. "No, no," she said. "You're working on something. I'll take care of this." She picked up the first title from Bernice's stack. "Oh! *Mystery on the Midway*. You're going to love this one."

"It looked promising to me," Bernice said. "I love carnivals."

Ashley trailed her mother behind the counter. But when she saw the unfamiliar image flickering on Mary's computer screen, she came over to investigate. "Are you watching your TV shows?" she asked.

Mary smoothed Ashley's hair, which Ashley tolerated about as well as Gus did. "It's not really a show," she said. "It's more like a video. You know. Like your father might take on your birthday? So you could remember the day."

"Oh," Ashley said. She studied the screen for another long moment and then turned to look at Mary. "What are you trying to remember?" she asked.

Mary laughed.

Behind her, the register dinged as Rebecca accepted Bernice's payment. "Good luck with that, Mary," Bernice said as she collected her books. "Whatever it is. I haven't been able to stop thinking about Amanda since she disappeared. I've been tugging on God's sleeve, asking Him to bring her home to us."

"Thank you," Mary said as Bernice went out.

"Honey," Rebecca said, calling Ashley away from her post by Mary's side, "come on. We need to let Mary work on something right now."

Reluctantly, Ashley let her mother lead her back out onto the floor of the shop.

Mary leaned back in her seat. She appreciated Rebecca's thoughtfulness. She just wished she really had something to work on. The truth was, she'd watched the bank video over a dozen times now. Not only had she not seen anything new in the footage that Steve had given her, but everything in the video was also now starting to blend together in her mind. The man loitered behind the parade crowd. A few heads turned to look at him. Then he darted across the parade route, off in the direction of Kemper's Alley. She'd been looking at it for almost an hour, and she still hadn't learned anything she hadn't already known when she'd left Steve's office that morning. Still, she wasn't ready to give up. Not while Amanda was still missing. No matter how fruitless it seemed.

She went back to the beginning of the clip, where the man first appeared, and began to watch again. As she did, Gus, exasperated with her inattention, leapt up into her lap and buried his gray head against her side.

Mary laughed. "Oh, all right," she said, petting him. On the screen, just as he had before, the mystery man vanished into the parade.

Maybe that's what she really needed—a break, Mary told herself, patting Gus's warm side as the video played. Just a few minutes to regroup, decide what tack to take next, and enjoy the simple things in life, like a friendly cat.

For the next few minutes, she gave Gus the attention he'd been demanding, while the floats and marchers drifted by on the screen. From time to time, someone shifted in the crowd, but for the most part, she could have been watching the parade on infinite loop for all the variety of the footage the bank security cameras had captured.

Finally, the parade ended, and the crowd began to dissipate. Dads wandered off with their toddlers still balanced on their shoulders. Elementary-age kids argued while they helped their moms gather up lawn chairs or fold the blankets they'd been sitting on.

Eventually, Gus got tired of all the attention and jumped off Mary's lap, but Mary continued to watch the bank security footage, fascinated by how quickly the crowd began to pack up after the parade cleared the area. Pretty soon, the street was almost completely deserted.

Then, from the direction of Kemper's Alley, came a group of kids, conspicuous on the now almost-empty street. They loitered in the empty intersection talking and laughing, obviously goofing off. One of them carried a plastic bag. As Mary watched, something fell out of it.

Mary gasped and hit a button to freeze the screen.

In the sharp focus and full color of Steve's surveillance footage, the object was unmistakable: a blonde wig.

Mary leaned forward to peer at the four kids, whom she'd only glanced at idly before. Was it her imagination, or was one of the girls strangely familiar?

She hit a button to start the video again, staring hard at the screen. As the kids sprang into motion, one of the boys in the group gave the girl a playful shove. She laughed and leaned against him, turning her head as she did so the camera caught a full profile of her face.

Mary drew in a sharp breath and tapped Pause again on her keyboard.

These kids appeared on the street within minutes of the time Amanda had vanished—around the time Mary had seen the blonde girl disappear between the fishing shanties. A blonde wig was still plainly visible, peeking out of the plastic bag that swung by the side of the boy who had been teasing the girl.

And the girl beside him, with her profile frozen by the camera, was just as unmistakable as the wig had been.

She was Mary's granddaughter Daisy.

TWENTY-FOUR

———◆◆◆———

"Daisy?" Mary called when she swept in the door. "Honey? You home?"

As she slung her purse down onto the table by the door, Jack emerged from the next room.

"Hey, Mom," he said, crossing the room to give her a kiss. Mary kissed him back, with a wide smile. No matter what was going on, it was always a pleasure to come home and find her strapping son there. She'd taken it for granted for years when he was growing up—when sometimes it seemed like he might never leave. But now each day she got to spend with him felt like a gift.

Jack smiled back at her, but his eyes seemed sad.

"Is everything okay, honey?" she asked.

"Oh," Jack said. "Sure, sure. But I'm afraid that Daisy's not home, if that's who you're looking for."

This didn't seem like it should be much of an announcement, but with her mother's eagle eye, Mary could see that Jack seemed to get sadder when he reported it.

"Do you know where she is?" Mary asked.

Jack nodded. "Yep," he said. "She went down to Seahorse Beach. A couple of her friends wanted to go."

"Well, that sounds nice," Mary said, calculating in her head. Seahorse Beach was a few towns east of Ivy Bay. And while Ivy Bay did have a small sandy beach, it was mostly a fishing village. But Seahorse Beach offered some real beach culture—miles and miles of sandy dunes, but also some interesting rock formations. "Do you have any idea when she might be back?"

"Actually," Jack said, "she only just left."

He looked so unhappy when he said this that Mary went over to give him a hug. "Honey," she said, her voice firm, "tell me what's wrong."

Jack hung his head as she led him over to the couch. "It's stupid," he said. "It's nothing."

"That's not what it looks like to me," Mary told him.

"Well," Jack said, pulling a pair of crisp cardboard tickets from the front pocket of his shirt, "I had these tickets to take Daisy fishing this afternoon."

"Did she refuse to go with you?" Mary asked, surprised. Daisy was her granddaughter, and she had a lot of sympathy with her—the frustrations of wanting to feel grown up, not being able yet to make all her own decisions, and being separated from her friends during what seemed like an important holiday weekend. But Daisy seemed to have been enjoying herself more in the past few days. And at some point, she needed to learn how to enjoy what was right in front of her, instead of acting like a spoiled child.

Jack shook his head. "No," he said with a rueful laugh. "In some ways, it was worse. I got these tickets because she always used to love to go out fishing with me. She's never been sure how she feels about hooking bait or cleaning a fish, but she's always loved being out on the water. I thought it might be some good father-daughter bonding time."

"But?" Mary said.

"Well," Jack said, "she was sweet about it, actually. She thanked me for getting the tickets and everything. And she said she'd go if it was important to me. But she didn't really want to. All her friends had this plan to go to the beach. And she wanted to go with them. She was just worried about hurting my feelings."

"So you let her go," Mary guessed.

Jack nodded. "I told her it was fine," he said. "She should just go along. Have a good time. But I guess it did hurt my feelings after all," he added. His voice was pretty steady, but Mary could see that his eyes were unusually bright.

He dropped his head. "See?" he said. "It's stupid."

Mary put her hand on her son's arm. "No, honey," she said quietly. "It's not."

Jack collected her hand in his, but continued to stare at his lap. "It's good that Daisy's making friends in Ivy Bay," Jack said. "We could never have expected that a few days ago. I should be happy."

Mary squeezed his hand. "That's true," she said. "But what you're doing is hard."

"It is," Jack agreed, finally looking up.

When Jack's eyes met hers, Mary smiled. "You want to know how I know that?" she asked.

Jack's lips curved into a smile as he nodded.

"Because I had to do it with you and Lizzie," Mary said.

"Well, I wasn't nearly as independent as Daisy," Jack managed to joke. "I think I had you doing my laundry until I was almost twenty-one."

"College graduation," Mary agreed. "That's when I cut you off."

Jack laughed.

"But you want to know a secret?" Mary asked.

Jack nodded again.

"It's one of the hardest things you can do, to let go of your child," she told him. "But it's also one of the best."

Jack shook his head. "I can't say I feel that way right now," he said.

"No," Mary said. "And that's because you're a good dad. Because you care about your daughter, and you love to spend time with her. But as you let her go, you'll also get to see her blossom into the amazing young woman God made her to be."

Jack grinned. "She is pretty amazing," he said. Then he put on a mock-serious expression. "But I still get to run background checks on any boy who wants to go on a date with her, right?" he asked.

Mary gave his hand a firm pat. "Absolutely," she said. "And if you don't, I will."

Now that her son was smiling again, her thoughts turned back to Amanda.

"How recently did you say Daisy left?" she asked.

Jack glanced at his watch. "I'd say…about half an hour ago," he said.

Mary calculated. In that case, the kids were probably just reaching Seahorse Beach now.

She rose and collected her bag. "I'm going to go see if I can catch up with her," she said. "I think she and her friends might have been in the area where Amanda disappeared. I'd like to ask them some questions."

"She was in the area where Amanda was?" Jack said, looking worried. "Do you think they were in any danger?"

Mary hesitated, thinking it over. To her, the presence of the wig suggested that the girl she'd seen might actually have been Amanda, and that for some reason, she'd left under her own power, not because anyone forced her to. "I don't think so," she said. "But I'm hoping they might know something that will help us find her."

"What happened to setting her free to fly?" Jack asked jokingly. "If she doesn't want to go fishing with her dad, how do you think she's going to feel about her grandmother crashing her beach party?"

Mary shrugged lightly. "We'll find out," she said. "But I'm not going down there to be her grandmother. I'm going down there to see if she can help us find Amanda."

She slung her purse over her shoulder again and pulled her keys out of it. They clinked in her hand.

"And if traffic is with me, I can be there in half an hour," she said.

TWENTY-FIVE

M ary pulled into a space facing the sea in the overlook parking lot that sat on the bluff above Seahorse Beach, cut the engine, and thought for a moment.

Despite her airy assurances to Jack, she didn't want to embarrass Daisy by showing up unannounced in the middle of her afternoon at the beach or upset her when she started to ask questions that pertained to Amanda.

But as she looked out at the blue horizon, she couldn't think of a plan that didn't, in some way, really just add up to showing up unannounced. And every minute that ticked past was another moment that Amanda was missing. Embarrassing Daisy probably wasn't even her biggest problem, Mary told herself as she got out of the car. First, she had to find her in the beachside crowd.

But to Mary's surprise, when she came to the top of the wooden stairs that ran down the bluff and looked down on the beach, half the beach was empty.

Or not exactly empty, she realized with a closer look. People had left their blankets and towels and chairs behind as they streamed toward a rock formation to the far right of the beach. A crowd had formed a large ring around something just out of sight. And if Mary's eyes weren't fooling her, she thought she made out the familiar form of her granddaughter for the second time that day in an unexpected place: smack in the middle of the ring, standing at the water's edge.

"Daisy!" Mary exclaimed. She hurried down the wooden steps, then picked her way through the maze of towels and blankets until she reached the crowd. Then, politely but firmly, she began to push her way through it.

"Excuse me," she said, returning bright smiles for people's irritated or curious glances at her. "Excuse me. Thank you. Yes. Excuse me." After a long push through the crowd, she elbowed her way around a bodybuilder type in bright-blue swim trunks and found herself in a clearing near the water's edge where she had last seen Daisy.

As she broke out of the crowd, she caught sight of her granddaughter, standing with some of her friends, barefoot at the water's edge.

"Daisy!" Mary said.

Daisy's head swiveled around to see who had called her name just as a sailboat puttered around the corner of the rock formation. Its sails were down, and it moved under the power of a small outboard motor mounted over its rudder. A policeman hunkered in the rear of the boat, guiding it through the shallow water.

Mary frowned. The Ivy Bay marina was full of boats. But this was a swimming beach. Sailors should know better than to sail this close to vulnerable swimmers.

"Grandma!" Daisy said and hurried over to Mary.

"What's going on here?" Mary asked, wrapping Daisy in a hug. "Are you all right?"

All of Daisy's grown-up bravado was gone. She looked like a scared kid who was glad to finally see an adult show up. "We found that boat!" she half whispered.

"What?" Mary said. A few people in the crowd turned to look at her, but most of them were craning their necks as the policeman steered the boat toward open water. As the crowd started to disperse, wandering back to their blankets and towels, Mary led Daisy off to the side, in the shadow of the big rock formation.

"Now," she said. "Tell me what happened."

She could see a few of Daisy's friends from Ivy Bay look around for Daisy as the crowd dispersed. Daisy waved to them. "It's okay," she said. "It's my grandma." She turned back to Mary. "We were just exploring," she said. Something about her abashed expression made Mary look around. Quickly, she picked out a sign on the rocks alerting swimmers not to proceed beyond that point.

"Past the sign?" Mary asked.

Daisy nodded. "I didn't think we'd really find anything there," she said. "I thought we'd just go over and come right back." But although she was trying to look remorseful, her eyes still lit up at the memory. "We found a cave," she said. "A big one."

"Big enough for a boat?" Mary asked.

Daisy nodded again. "I wasn't going to go in, but Brian did. He came back and said there was a boat back there. None of us believed him, so he said we should come and look. Then all the rest of us went too. And then Celia recognized whose it was."

Mary felt a chill as pieces began to fall together in her mind. "Whose boat was it?" she asked, even though she was almost certain she knew.

"Celia said it was Jared Wilson's," Daisy said. "I mean, actually, his parents'."

"And you...told the police?" Mary guessed, trying to work out the series of events that had led up to her finding her granddaughter at the water's edge, involved in what might or might not prove to be a crime scene.

Daisy shook her head. "We told the lifeguard on duty," she said. "She called the police. Brian told them it was Jared's parents' boat. They didn't believe us at first, but then they ran the number, and they did. I guess they're going to Jared's house now, to talk to him about it."

Suddenly, Daisy enveloped Mary in a hug, her arms tight around Mary's waist. "I'm glad you're here," she said.

"Me too," Mary said, patting her back. "Me too."

A moment later, Daisy released her grip and stepped back. Some new idea seemed to have occurred to her. "But wait," she said. "Why *are* you here? Did they hear about the boat already in Ivy Bay? But we only just found it a little while ago. You must have left before we even told anyone where it was."

Mary smiled at this evidence that her granddaughter was growing up with some sleuthing skills of her own. Then she shook her head. "I didn't know anything about the boat," she said. "I came to ask you about something else."

"About what?" Daisy asked.

Mary looked around the beach. It was almost back to normal now, with most people having returned to whatever place they'd staked out when they first arrived that day. Even Daisy's friends had trailed back to a set of blankets not far off. Then she looked at Daisy, trying to gauge how much excitement her granddaughter could handle in one day.

"The night of the fireworks...," Mary began. "Were you down by the docks?" The footage of the security camera couldn't tell her for certain where Daisy had come from that night, but Mary had seen the blonde woman by the docks, and she was gambling that that was where Daisy had collected the wig.

Suddenly, Daisy looked a little wary. And maybe, Mary thought, even a little guilty. "For a little while," she said, cautiously, trying to read her grandmother's face. "Why?"

"I saw some footage of you on the security camera from the bank," Mary told her.

"Security camera?" Daisy said, sounding alarmed. "We didn't do anything at the bank! I promise."

"No, no," Mary assured her. "Of course not. But one of the boys you were with seemed to be carrying something in a bag. Do you know what it was?" She deliberately didn't mention the wig, to keep from putting words in Daisy's mouth. There was still a chance that she'd misjudged the object the kids were playing around with in the video. Maybe there was still some other perfectly reasonable explanation.

"Um," Daisy said. "That was a while ago. I'm not sure what you're talking about."

"Daisy," Mary said. "You're not in trouble. And this could be important."

Daisy gave her a long, measuring glance. Then she dropped her eyes. "It was a wig," she said.

Even though Mary had known this answer, she felt a little jolt of excitement. "And where did you find it?" she asked.

Daisy looked up. "On the docks," she said. "We were just playing around with it. First, Ginger tried it on and pretended she was some kind of movie star. Then Brian put it on and pretended he was a singer in a rock band. It stayed on pretty good," she added. "I would have thought it would fly off, the way he was banging his head around." She giggled a bit at the memory.

"You said you found it," Mary said, trying to keep her voice steady. "Where did you find it?"

"Well," Daisy said, reluctance creeping into her tone again, "we didn't exactly find it. Someone dropped it."

Mary's heart leapt. "Who?"

"A girl," Daisy said. She met her grandmother's eyes. Since she didn't see any anger or judgment in them, she decided to confess. "That's why I didn't really want to talk about it," she said. "We probably should have run after her to give it back. But when Brian found it, he was so excited it was hard to get him to listen."

"What did she look like?" Mary asked.

"Um," Daisy said, "I didn't get a really good look. She seemed like she was in a hurry."

"Do you remember anything?" Mary pressed. "Anything at all?"

Daisy bit her lip. "She had dark hair," she began.

Mary realized she was holding her breath, listening. She wasn't sure whether to be elated or deflated at this. It could mean that the girl was Amanda, after all, with her true hair color revealed after doffing the wig. But it could also mean that the person was a total stranger, just another one of the many clues or false leads she'd gathered over the past two days, but had been unable yet to fit together. "Anything else?" Mary asked.

Daisy nodded. "She was wearing a tank top," she said.

To Mary, that clinched it. Now she wasn't the only person who had seen the mysterious girl shortly after Amanda's disappearance. And the blonde wig and the fact that the girl had dark hair only strengthened her case.

"Where were you?" she asked. "When you saw her?"

"Near the pier where Sam's Seafood is," Daisy said. "That's where she was headed. We were just on the shore road. She dropped it before she got out on the pier."

"Was there anything else in the bag?" Mary asked.

Daisy shook her head. "Nope," she said. "But I guess it was kind of a funny bag. Brian recognized it. It was from the hardware store, I think. He was joking about how he was going to ask Johnny or someone if he sold wigs now."

"Jimmy," Mary said.

Daisy's eyes lit up. "That's it," she said. "Jimmy." Then her brow furrowed. "How did you know that?"

Mary didn't answer for a moment, trying to understand what Amanda could possibly have been doing, walking away from the parade in a blonde wig...and how the wig had ended up in a bag from Jimmy's store. That didn't prove Jimmy was involved though, she knew. It would have been easy enough for Amanda to snatch up a bag of his at any time during the making of the float or the preparation for the parade.

During her silence, Daisy's expression turned serious. "Grandma," she said, "is all this important?"

"I'm not sure, honey," Mary said, putting her arm around her granddaughter.

"Does it have something to do with Amanda?" Daisy asked. "I'm sorry. I didn't realize it was important. I would have told you before."

"That's all right," Mary said. "You didn't know. And you told me when I asked."

Daisy kicked at the sand near the rock formation that led to the mouth of the cave where the boat had been hidden. "I guess so," she said.

As she did, something flashed in the sand.

"What's—?" Mary and Daisy both chorused together. Then they broke into laughter. Daisy bent over and retrieved the shiny object.

When she straightened up and dusted it off in her hand, Mary could see it was a key. A brand-new key, with a novelty handle in the shape of a ship at full sail.

"It's so big," Daisy said, turning it over in her hand. "I wonder what it goes to. Or how you could even use it."

She blew a puff of sand away from the metal and looked up at her grandmother. "Have you ever seen anything like this?" she asked.

Slowly, Mary nodded. She had seen one like it before. Just the day before, in fact. Hanging on the wall with the collection of novelty keys at Jimmy's Hardware.

"Where?" Daisy asked. When Mary didn't answer, she closed her fingers around the key. "Grandma?" she said.

"It's time for us to go back to Ivy Bay," Mary told her.

Daisy didn't even put up a protest. She just went over to her cluster of friends, collected her towel and bag, and made her excuses. Then she joined her grandmother and started across the beach toward the wooden stairs that led up to the lot on the bluff.

When they reached Ivy Bay again, about half an hour later, Daisy looked up as Mary began to park on Main Street before they had reached home.

"Where are we going?" she asked.

"Jimmy's Hardware," Mary told her. "I have a few questions to ask him."

But just as she parked her car, Mary's phone began to ring. When she fished it out of her bag and looked at the incoming number, she got another jolt. The screen of her phone read "Amanda."

It took her a moment to realize that it likely wasn't Amanda herself, but someone calling from Amanda's house.

When she answered, she discovered she'd been right. It was Heather, Amanda's mother, her voice high and breathy with excitement.

"Oh, Mary," she said, "you've done so much to help us, I just had to call."

"Is everything all right?" Mary asked.

Heather's voice cracked with emotion when she answered. "Yes, yes," she said. "Amanda's back. She escaped and came back. And you won't believe what happened to her."

TWENTY-SIX

❖◆❖

Mary pulled up to the curb outside of Amanda's house just minutes later, behind a new collection of private vehicles and police cars. But before she went in, she pulled her phone out and dialed.

A moment later, Jack answered. "Mom?" he said. "Is everything okay?"

"Everything's fine," she said. "Amanda's back home."

"Oh, thank God," Jack said.

Amen, Mary prayed.

"But that's not actually why I'm calling," she said. "I picked Daisy up from the beach and brought her back to Ivy Bay. I'm at Amanda's now, but I dropped Daisy off at home. I just thought you might like to know that your daughter's in town now and might enjoy some company from her dad after all."

"That's great," Jack said, his voice softening. "Thanks, Mom."

"Love you," Mary told him and ended the connection.

As she walked up to Amanda's house, the door swung open before she even reached it. A police deputy stood in the doorway, blocking the entrance. Mary heard a voice call out over his shoulder—Heather's.

"Oh, it's Mary," she said. "It's fine; it's just Mary. Please, let her in."

The deputy stood aside to let Mary pass.

When Mary stepped into the living room, it was crowded with people. Heather sat on the couch, just where Mary had first found her when she came over after Amanda's disappearance. Her two friends were there as well. The police deputy remained by the door. Standing with his back to the front window was a man who Mary didn't remember meeting, but who seemed familiar. It took her a moment to recognize where from. Then it hit her: the collection of papers Amanda had been keeping about her father. This was Hank Branson, about twenty years older than his high school yearbook photographs, but still unmistakable.

But Mary only glanced past all these figures, because beside Heather on the couch was Amanda herself. She was wearing a plaid flannel shirt and a pair of loose-fitting blue jeans. Her hair was tousled, and her face was dirty and tracked with tears. But other than that, she seemed to be unharmed.

Relief struggled with outrage in Mary's chest. She wanted to go over and gather Amanda in a hug, but something about the way that Amanda sat huddled on the sofa restrained her.

"Oh, Mary," Heather said, "thank God you're here. You even beat Chief McArthur. I guess he was almost an hour up the coast, investigating some lead or other. But we have Amanda back. Can you believe it? She escaped all on her own, and she came back." Her voice broke, and tears began to roll down her face.

"Escaped?" Mary asked, stepping farther into the room. "Escaped from where?"

"Someone took her!" Heather exclaimed, her voice breaking again as it rose. "Right from the float. When the parade got caught up in the confusion at the end of the route. She would have screamed, but they told her they'd hurt her if she made any noise. And then they dragged her off."

Mary glanced at Amanda to see her expression as Amanda's mother repeated the story that Amanda must have just told to her herself. Amanda gazed steadily at the floor in front of her. It would be hard, Mary thought, to hear the story of your abduction told again, especially just after you'd reached safety. But something about the details of it didn't add up, even allowing for the way Heather might have scrambled them in translation. How would somebody have climbed up on the float to capture Amanda, in the middle of a busy parade route, without anyone in the crowd noticing, no matter how much confusion? She glanced back at Heather.

"I just came from Seahorse Beach," Mary said. "They found the Wilsons' family boat in a cave just off the public access area."

Heather looked perplexed. Amanda looked up. "They put me in a boat," she said. "It could have been Jared's. I don't know. They had me blindfolded, so I couldn't see much of anything."

Hank Branson shifted uncomfortably at the window.

Heather's face stretched with pain. "And then," she went on, "they took her to an abandoned cabin and kept her there till this morning."

"What kind of cabin?" Mary asked.

Amanda shook her head again. "They didn't let me see anything," she said. "They kept a shirt over my head all the time. I could hear things, but I couldn't see."

"But when you escaped," Mary said, "could you see anything then?"

Amanda shook her head again. "It was dark," she said. "That's how I got away. One of them went out, and the other one fell asleep. I was only tied up with a rope, and I got my hands free, and I wasn't very far from the door. So I made it there and ran out."

"You couldn't see anything at all?" Mary said.

"Not for a while," Amanda said. "It was the middle of the night, and there were clouds over the stars. I know there was a pine forest," she said. "I could smell it and hear the needles underfoot. It seemed to go on for miles and miles."

A pine forest outside a cabin only narrowed it down to just about anywhere on the entire Cape, Mary thought. And if Amanda had escaped before first light this morning, how had it taken her this long to make her way home?

"It must have taken you a long time to find your way back," Mary said.

Amanda glanced at her, then resumed looking at the carpet again. She nodded and gave a slight shudder. "I didn't know where I was," she said. "And I was so scared." Her voice broke, and she gave a slight shudder. Her mother wrapped her arm around her daughter's shoulders protectively.

Mary glanced at Hank again, expecting to see some strong emotion on his face. If Jack was as worried as he was about Daisy starting to grow up, she couldn't imagine what it must be like for a man to listen helplessly to the story of his daughter's abduction. But if Hank was struggling with Amanda's story, Mary couldn't read it on his face. If anything, he looked uncomfortable, as if he couldn't wait for all of this to be over. But she did see real tenderness in his eyes when he glanced at Amanda.

Mary's brow furrowed.

"So how did you make it home, finally?" she asked.

"Well," Amanda said, "I wandered in the woods for—" She broke off and shook her head. "I'm not sure how long. And finally I found the water. And I recognized it was the bay. So I went to someone on the shore, and I asked if I could use their phone."

"She called me right away," Heather said. "And Hank was already on his way down."

"Chief McArthur had called me this morning," Hank explained. "He thought he had a real good lead with this mystery man he'd been tracking. He wanted me to come down. Just be nearby in case they found something."

"I wasn't in any shape to go out," Heather said, "so Chief McArthur called Hank to go get her while he came back to town. And here she is." Heather squeezed her daughter in a tight hug.

When Heather released her, Amanda gave her a grateful smile, but Mary noticed that she barely glanced at Hank. That was strange, Mary thought, for a girl who had never met her father before and spent the last several months collecting any scrap of information about him she could find. Wasn't she curious about him at all?

She didn't want to believe Amanda could be lying about her disappearance, but nothing she'd said so far seemed to match the facts that Mary had spent all weekend sleuthing after.

"You know," Mary said, "I was down at the docks around the time you disappeared. I was afraid I might have seen you, but not realized it. The girl I saw was wearing some kind of blonde wig. And some local kids found one later, near the docks. Was that part of how they got you away from the parade without anyone seeing you? Did they make you wear some type of disguise?"

Amanda, she realized, actually looked more frightened now than she had while telling any other part of her story. "No," she said quickly and shook her head. "No, there was nothing like that. No wig. They just took me." Her voice rose as she said it. To Mary, it was an almost eerie imitation of the way Heather had been ascending into hysterics over Amanda's disappearance over the course of the weekend. "They took me!" Amanda said. "It was awful! I was afraid I was never going to come back!"

She collapsed into her mother's arms and buried her face in her mother's neck.

"Oh, honey," Heather said. "It's okay. Don't cry. You're safe now. You're back. It's all right."

"You know," the deputy said, "it might be better not to talk about this too much. At least not until Chief McArthur gets here and we can take a formal statement."

Heather looked at him somewhat indignantly. "Are you trying to tell me my daughter shouldn't tell her mother what happened to her?" she said. "When she's been missing for days?"

The deputy crossed his arms over his chest, cowed. "No, ma'am," he said. "It's just—"

"It's okay, Mom," Amanda said. "I don't really want to talk about it now."

"Well, that's all right too," Heather told her, her arm around Amanda's shoulders. "You don't have to, if you don't want."

For a long moment, nobody said anything. Heather's friends looked at each other. The deputy looked at the ceiling. Hank looked at the floor. Heather held Amanda's hand, toying with her fingers.

Mary took a long breath. Until she had mentioned the wig to Amanda, she had been willing to believe that the confusion in her story was the honest result of a traumatizing experience. But she knew now that she wasn't the only one who had seen Amanda down on the docks during the window of time after her disappearance, wearing the blonde wig. Daisy had seen her too, and so had all of Daisy's new Ivy Bay friends. Even if Amanda had given a flimsy explanation for what Mary had seen, Mary might have been willing to accept it. But for Mary, Amanda's denial of the wig, after both she and all of Daisy's friends had seen it, threw Amanda's whole story into question. And Amanda's hysterics every time Mary pressed her didn't help.

Mary was sure Amanda wasn't telling the whole truth. And she was still afraid of something. But what? And why?

Mary opened her purse, searched in it for a moment, then pulled out the key that Daisy had unearthed on the beach near where Jared Wilson's boat had been abandoned.

Before she even thought of what to say, she could see Hank Branson start. When she glanced at him, he was staring fixedly at the unusual key in her hand. As soon as he recognized that she'd seen him, he dropped his gaze to the floor again.

"It's an unusual key, isn't it?" Mary said, as if she were just showing off some interesting little item she'd just brought home from the store. "Daisy and I found it in the sand. Near where the Wilsons' boat was left, by Seahorse Beach."

"A key?" Amanda said, in a weak voice. She lifted her head from her mother's shoulder. When she saw the key in Mary's hand, her eyes widened. She stared for a minute, then buried her face in her mother's shoulder again.

"It's so unusual and distinctive," Mary said. "Daisy was saying she'd never seen anything like it before. But that got me to thinking. Because I have. I was just in Jimmy Shepard's store yesterday. And he had one just like it. He said he'd only made a few for him and his friends. So I can't help wondering," she finished, with a glance at the deputy, "if he might have had something to do with this."

Amanda's hands opened and closed on the hem of her oversized shirt, but she didn't say anything.

Then Hank Branson spoke up. "Jimmy Shepard's got nothing to do with this mess," he said.

TWENTY-SEVEN

To Mary's surprise, she didn't even need to ask the next question.

Her eyes flashing, Amanda's mother asked it for her. "And how would you know that, Hank Branson?" she asked. "You might have been thick with Jimmy back when you were both high school sports stars, but as far as I know, you haven't set foot in this town in years."

Hank folded his arms, even more uncomfortable, and now agitated as well. "Jimmy wasn't a fool then. And he isn't a fool now. I'm not saying we're best buddies these days or anything. I'm just saying I don't think the man I knew back then would ever have anything to do with this kind of nonsense. Even if time does do some things to change a man."

"Oh," Heather said, "I can hear it all now. It's all so familiar. Always defending your friends. But not a thought for your daughter. Have you thought about *her*, Hank?" she asked. As she spoke, she gave Amanda's small frame a shake, as if she'd forgotten that Amanda was a living girl and not a doll she'd been playing with. "What about Amanda? What about your family? Aren't you worried about her? Don't you want to catch the man who did this? Aren't you at all interested in what a key from Jimmy's shop might have been doing at the scene of the crime where your daughter was stolen from us for *two whole days*?" Her voice rose in its familiar crescendo of dramatic anxiety.

Hank stared across the room at his ex-wife, his gaze steady. "Two days," he said. "You're right. That's a long time. It must have felt like years. But you wouldn't know anything about what that feels like to miss your daughter for years. I'm the only one in this room who knows that."

"That's right, Hank," Heather said bitterly. "It's all about you. This whole kidnapping; it's all about you. That's the only thing that's ever really mattered to you. Not me and Amanda. Just you and your good-for-nothing friends. Who cares if we ever find out who did this to our daughter? Just as long as nobody points a finger at some buddy of yours who you haven't seen in years. You're so selfish, Hank. And you haven't changed a bit. This is exactly why I left."

"Of course, Heather," Hank said. "I'm sorry. You're right. You always are. That hasn't changed either, I see."

The two of them continued to bicker back and forth while the policeman shifted restlessly by the door, but Mary had frozen. When Heather had told her the story of her breakup with Hank before, she'd always stressed how he abandoned the family, leaving her a single mom with a young daughter to take care of. But now she was directly contradicting herself by saying she was the one who had left. It was a crucial slip in the story, but still, Mary hesitated to say anything. Did it have anything to do with Amanda's disappearance? Or was it private family business, something she didn't have the right to pry into?

Lord, Mary prayed, *am I the only one who noticed this? Should I say anything?*

As she was praying, Amanda raised her head.

"Wait," she said, breaking into her parents' argument. "Mom."

Both of Amanda's parents fell silent for a moment. They turned to look at her.

"What do you mean, 'I left'?" Amanda said. "You always told me that Dad left us."

Mary half expected Heather to burst into a new fit of hysterics, working herself up into a state where nobody could expect her to answer the question. But instead, she simply turned very still. Her hands came to rest on her knees. Her mouth shut. And her eyes locked on her daughter's face.

Amanda looked over her shoulder at her father. He shrugged and folded his arms.

The radio receiver on the deputy's belt squawked and then pinged. He pulled it from its holster and glanced at it. "That's Chief McArthur," he said. "He's not far out. I'll tell you what. If you folks just want to settle down, you can tell him all about it when he gets here. And he can decide what to do about Jimmy."

At this, Amanda whipped around in her seat to face her father. "Dad!" she said. "Jimmy didn't do anything. What should we do?"

Hank Branson shifted uncomfortably from one foot to the other. "Well, honey," he said, "I think that's up to you."

Something in the way they interacted with each other felt strange to Mary. In fact, it had since she walked in the room, she realized. If Amanda hadn't spoken to Hank since she was small, why was she acting so familiar with him? And why was she so much more interested in what might happen to Jimmy than in finding the person who had kidnapped her or getting to know her own father?

"Amanda," Mary said gently, "how can you be so sure Jimmy didn't have anything to do with this?"

"We can't," Heather broke in, seeming grateful for the distraction from the question she'd been avoiding. Her voice turned harsher as she went on. "I wouldn't put anything past him. After all, he was driving the truck. He would have been in the perfect position to scheme with someone about taking Amanda. Why else would the truck stop in the middle of the parade? So someone could sneak onto the float? I bet he was in on it."

"No, Mom!" Amanda said, her voice rising in volume and intensity to match her mother's.

Heather patted Amanda's hand. "You don't need to think about this," she said. "You've been through enough. You just put it out of your head. We'll let Chief McArthur deal with it when he gets here."

Amanda swiveled to look entreatingly at her father again.

"Dad?" she said. "Tell them!"

"Tell them what, honey?" he said, almost as if he were asking her.

Amanda threw herself back against the couch and crossed her arms. She looked like she was on the verge of tears again.

Mary's mind raced. Now that she knew that Jimmy and Hank had been good friends once, everything she'd discovered over the past few days had begun to fit into place: the wig, the key, the stalled float—everything. The only piece that didn't fit was the story Amanda had just told them, of her abduction by a stranger and escape from an unidentified cabin in the pines.

"Amanda," Mary said, "do you remember anything that you haven't told us?"

Amanda bit her lip and looked down at her lap.

She seemed to be struggling with a powerful emotion, but Mary knew that the mention of Jimmy seemed to be a flash point for her. Maybe she could use that to get at the truth. "Anything that might keep Jimmy from being in trouble with the authorities?" she pressed. "I know Jimmy too. I can't believe he'd have anything to do with you being abducted. But your mom's right that it may look suspicious. And it'll be Chief McArthur's job to do anything he can to find the person who did this to you. After all, we've all spent the last few days worried sick about you. And he's brought in people all the way from Boston to help solve this case."

She had a sense that, whatever Amanda had been up to, she hadn't realized the seriousness of the trouble it had caused everyone. And as she mentioned the upheaval Amanda's disappearance had thrown the town into, she could see Amanda wring her hands in her lap.

"I didn't think anyone would care so much," she said. "I mean, I'm back. I'm okay. It's not such a big deal."

"It is, honey," Heather said, wrapping her arms around Amanda and squeezing her tight. "You don't have to pretend it's not. You've been through a horrible experience. And so have we all. These have been the worst two days of my life, not knowing where you were."

Amanda looked at her, stricken. She seemed even more upset than she had when she was describing her own abduction. Significantly more upset, Mary observed.

"And don't forget," Mary said, "the people who did this to you might still be out there. There's nothing to say they won't come after you again. Or after someone else in Ivy Bay. Or anywhere else. Chief McArthur won't be able to stop looking until they've got some answers. It wouldn't be safe for you. Or right for anyone else."

Amanda stared down at her own hands again for another long moment. Then she looked up at her father. Now tears were streaming down her face. "I don't want anybody to get into trouble," she told him.

Hank, his eyes troubled, gave her a nod. "You do what you need to, sweetheart," he said.

Amanda looked down at her hands again.

"Amanda?" Mary said. "Is there anything you'd like to tell us?"

Amanda took a long, trembling breath.

Then she nodded.

TWENTY-EIGHT

———◆◆◆———

I just wanted to talk to my dad," Amanda said, so quietly that it was difficult to hear her.

"What did you say, honey?" Heather said.

"She wanted to talk to her dad," Hank repeated. He spoke clearly, but there was no recrimination in his voice as it had been when they were arguing earlier. He sounded worn out but matter-of-fact.

Heather looked from one of them to the other, shocked. "But why?" she began. "After everything he put us through. He's never been there for you. Would you really rather have him than me? After everything I've—"

Before she could really get started, Amanda raised her hand and nodded. "I know, I know," she said.

Heather stopped and looked at her. "I knew you'd say that," Amanda told her. "That's why I couldn't ask you about him. But I had to know. He might not be perfect, but he's my father."

"Well, I don't—" Heather began.

"I'm her father," Hank repeated. "You can at least give me that. She didn't even say if I was good or bad."

"I didn't want to seem ungrateful," Amanda said, taking her mother's hand. "I know everything you've done for me. More than anyone does. You don't have to tell me."

Now tears began to roll down Heather's face too. "You're the best thing that ever happened to me," she said. "I'm the one who's lucky to have you."

"We're both lucky," Amanda said. But she glanced over her shoulder at her father. "But I had to know who my dad was," she said. "And I was afraid to ask you. You always got so upset when I asked about him."

Heather stared at her daughter, biting her lip.

"So I started trying to find out little things about him," Amanda said. "There was a picture of him at school. In the trophy case."

"From his senior-year football team," Heather said.

Amanda nodded. "I guess so," she said. "I used to see it all the time when I went by. And I'd stop and look at him and wonder why he didn't care about us. And just…who he was," she finished. "So then I thought, maybe there were other things. Around town. Or at school. I found some things down at the library. Some articles he'd been in, for sports and things."

"He was a big star," Heather said. "For a while, it seemed like he was in the paper every week."

Amanda nodded. "That's what I saw," she said. "And when I worked in the school office, I went back through his file and found his grades. He never got in any trouble or anything. He seemed like he might have been a good person. Or at least not a bad one."

Hank let out something that sounded like an involuntary sigh.

Heather glanced at him. Then her eyes locked again on their daughter.

"And then I found an old yearbook," Amanda said, looking over at her mom. "It had pictures of you and him. You looked...happy."

Heather's lip twisted. Her eyes filled with tears.

Amanda glanced at Hank. "And I also found some of him and Jimmy. It looked like they were real friends. I mean, it wasn't just one picture. So I thought, if I can't ask Mom, maybe I can ask Jimmy. Maybe he'll still know something. So I went down to the hardware store one weekend, and I asked him."

"You...what?" Heather said.

"I just asked him," Amanda said. "About Dad. And he told me that Dad loved me a lot. He told me it'd been the worst thing that ever happened to him, when you left him. He said Dad pretty much went crazy. And then when he straightened out, a few years later, he thought it was probably too late. Jimmy knew the kinds of things you'd been saying about Dad around town. Dad figured you'd probably been saying even more to me. And he didn't want to fight anymore. So he just stayed away."

Heather took a sideways glance at Hank, but she couldn't seem to hold her gaze, as if she were looking at something that was too bright for her eyes.

"But Jimmy knew where he was," Amanda said. "He never gave up on Dad. Not even when he was such a mess, after you two broke up. So he talked with Dad from time to time. And he gave me Dad's number."

"And you told her to...what?" Heather said. "Run away from home?"

Hank shook his head and opened his mouth, but before he could speak, Amanda interrupted. "This wasn't his idea," she said. "It wasn't even mine at first. I talked to him a few times. It was nice. But I couldn't really tell on the phone. It just made me more confused. I wanted to get to really see him and talk to him. To know what it looked like when he laughed, or how it seemed like he felt when I told him about things. He doesn't really talk that much."

"He never did," Heather said, with what might almost be a trace of wistfulness.

"I really wanted to see him," Amanda said. "But I didn't think...I just thought you—"

For once, Heather didn't escalate the tension in the room. She just squeezed her daughter's hand. "Oh, honey," she said.

"And then I found out about Jared," Amanda said.

"Jared?" her mother said. "What did he have to do with this?"

Amanda's lip quivered. "He..." She hesitated, searching for the words. "He found this other girl," she said. Her voice broke. "We'd been together for so long. He was the person I felt safest with. And all of a sudden, I didn't know who I could trust. And I just really wanted...I just really wanted to see my dad. So I came up with this plan. Jimmy didn't like it, but I told him I was going to do it whether he helped me or not, and he said he'd rather he helped me than have me trying to get up to Boston all on my own."

"So the kidnapping—" Heather began. She seemed to only be putting it together for the first time.

"It wasn't real," Amanda said. "I know it sounds crazy now. I just didn't know how to tell you."

Heather's eyes widened in shock. Then anger flared in them. She turned to Hank. "And you thought this was a good idea?" she said. "Letting your daughter fake her own kidnapping? And you wonder why I had reservations about her having you in her life."

"I told her I didn't like it," Hank said.

"He told me, the same as Jimmy," Amanda said. "And I told him the same thing I told Jimmy. I was going to come up to try to find him, whether he gave me permission or not."

"I was trying to keep her safe," Hank said. "I didn't want her getting into any trouble if I could help it. And..." For a minute, it almost seemed like his voice was about to break. Then he mastered himself. "I wanted to see my little girl," he said after a minute. "It had been almost sixteen years. If she wanted to see me, I wasn't going to tell her no. No matter how she wanted to make it happen."

"So what...?" Heather began. "How—?"

"Jimmy built the tree with a trapdoor," Amanda said. "The trailer was high, so there was no danger from the wheels. You could pretty much drop through it anytime on the parade route and come out safe. Even if the truck was moving. But we planned that I'd drop out sometime near the end. So it wouldn't attract too much attention. I had a wig I changed into when the throne went inside the tree, and I switched out of my dress into an outfit I had on underneath. And then I went through the door and knelt down on the pavement. When the trailer moved up, I just looked like I'd been marching in the parade and stopped to tie my shoe.

The trapdoor jammed the tree, but Paige took a look at it so Cindy wouldn't figure out what was going on."

"She knew about this?" Heather said.

"Just her and Jimmy," Amanda said.

"Not Jared?" Heather asked.

Amanda shook her head. "He knew I was looking for Dad," she said. "But I never really told him the plan. I was thinking about telling him, but just before the parade, we had a big argument. He thought I was keeping something from him, and I told him I knew he was keeping something from me. He tried to pretend like there was nothing happening. That was actually worse than if he'd just admitted something was. So I took the key to his parents' boat off his key chain. I was just going to ask him for it, but instead I took it."

"You took the Wilsons' boat?" Heather asked, disbelieving.

Amanda nodded. "It's fine," she said. "I was real careful when I brought it up on shore."

"At Seahorse Beach," Mary said.

Amanda nodded again. "It was all fine," she said. "Until you caught me down by the docks."

"It *was* you," Mary said. Despite all the wild revelations of the past few minutes, she couldn't help feeling a little satisfied that she had been right all along.

Amanda nodded. "I'm sorry, Mrs. Fisher," she said. "I felt terrible about that. But I couldn't tell you it was me. I had to get away."

Mary shook her head. "All I wanted was to bring you back safe and sound," she said. "I'm just glad to have you here in one piece."

"So I hid for a while," Amanda said. "Between the fishing shanties. And then I slipped out and took Jared's boat out."

"And hid the clothes you wore on the float by his dock," Mary filled in for her.

Amanda nodded.

"Why did you leave them?" Mary asked.

"I was trying to leave a clue," Amanda said. "To back up the kidnapping story. I guess it didn't work so well."

Mary shook her head. "I just couldn't understand why a real kidnapper would leave behind a clue like that," she said. "Where did you go then?" she prompted.

Amanda sighed. "With the fireworks," she said, "it wasn't hard to slip away through the bay. There were so many other boats already on the water, watching and moving around. I got up to Seahorse Beach in a little over an hour. We chose it because we didn't want Daddy to be recognized, picking me up from a stolen boat in Ivy Bay."

"That's where I met her," Hank said. "I didn't want her trying to make her way all the way up to Boston on her own. So I came down and met her on the coast. Helped her get the boat all squared away."

"And that's where you lost your key," Mary said. "In the sand."

Hank nodded. "Jimmy gave me that one time when he came to Boston to see a game. He thought it was real funny. Of course, it's no good as a key. But he said it'd be a good luck charm."

"And then you took her back to Boston in a delivery van," Mary said, thinking back to the mysterious late-night delivery Hank's workman had complained to her about.

Hank nodded. "That way, nobody could recognize my private vehicle," he said. "It was just one of a million industrial rentals in Boston."

"So that's where I was," Amanda said, turning back to her mom. "I went up to Boston to meet my dad. And then he brought me back down here today. And here I am."

"Well," Heather said, clearly struggling to take it all in, "I guess that's all that matters."

"No, Mom," Amanda said, her voice gentle but insistent. "It isn't."

"What do you mean?" Heather said.

"You always told me one story," Amanda told her. "Actually, you didn't really tell me the story. You just told me things. Like that Dad didn't care about me. Or I wouldn't want to know him. Or we were better off without him."

Heather watched her, her eyes wide. "Yes, and—"

Amanda cut her off with a shake of her head. "But that's not what Dad told me," she said. "He says that he always loved me. And he loved you. But you made him move out. And you told him I was afraid of you, and that I cried when I heard his name, and that I never wanted to see him again. And he didn't want to hurt me, or hurt us, so he just...gave up. But he always hoped and prayed that I'd come looking for him."

Mary glanced at Hank. His gaze was inscrutable, but his eyes were suspiciously bright.

"Mom," Amanda said, "is it true? You always said he left us. But that's not what he says. And it's not what you said just now. Is it?"

Despite everything that had happened, and everything both Mary and Amanda had learned in the past two days, it was clear that Amanda still needed to hear the truth from her mother directly.

And Mary wasn't sure, at first, if Heather was up to the task. She stared into her daughter's eyes for a long time. Then she glanced over at Hank. The look that passed between them had a strange intimacy to it, just as Hank had for his daughter. He nodded at Heather.

Tears began to stream down her face. She took both of Amanda's hands in her own. "Honey," she said, "I'm sorry."

"For what?" Amanda asked, her voice barely above a whisper.

Heather shook her head. She didn't seem to know what words to use herself. "I just—" she began. Then she took a deep breath. "Your father and I were very young when we got married," she said.

"Just out of high school," Amanda said, as if repeating a piece of information she'd learned well, for a test.

Heather nodded. "That's right," she said. "And probably we should have waited awhile. But we didn't. I thought your dad was special because he had so many friends, and everybody loved him, but after we got married, he still wanted to go out and see them. I just wanted him to stay in with me. He couldn't understand why I wouldn't go out with him. And... it all seems so silly when you say it out loud. But it just got worse from there. We were just real young. We didn't know how to be married. And it's not easy to get married."

"Or to have a baby," Amanda said.

"No!" Heather objected. "You weren't the problem. You were actually the one thing we agreed on. But by then, it was already too late. Or at least it felt that way to me. I wasn't happy. Hank wasn't happy. I didn't see why we should spend the rest of our lives making each other unhappy. So I pushed him away."

Hank shifted over by the window. Mary glanced at him. Now his eyes were unmistakably bright.

"And this might sound crazy," Heather said, "but then I missed him. It hurt a lot to have him go, even though I was the one who asked him to stay away. And so I guess I got—" She paused again, searching for words to express things she'd never said out loud before. "I guess I just got scared," she said. "I got scared that maybe everything I love, I'd lose. And there was nothing in the world that I loved more than you. And I started to worry that maybe one day, he'd take you away from me too. But I figured, if I could cut off contact with him, he could never do that. And you were so little. I figured as time went by, you'd just forget, because you barely even knew him. I thought I could build a world that would be enough for you, just the two of us. Because I loved you so much."

"I love you too, Mom," Amanda said, leaning in to hug her mom's neck.

Heather broke out in a sob at this. "I'm sorry," she said. "I didn't realize how much you missed him. I should have never kept you away from your father for so long. I didn't understand how that would affect you."

Amanda kissed her mom's cheek. "Thank you, Mom," she said.

Heather wiped her eyes and looked up at her daughter, surprised. "For what?" she asked.

"For telling me the truth," Amanda said.

Then she rose from the couch, went over to her father, and gave him a big hug as well. Hank bowed his head over his daughter's and closed his eyes.

"Hank," Heather said, getting to her feet, "I'm sorry. I don't know if you can forgive—"

Hank cut her off with a shake of his head. "Neither one of us was perfect back then," he said. "There's a whole lot of water under our bridge since then. I'm just glad to have my daughter in my life now. And now that I've got her, I'm not ever going to let her go again."

Amanda gave him a squeeze.

Outside, Mary heard the sound of a car door slam. A moment later, there was a brisk rap at the door. The deputy jumped to open it, and Chief McArthur stepped in.

He stopped and shook his head when he saw Amanda. "Amanda Branson," he said. "I don't know that I've ever been so glad to see anyone in my life."

"Hi, Chief McArthur," Amanda said, trying to dry her eyes with the back of her hand.

Chief McArthur slapped his deputy on the arm as he came into the room. He took off his hat and planted his feet. "Now, tell me," he said, "what did I miss?"

TWENTY-NINE

———◆◆◆———

"Well," Chief McArthur said as he and Mary walked out of Amanda's house, "I guess I'm going to have some explaining to do to our out-of-town guests."

"I'm sorry," Mary said sympathetically.

"I'm not," Chief McArthur said. "I'd much rather this turned out to be some kind of harebrained scheme by a half-baked teenager's brain than an actual kidnapping case. This was a bit of trouble. The other might have been a tragedy."

"I guess you're right," Mary said. She didn't tell him, but she had the sense that this situation was actually just the opposite. Amanda wasn't just safe at home, just the way she'd been before. She'd learned some hard truths in the past few days, but Mary had the feeling that they might be just what Amanda needed to face in order to grow up into the woman she was meant to be.

When they reached their cars, Mary was reminded of what Heather had said when she explained Chief McArthur's long absence: that he had been following up a lead.

"What clue were you chasing down when you got the news?" Mary asked.

"Oh," Chief McArthur said. "There was a man we caught on video—"

"By the bank," Mary said.

Chief McArthur looked at her in surprise. "How did you know that?" he asked.

"Your deputy," Mary said. "He told you about him while I was standing there on the curb by the warehouse...."

Chief McArthur smiled and shook his head. "Mary Fisher," he said, "you never cease to amaze. And I have to admit, with all my high-tech equipment and police training, you wound up getting to the truth before I did."

Mary waved his admission away graciously. "But I'm still curious," she said. "Did you ever trace that man? Did he explain what he was doing lurking around the bank like that?"

"Well, I'll tell you," Chief McArthur said. "It's an interesting story." He leaned against the door of his car as Mary wandered the few steps to hers, then turned back to hear.

"Owen's got that facial-recognition software on his computers at the bank," Chief McArthur told her. "Which gave me an idea. We weren't able to identify the guy from any features of his bearing or dress. But we did have his face. And I had all these fancy friends down from Boston, with more technology than they knew what to do with. So I gave them the bank security disk. Took them about a day, but this morning, they came back with a name. It's pretty convincing too. We punch it into the Internet and get some hits of a guy who looks just like him. Problem is, he hasn't been to work in three days. And he isn't answering his home number. Or his cell."

Mary could see why Chief McArthur would have thought this was a good lead. Amanda was safe inside the house, just across the small lawn from them, but even so, Mary could feel gooseflesh rising on her arms.

"That doesn't sound good," she said.

"It doesn't, does it?" Chief McArthur said. "Especially not with footage of him loitering around the site of a girl's disappearance not two days before. So this seems to be reasonable cause to run a trace on his credit card. And when we do, we find he used it to pay for a hotel up the coast. Not far. Maybe half an hour."

"Sounds like he didn't get very far," Mary said.

Chief McArthur shook his head. "Right. So I take my team, with a little company from the Boston SWAT team, and we go up there and knock on his door."

"Was he there?" Mary asked.

"Yep," Chief McArthur said. "With his new wife."

"His *wife*?" Mary repeated.

Chief McArthur's face finally cracked into a smile. "That's right," he said. "You know Melissa Barometti? Cooks at the Pizzeria Rustica?"

Mary nodded.

"Apparently, they were high school sweethearts," he said. "Hadn't seen each other in years, but they met up again recently. Decided it was true love all along. And then figured they'd get married over the long weekend."

"You brought a SWAT team to their honeymoon?" Mary asked, trying to stifle a smile.

It was no use. And by this time, Chief McArthur was grinning too. "Sure did," he said. "Melissa was actually real sweet about it. She told him if they could make it through a SWAT team visit on their honeymoon, they could make it through anything."

"So that's why he looked so nervous," Mary mused.

Chief McArthur nodded. "I've seen a lot of criminals in uncomfortable situations," he said. "But the most nervous men I've ever seen are grooms, right before the wedding."

"Amazing," Mary said. Then she remembered something else. "So what was in the package he was carrying?" Mary asked.

"A big picture," Chief McArthur said. "Of a spot they used to go to when they were kids. He painted it himself. As a wedding present. He had it all wrapped up in that brown paper for travel, but then I guess he pulled off all the paper right before he met up with her..."

"And left it in Kemper's Alley," Mary finished for him.

"How did you know that?" the chief asked.

Mary smiled. "I found the paper," she said. "You actually got to see this painting?" she asked.

"You couldn't miss it," Chief McArthur said. "It was right there in the hotel room, with all their luggage."

"Well," Mary said with a smile, "I can't say I'd have done anything different than you did."

"That's kind of you," Chief McArthur said, putting his police hat back on as he opened his car door. "But the fact of the matter is, you did. And you wound up here, with Amanda safe at home, while I wound up knocking down the door of some innocent guy on his honeymoon."

"We both worked on it together," Mary said. "And we all just wanted to bring Amanda home."

"Well, that's where she is now," Chief McArthur said. "Thank God. And maybe next time, I'll pay a little closer attention to your hunches, Mrs. Fisher."

Mary smiled.

He tipped his hat, got in his car, and drove away down the quiet street.

THIRTY

———◆◆◆———

I never get tired of it," Jack said, staring out at the water. Then he turned to Betty, who was sitting beside him on the giant picnic table the family had occupied on the beach at the annual Fourth of July weekend lobster bake. "What about you, Aunt Betty?" he asked. "Does it ever get old?"

"I've been here forty years," Betty said with a smile. "I can't say I've ever gotten tired of it."

"It's been a perfect weekend," Christa said, polishing off the last delicious bite of her lobster.

Mary glanced at Daisy to catch her reaction to this. Daisy didn't nod in agreement, but she didn't give the scowl they might have expected a few days ago either.

"Well, it is since Amanda came home," Betty said. "I don't think anyone would have called this a perfect weekend if she was still missing. No matter how beautiful the sunset is."

"Amen to that," Jack said.

"I'm just so glad she made it home," Christa said. "Her mother must be so relieved."

"She was," Mary said. "And I think Amanda was relieved to be home too."

"I bet," Betty agreed.

"It's such a strange story too," Christa said. "Running away and going through all that trouble. Just to meet her dad. It seems like there must have been some other way."

"There were about a hundred other ways," Mary said. "But sometimes teenagers don't always see that."

"It's not just teenagers," Jack said. "I think all of us get that way, from time to time. We get tunnel vision. We can't see any way but our own."

"That's true," Christa said.

"And she caused everybody so much trouble," Betty said. "The police. The whole town. Everyone so worried."

"Yes," Christa said. "But to me, there's still something sweet about the story."

"Really?" Betty asked.

Christa nodded. "That little girl loved her father so much. Even though she barely remembered him," she said. "To me, there's something beautiful about that."

"*Hmm,*" Betty said.

Mary saw a slight motion under the table, near where Daisy sat beside Jack. When she tilted her head to see better, she caught a quick glimpse of Daisy putting her hand in Jack's. Jack tried to play it cool, just like Daisy seemed to want to, but a big grin spread across his face anyway.

He looked out again at the bay, where the sun was sinking down the horizon in a gorgeous symphony of color: deep violet at the top of the sky, with navy below it bleeding into true sky blue that then became streaked with bands of gold, as the pink sun trailed down the sky.

"What about that?" Jack said, putting his arm around Daisy. "They don't make sunsets like this in Chicago, do they? You have to come to the Cape for this."

Daisy wrinkled her nose at this, but she was still smiling.

"We have sunsets in Chicago," she said.

A flock of Cape gulls wheeled through the sunset over the masts of the boats that crowded the bay.

"But what about those gulls, huh?" Jack asked. "Look at this. It's like a painting."

"We have seagulls in Chicago," Daisy insisted. "One of them stole Mike Davies's hat at Navy Pier last month."

"I'm not sure that's something I'd brag about," Jack said.

"That sounds like a Chicago seagull to me," Betty said wryly.

Jack sighed, his arm still around Daisy. "So what are you telling me?" he asked. "You don't think there's even one thing here in Ivy Bay that we couldn't find right back home in Chicago?"

Daisy thought for a moment. Then her face broke out in a wide smile.

"Well," she said, "there is one thing I wouldn't have had back in Chicago this weekend."

"Amen!" Jack said. "I can't believe it. And what's that?"

Daisy caught him around his waist in a big hug, burying her face against his blue chambray shirt. Mary smiled at the picture of her granddaughter happily hugging her son.

Amanda wasn't the only girl in town who was finally back where she belonged.

After a minute, Daisy looked up at Jack.

"So what is it?" he teased. "The only thing that this weekend in Ivy Bay has that might possibly beat the adventure you could have had in Chicago?"

Daisy grinned. "My dad," she said.

ABOUT THE AUTHOR

Vera Dodge is a lover of books and the Cape and is delighted to blend both her passions in the series Secrets of Mary's Bookshop. She grew up in small towns in the Midwest.

A CONVERSATION WITH VERA DODGE

Q: *What's your favorite vacation spot?*

A: I have something in common with Mary when it comes to vacation spots: Cape Cod has been one of my family's favorite places to get away since I was a child. My parents loved to take us there because the Cape offers both the drama of the Atlantic coast and the relaxing calm of the many freshwater ponds, which turn almost bathwater warm in the summer sun. I still love to get away to the Cape whenever I can, and one of my favorite things about it is returning to places that have been there since I was a child—everything from my favorite pizza place to the familiar curve of the coast sweeping off into the distance.

Q: *What are your favorite memories of the Fourth of July?*

A: For me, the Fourth of July holiday is all about family. You don't have to worry about presents, like you do at Christmas, and no one even has to go through the production of making a big fancy meal, like at Thanksgiving. My family always got together on a little lake we loved to visit. Everyone brought their favorite dish: fancy breads from my cousin, big plates of barbecue from my aunt, giant bowls of salad from my grandmother, and a watermelon cooling in the lake. No one had to dress up or do too much work—it was just a time to enjoy each other and plates and plates of delicious food.

Q: *If you could go to Ivy Bay, what shop would you visit first?*

A: That's easy! In pretty much anyplace I visit, I make a bee-line for the nearest bookshop. So I'd be one of Mary's customers. Once I discovered what a great bookshop she runs, I'd probably be there more than once before I left town. And after striking up a conversation with her, I'd almost certainly hear about her sideline as an ice-cream inventor and take myself down to Bailey's to get a cone to eat while I enjoyed the first pages of my new book.

Q: *Do you have any pets? Have they ever helped you solve a mystery like Gus helps Mary?*

A: My dog is curious about just about everything, but he's never actually helped me crack a case, like Gus helps Mary. (That may have something to do with the fact that I don't solve nearly as many real-life mysteries as Mary does.) But I do feel like my pets have often helped me to solve mysteries of life—not because they give me the answers, but because, just by sitting next to me or laying their chin on my knee, they give me a sense of peace that allows my mind to settle down so that I can see the answers that were always in front of me.

Q: *Mary often goes to the library when sleuthing out a mystery. What's the library like in your hometown?*

A: The library in my hometown was created in one of the town's oldest Victorian brick homes, complete with gingerbread trim on the roofline. When I was young, the layout of the original home was still evident among the stacks, with a parlor in the front and several other rooms in the back, and a beautiful staircase up to the second floor, where the librarian had her office. Today, the town has grown, but we still care about books, so the old building has been renovated into one of the best small-town libraries in America. The old walls still stand, but the interior has been renovated into a soaring atrium, and new construction has been built in the back to hold the growing collection.

Q: *What's your favorite type of book to read?*

A: I read anything and everything, and usually all at the same time. Right now I'm reading a collection of writers who died during World War I, a book of ghost stories edited by the inimitable Edward Gorey, a short story collection by Mark Richard, a history of the second scientific revolution during the Romantic period, a George MacDonald novel, *War and Peace* (for the second time), Ralph Ellison's unfinished final novel, a history of Detroit, C. S. Lewis's *Perelandra*, *The Art of Disappearing*, a forgotten and forgettable novel from the early part of the last century by a Catholic priest who apparently sidelined as a popular novelist, a biography of Bing Crosby, and the Bible. It's great fun to jump from title to title, and the connections between them are often illuminating, especially when various books give you multiple perspectives on the same event, like reading a Scott Fitzgerald story about young men struggling through the Jazz Age after their return from World War I side by side with the writings of soldiers who were lost in that same war.

Q: *Mary loves to snuggle up with a cup of tea or a quilt and read at the end of the day. How do you like to spend the quiet hours of an evening at home?*

A: Mary and I would get along very well in the evenings. I also love to spend time curled up with a book, but I also enjoy a great meal with friends and family. I find you can learn all sorts of things from people that you couldn't learn the same way from books—because a book doesn't (usually) argue back and forth with you or stop to explain if you get confused. But I also love to combine a delicious snack with my more solitary reading. One of my favorite things is to make a little plate of fruit, cheese, and chocolate to enjoy as I'm flipping through the pages of a new story.

PEANUT BUTTER AND JELLY ICE CREAM

1 half-gallon commercial vanilla ice cream
1 cup peanut butter
1 cup jelly of choice

Allow ice cream to soften outside freezer until soft but not melted. Mix in peanut butter until fully blended. Swirl jelly through blend of ice cream and peanut butter. Refreeze until normal consistency. Scoop and serve!

FROM THE GUIDEPOSTS ARCHIVES

Shall I come to you with a rod, or with love in a spirit of gentleness?
—I Corinthians 4:21 (RSV)

We were visiting my husband Paul's parents in Ohio, and Grandma thought we'd enjoy watching the Fourth of July parade in a neighboring town. But when we arrived, the main street was empty. She had misread the time of the parade in the newspaper, and we had missed it. All we could do was turn around and head home. My daughter Maria, who'd been jabbering to her brother like a typical six-year-old, didn't realize what had happened until Grandpa turned the car onto their street.

"We're going home?" Maria asked. "But what about the parade?"

"I goofed," Grandma answered, sounding sad and a little embarrassed. Nobody said anything. I knew that whatever happened next to fill the silence would set the mood for the entire day. *Help me say the right thing*, I prayed. Then an idea that didn't even take the time to pop into my head first popped out of my mouth: "Let's have our own parade."

Everyone jumped on the idea. "I'll drive the lawn mower, with Maria in the cart in back," said my twelve-year-old son Ross, running off. "I'll push Dan," Paul said, helping his big brother out of the car and into his wheelchair. "We need music," Paul's brother Tom said, heading to the garage and returning with an old plastic horn, a metal bucket and some sticks. "I'll get the camera," Grandpa said, while Grandma ran into the house and returned with a toy piano and a huge smile. Tom's wife Ann brought their dog Randy out on a leash, and I grabbed the big American flag from the front porch to carry myself. We marched our horn-blowing, bucket-banging parade around the neighborhood, laughing and waving, bringing neighbors out to cheer and laugh with us.

Later, I wondered how many of those decisive moments I have faced unawares, especially when someone's feelings were involved. I can't always control what happens, but I can control how I react when things don't turn out right. By bringing love instead of scorn, and with the help of God's joyful Spirit, I can do more than make the best of it—I can have a parade.

Lord, help me to think first, then speak with Your wisdom, Your joy and Your love. —Gina Bridgeman

A NOTE FROM THE EDITORS

We hope you enjoy Secrets of Mary's Bookshop, created by the Books and Inspirational Media Division of Guideposts, a nonprofit organization. In all of our books, magazines and outreach efforts, we aim to deliver inspiration and encouragement, help you grow in your faith, and celebrate God's love in every aspect of your daily life.

Thank you for making a difference with your purchase of this book, which helps fund our many outreach programs to the military, prisons, hospitals, nursing homes and schools. To learn more, visit GuidepostsFoundation.org.

We also maintain many useful and uplifting online resources. Visit Guideposts.org to read true stories of hope and inspiration, access OurPrayer network, sign up for free newsletters, download free e-books, join our Facebook community, and follow our stimulating blogs.

To learn about other Guideposts publications, including our best-selling devotional *Daily Guideposts*, go to ShopGuideposts.org, call (800) 932-2145 or write to Guideposts, PO Box 5815, Harlan, Iowa 51593.